HER ALIEN BOSS
STRANDED ON EARTH
BOOK FOUR

IVY KNOX

Copyright © 2023 by Ivy Knox

This is a work of fiction. Names, characters, organizations, places, events, and incidents are either products of the author's imagination or used fictitiously. Any resemblance to actual persons, living or dead, or actual events is purely coincidental.

All rights reserved. No part of this book may be reproduced in any form or by any electronic or mechanical means, including information storage and retrieval systems, without written permission from the author, except for the use of brief quotations in a book review.

Cover art: Natasha Snow Designs

Edited by: Chrisandra's Corrections, Mel Braxton Edits, & Owl Eyes Proofs & Edits

❦ Created with Vellum

To Mom,
You were always too good for this world.
See you on the other side.

CONTENT WARNING

If you don't have any concerns regarding content and how it may affect you, **feel free to skip ahead to avoid spoilers**!

This book contains scenes that reference or depict suicidal ideation from FMC, sexual harassment, physical abuse, police abusing their power, narcissism, c-section birth (successful and non-graphic), systemic racism, as well as graphic violence which may be triggering for some. If you or someone you know is in need of support, there are places you can go for help. I have listed some resources at the end of this book.

CHAPTER 1

NAOMI

This would be a great way to die. The water beneath the abandoned bridge shimmers like black diamonds against the moonlight, and the current seems strong enough to carry my body miles from where I stand. There's enough distance between the rusty guardrail I'm peering over and the water below that hitting the surface alone could do me in, and I wouldn't have to worry about drowning.

On the list of potential ways to die, drowning will always be at the bottom for me.

Not that it matters anymore. If I jumped off this bridge, I wouldn't die. It would be freezing and deeply unpleasant, but I'd survive. Now that I'm a vampire, I'm practically immortal.

A stake through the heart is the only thing that'll take me out. I know because I've tried everything else.

If a human wanted to opt out of their future, they could just drink too much water in a short period of time, or eat something they're allergic to, or get a splinter and never have it removed, letting the infection grow and fester until it found its way into the bloodstream. The most innocuous things can take a person out.

This isn't something I realized until I was turned, and dying became close to impossible.

Not because death was a foreign concept to me when I was human. Working in the medical field put death right in front of me, and it was my duty to step between it and my patients, protecting them from death's icy grip. I was a successful OBGYN in Seattle and had just joined an incredible all-female practice that was a five-minute walk from my large and remodeled Tudor-style house. A house that I bought with cash. My mom and I had finally reached a place of mutual acceptance—my mom accepted that I'd never settle for plain fruit as dessert, I accepted that she would always offer it anyway. I had wonderfully supportive friends, and I had just started dating the smoking hot anesthesiologist at the hospital that I'd been crushing on for months.

Then I lost everything.

Tears fill my eyes at the memory of that awful night. The eve of my thirty-third birthday. If only I had chosen to get a ride instead of walking home from the bar, then maybe I wouldn't have woken up in a stranger's apartment, thousands of miles from home, my heart no longer beating, and the thirst for blood so strong that my throat burned with the heat of a thousand suns.

Maybe I wouldn't be the monster I am today.

I swipe my cheeks, anger and defeat filling my chest as I lean heavily against the guardrail. It doesn't matter what could've been. This is my life now—languishing in a shoddy trailer in a tiny town in the middle of New Hampshire that most people have never heard of, expending too much energy trying to get the members of my cell to like me and failing miserably every time I refuse to hunt with them.

A flutter of wings to my right grabs my attention, and a crow lands next to me on the guardrail.

"Good evening, Felix," I say with a smile as I lean my cheek against my palm. I gave him a name because of how frequently the little bugger shows up. It's always when I'm in a sour mood, longing for my past. I like to think he's here because he wants to brighten my day, but he's a wild bird, so who knows? "I brought you something." Pulling my hand from the pocket of my cardigan, I place a dime on the guardrail next to him.

He caws in response before dipping his head and gently taking the dime into his beak. A few days ago, he showed up on my kitchen windowsill with a paperclip. After thanking him for his generosity, I waited until he flew away before tossing it in the trash. I know crows bring gifts to their friends, so I hope continuing this exchange makes him one of mine. I don't have many at the moment.

"Naomi!" Wyatt shouts from the edge of the forest. "Where are you?"

"On the bridge," I yell back.

Felix launches himself into the air a few minutes later when Wyatt clears the trees, and I swallow my nerves as I narrow down the possible reasons he could be looking for me. It could be a booty call, but the odds are greater that Elaine sent him to retrieve me.

"There you are," he says, his heavy gait making all kinds of noise in an otherwise peaceful setting. He steps onto the bridge, and the rusted decking creaks beneath his weight.

"What's up?"

"Elaine needs to see you," he replies as he crosses his thick farmer boy arms over his broad chest.

Fuck. I knew it. Elaine needing to see me is a bad sign. She only ever sends for me when she's inclined to berate me over what a terrible vampire I am and how disappointed my maker would be to see how little progress I've made since he dropped me at her doorstep.

I let out a wary sigh as I follow him through the woods toward the light brown, split-level house he shares with Elaine and Mike, the other two members of our cell. When I joined, Elaine didn't want me in the house, so she bought a repossessed trailer home at a police auction and parked it as far from the house as possible without going over the property line. We're not exactly besties.

"What is it this time?" I ask Wyatt, trudging behind him.

"She didn't say much," he mutters over his shoulder, "just something about an assignment."

An assignment? That sounds ominous given that the only place I'm allowed to go without vampire supervision is the Dunkin' Donuts on the edge of town.

When we enter the house, Elaine is sitting in her recliner watching HGTV, and Mike is reading an old, dusty phone book on the couch next to her. I have no idea why, and I don't bother to ask. The man looks like he stepped out of a Pinterest page for steampunk fashion. Why he chose to settle in the sticks when he could've stayed in London is beyond me.

These three aren't the sharpest tools in the shed, and somehow, they seem to be getting dumber each year.

"Got her," Wyatt says, pointing to me.

"Ah, there she is," Elaine adds, clapping her hands together. Her cheerful expression immediately puts me on edge.

"Salutations, Naomi," Mike says, temporarily removing his pipe.

"Hi," I mumble quietly. If my palms could still sweat, they'd be drenched right now.

"Did you order a printer?" she asks. Waving me over to her side.

"No," I tell her. There's no way I could even fit one in my trailer. Not that I even have use for one if I could.

She shakes her head as she stares at her phone. "I got this email from Circuit City saying that the printer I ordered is ready for pickup, but the payment method needs to be updated. Did you—"

"That's a spam email," I tell her. "Don't click on anything and don't provide any payment information."

"If there's no printer, why would they send me this email?"

"Because they want to steal your money," I spell out for her. "Also, Circuit City closed in 2009." It's such an obvious scam. How can she not see that?

Elaine sighs as she deletes the email.

"Um, Wyatt said you were looking for me."

"Yes," Elaine says, her blue eyes gleaming with excitement. "I have a very important assignment for you." She uses her kitten-heel-covered feet to close the footrest on her recliner. When she reaches me, she swipes through several pictures on her phone before turning it around. "Do you recognize him?"

The man in question has the sharp, angular features and lean-but-cut build of someone who models tuxedos for a living. His hair is light brown and somewhat long, but styled with enough gel to keep it brushed back and off his pale face, and he's dressed in a crisp, white button-down shirt, a gray-checkered tie, and matching gray slacks that look perfectly tailored to his body. All the photos seem to have been taken as he's leaving a corporate building and about to cross a busy street. His brow looks permanently furrowed, as if he's carrying the weight of an entire planet on his shoulders, when, in reality, he's probably stressed over a quarterly earnings report, or an upcoming shareholder meeting, or something else that rich white guys like him take way too seriously. He's pretty, I suppose, if you're into the whole arrogant CEO vibe.

"No, I've never seen him," I tell Elaine.

Elaine chuckles. "Well, he's about to be your new boss."

"My...boss?" I stammer, confusion making me slightly lightheaded. "You got me a job? I thought I wasn't allowed to have consistent access to humans until my twentieth fangiversary."

"You've shown impressive restraint for such a young vampire," Mike says with a proud nod.

Translation: I haven't killed anyone since I turned, so I'm not as much of a threat as most young vampires would be.

I'm caught off guard by the compliment. Mike is certainly nicer than Elaine, but he rarely offers support of any kind.

Elaine tilts her head to the side. "That's one way to put it. Another way would be," she pauses, chewing on the inside of her cheek, "since you refuse to embrace your instincts and contribute to our food intake, we've found an alternative way for you to live among us without being such a mooch."

Ouch. Though I suppose my refusal to hunt with them has been the biggest source of tension since I arrived. They don't understand why I won't drain or kill a person for blood. To me, the reason is obvious. I spent my entire adult life in the medical field, trying to help or heal the patient in front of me. It doesn't matter what I am now, or that I need to consume blood in order to survive. I'm not about to desecrate the Hippocratic oath like some selfish asshole.

My maker, Xavier, insisted it was a temporary affliction that only baby vampires suffer from. "Once everyone you know is dead, you stop caring about who you hurt in order to feed."

That was one of the last things he said to me before he shoved me out of the car in Elaine's driveway, followed by, "I'll come back for you once you've outgrown this pitiful state."

I hope he never does. And I really hope he's wrong. Maybe it's counterintuitive to the way most vampires think, but I like knowing that I'm still me. That I care about the safety and well-being of others. I don't want that to change.

"You have a Zoom interview tomorrow with the company's COO. I think her name is Thea," Elaine says, interrupting my thoughts. She hands me a piece of paper. "Thea…something. I don't remember. Here's your résumé. Don't fuck it up."

"Wait," I choke out, my mind racing with all the unanswered questions. "What position am I applying for?" The paper in front of me has my name at the top and lists a bunch of jobs that I've never had. "This résumé is completely inaccurate, by the way."

Mike and Wyatt start packing a duffle bag that's sitting on the bench next to the front door.

Elaine sighs, looking annoyed. "You're going to be the CEO's executive assistant. His name is Kyan Monroe, and we need you to get close to him. Spy on him. Figure out what he's hiding in that big, fancy building he owns and runs the company out of. And see what you can find out about his brothers too."

"His assistant?" I ask. "I've never had a job like that. This résumé says I have fifteen years of experience as a receptionist and assistant to top executives. How am I supposed to fake that?"

Wyatt tosses a rope and duct tape into the duffle, along with three empty stainless steel water bottles. Elaine tosses a change of clothes on top and zips the bag closed. "It's answering phones and scheduling meetings. How hard can it be? Just act like this is a role you're comfortable in, and you're eager to make Monroe's life easier. That's all he wants."

I can probably pull that off. Something still seems off about this plan though. "What do you have against this guy?" I ask Elaine. "Is he threatening to go public with what we are?"

She hands the bag to Mike and frantically fluffs her blonde ringlets, a move she always makes when I'm on her last nerve. "You know that old cop who sends us information on all the newly released convicts? Officer Burton? He wants us to spy on Kyan. Apparently, him and his brothers have been causing trouble around town, and Burton is desperate to get at least one of them behind bars on a charge that'll stick. He says he won't give us the monthly convict lists until we can provide information on Kyan that he can use to make an arrest."

That seems flimsy as fuck. "Why does he even need us? Can't

Burton plant drugs in his backyard or pull him over for a broken taillight and then claim Kyan's resisting arrest?" Straight out of the bad cop playbook.

"Officer Burton has kept us fat and happy for decades, and now he needs us to return the favor. It's the least we can do," she snaps. "Burton even told me he suspects the Monroe brothers aren't human. He doesn't know what they are, just that they're incredibly dangerous. And now they're fucking with our food."

Hm. That's a new one. "We're sure they're not vampires?"

She rolls her eyes. "Obviously not. I'd know if another cell had moved into our territory."

I chew on the inside of my cheek as I consider this. It still seems like a strange mission to take on, considering we have no proof these guys are dangerous. And given Burton's track record of giving Elaine names and addresses of ex-cons and covering up their murders once Elaine has sucked them dry, he certainly isn't a Boy Scout, so why would she trust anything he tells her?

She huffs a breath at my lack of enthusiasm. "Well, if that won't motivate you to put some fucking effort into this task, try this one on for size. If you don't track this guy's every move from the moment you're hired and report back to me, I'm going to send you back to Xavier."

The only reason Elaine took me in was because she owed Xavier a favor from years ago. If she calls him and tells him she refuses to keep me as part of her cell, I'm screwed. The things I witnessed Xavier do to people after he turned me still give me chills. He doesn't just kill to eat; he tortures humans for fun before draining them. That man is a twisted, depraved motherfucker, and I don't want to be anywhere near him.

"Okay, I'll do it," I tell her with a shaky nod.

She grabs a set of keys from the hook by the door and tosses them to me. "His office is in Manchester. You can use the station wagon for your commute."

Gee, what a generous gift. A car that's thirty years old and barely runs. "I thought the brakes needed to be replaced?"

"The brakes are fine," Elaine replies with a dramatic eye roll. "It's not like a car crash would kill you anyway. What are you worried about?"

Oh, I don't know, killing someone else on the road? I don't bother saying this to her, though, because she doesn't care. Given her ability to glamour people into doing whatever she wants, you'd think she could show up at a car lot and leave with however many cars she felt like getting for exactly zero dollars. She's certainly done that for Mike and Wyatt. But she'd never waste her powers on me like that.

Mike heads out the front door with a stack of books under one arm and the duffle over his shoulder. Elaine stands in front of the hallway mirror and touches up her matte red lipstick with expert precision.

Wyatt puts on a backpack and shoots me a boyish grin. "Want to come along this weekend? We're hunting college students up north at Plymouth State. I'm sure you could do your Zoom interview from a Starbucks or something."

I appreciate his continued efforts to include me. He's the only one who seems to like having me around. When I first joined their cell, we had a bit of a fling. I was lonely, and he had a calming presence and kind eyes. We haven't hooked up in over a year though. He's offered, but I haven't had any interest. Maybe my depression has killed my supercharged vampire sex drive.

"Thanks, but I have a group meeting tomorrow night. I don't want to miss it."

"Aww, another gathering for you and your anti-sucker pals?" Elaine says mockingly as she holds my gaze in the reflection of the mirror. "Do you all sit in a circle and cry about how precious human lives are?"

"It's a Sippers Support Group, actually," I quietly correct her.

We hate the "anti-sucker" label, and Elaine is very aware of this. "We mainly talk about how difficult it is to live in a world where we're constantly shamed for our lifestyle."

I wish I had the guts to stand up to her, but she's older than me by over a hundred years. Since vampires get stronger as they age, that would make her the equivalent of The Hulk and me a fruit fly. Plus, she knows she doesn't even have to touch me to hurt me. She can threaten to send me back to Xavier, and I'll cave and do whatever she wants, short of draining a human.

Wyatt must see the anger in my eyes because he nudges Elaine toward the door. Then turns to me with a sympathetic expression and says, "Have a good weekend, Naomi. Good luck with your interview."

I hear Elaine yell, "You better fucking get the job!"

The door slams behind him, and I let out a long sigh of relief. It's not like I have much time to relax though. I need to start prepping if I want to land this job in order to spy on the mysterious CEO Elaine has deemed her nemesis.

I like him already.

CHAPTER 2

KYANSSANAI "KYAN"

This is unacceptable. How dare Thea hire an assistant for me? I don't need one. Even if I did, I would insist on meeting this person before hiring them. Thea didn't even give me the chance to do that. She can't go over my head like this.

My work phone rings, and I let out a groan when I see that it's Donnie from development.

"Yes?" I answer, my tone curt. "What is it, Donnie?"

"We have a call right now to discuss the updates to the company website, sir. Does this time still work for you?"

Thea enters my eye line through the floor-to-ceiling windows that make up the front wall of my office. She's chatting with the head of HR at the large round table that fills the common area next to the kitchen. I need to talk to her before the person she hired shows up.

"Are you there?" Donnie asks. "We have the entire dev team on the line."

"Uh, no," I mutter. Damn, I forgot he was still on the phone. When did I schedule this meeting? And why are we making updates to the site? I don't recall requesting any changes. I'm also too distracted thinking of how I'll be able to convince Thea to fire my assistant before she begins her first day on the job to continue this conversation. "Sorry, Donnie. This isn't a good time. Let's reschedule. Anytime next Wednesday. Thanks. Good work, team."

I drop the phone on my desk as I scramble to my feet and race out of my office. "Thea, good morning. You need to call off my new assistant."

Thea turns to face me with her signature lopsided smirk, which I found interesting when she first started working here, but I've since noticed it's a face she makes when she thinks I'm acting ridiculous. It's a face I now resent.

"Get her on the phone and tell her our needs have changed and her services are no longer required," I add. "And make sure you do it before she arrives. I don't want her commute wasted on a job that no longer exists."

"But Ky—" she interjects. She wants to argue the many reasons why me having an assistant is necessary, but she's wrong, and I'm not interested in discussing it further.

"No. That's my final decision," I say. "We can revisit this in a month or two."

Thea clears her throat as she takes a step to the right, revealing a short Chinese American woman with a bright smile and shoulder-length black hair that looks impossibly soft. She wears a black cloche hat and a powder blue wool coat that reaches her knees, with a sensible office ensemble beneath it. Her dark brown eyes are wide-set, and despite her friendly demeanor, her gaze is penetrating, and I feel naked beneath the intensity of it. In her small hands she holds a tray containing muffins. Steam still rises from their moist tops, and the scents that fill my nose are of warm sugar and blueberries. My mouth fills with saliva, and my stomach reminds me by way of a growl that I didn't eat breakfast this morning.

The corner of Thea's lip quirks up a bit higher as she says,

"Kyan, allow me to introduce you to Naomi Zhao, your new assistant."

Shit.

"She has extensive experience, and her references are impeccable," Thea adds.

I can tell she's enjoying the cocoon of embarrassment I've trapped myself in.

"I think you two will make a great team." Thea gestures to the desk just outside my office door. "This is yours, Naomi."

Naomi drapes the strap of her bag over the back of her chair and puts the muffins down next to her laptop.

"Why did you bring those?" I ask, not knowing what else to say and eager to pretend the previous few minutes never occurred.

Naomi sits down in her chair, smoothing the skirt of her navy-blue dress, and adjusts the height and back support. "Because it's my first day, and I wanted to make a good impression. Can't hate the muffin girl, am I right? Would you like one?" She lifts the tray toward me, and I can't resist the offer.

"Thank you," I tell her as I take a bite. A blueberry explodes on my tongue, the juice hot and sweet as chunks of granulated sugar crunch between my teeth. The muffin practically melts in my mouth, warming my throat as I swallow. It feels as if someone has draped a thick blanket around my shoulders on a cold, rainy morning—safety and comfort in just one bite.

"Good, right?" Naomi asks, beaming with pride as she rests her elbows on her desk.

I shrug. "Fine." I probably should've been honest and told her that I've never tasted anything as exquisite as that muffin, but I don't want Naomi to get comfortable here. If I'm constantly showering her with praise, she'll start thinking I can't run this company without her by my side. If I get my way, this will be her first and only day of employment at Monroe Media Solutions.

Naomi's gaze narrows as I take a second bite, and I worry she sees right through me. My phone rings, and my new assistant gets to her feet, pausing at my office door. "May I?"

Thea answers for me. "Go right ahead."

She answers the phone with, "Mr. Monroe's office, how can I help you?" followed by a series of head nods and "uh-huhs" before telling the person I'm currently in a meeting, and I'll get back to them later.

I can't remember a time when my phone rang, and I didn't answer it, which inevitably leads to a lengthy conversation that should've been an email. Yet Naomi prevented that from occurring just by telling whoever it was that I'm busy, and she did so to allow me to enjoy my muffin in peace. I feel the tension leave my shoulders and a sigh of relief escapes me.

Naomi writes the message down on a yellow sticky note and puts it on the corner of my computer screen.

"That was Jack Dovarro from EPL DataWorks. He said he wanted to discuss changes to their contract."

"Oh, right," I say, tossing the crumpled wrapper of the muffin into Naomi's trash bin. "His contract is up for renewal soon, and he wants his monthly bill reduced, but I think there's a chance to lock him into a bigger package." My mind becomes a jumbled mess of strategy as I figure out how to upsell him without him even realizing it. "I should call him sooner than later." That muffin break was nice, but I can't afford to wander about eating fresh baked goods. This is my company, and it requires my full attention. I reach my office door and turn around to face Naomi and Thea. "Thank you, Naomi, for taking that call and for the muffin. But to be honest, I don't think answering my phone is a full-time job. I'm perfectly capable of managing my time. I've been running this company for thirteen years and have never had an assistant..."

Naomi is staring at me in a way that makes me lose my train of thought. She pulls a tissue from the box on her desk and hands it to me. In a quiet voice, she says, "You have a massive eye booger in the corner of your left eye."

Blood rushes to my cheeks as I rip the tissue from her hands and frantically wipe at the corner of both eyes. She said the left, but I need to be thorough. What a horrifying thing to be made aware of. How long would Thea or my other employees have let me walk around like that?

Naomi smiles, and warmth spreads through my chest. "Don't worry. It just means you're human."

I hope she isn't around long enough to learn how wrong she is about that.

Uncomfortable and frustrated with how this interaction has gone, I straighten my tie and tug on the cuffs of my dress shirt. I wanted her and Thea to see how much better off I am on my own. That I'm a confident, successful man in peak physical condition, with a mind that never runs out of brilliant ideas. And I wanted to intimidate her a little bit. Not frighten her, exactly, but to make the hierarchy between us clear in a nonverbal way.

Isn't that how most assistants see their superiors? Through a lens of admiration and fear?

"Oh no, you got some blueberry juice on your tie," Naomi says, showing me the blueish-purple splotch on the bottom of my tie. She scurries over to the bag slung over her chair and digs through it. Her movements are so smooth, it's like her feet are gliding across the drab gray carpet. "Ah! Found it."

With what looks like a bright orange marker in her hand, she comes back over, grabs my tie, and presses the end of the marker into the stain.

"I never go anywhere without a Tide pen. These things always come in handy."

Thea chuckles. "You're welcome," she mouths to me before turning on her heel and heading toward the elevator.

Naomi leans in to focus on removing the stain, closing the distance between us, and I can't keep myself from inhaling the scent of her hair as it falls over her cheek. I expect the scent to be fresh. Calming even, like the sea, but…there is nothing. Slowly, I take another breath in, certain I'm mistaken. Humans always have a strong scent, and it's usually dreadful. Even the good-smelling mortals tend to wear too many fragrances at once, making the overall scent impossible to enjoy, much like stepping into a candle store.

How is it possible that Naomi doesn't have a scent? Not even a bad one? I don't detect any kind of shampoo, deodorant, soap, or perfume on her skin. My nose is so strong that normally I can determine which products a human has used and how long ago. If it was too long ago, the scent of unwashed skin becomes overpowering. But Naomi doesn't smell unwashed or washed. There's nothing there. It's unnerving.

"See? All better," she says with a proud grin as she holds up my tie.

"Thank you."

Well, I'm stuck with her now. She has proven herself to be far too useful for me to fire. I suppose I'll have to wait for her to make a mistake. As soon as that happens, she's gone.

The rest of Naomi's first day is filled with visits from people trying to help her get settled into her new role. I know because I spend my entire morning and afternoon watching the flurry of activity through my office window. It's frustrating how quickly my employees seem to take to her. Anyone who passes her desk gives a smile and an introduction, and then I hear them offer to help her whenever she needs it. It's not as if I want them to bully her, but the more connections she makes and the more favors she banks, the longer she'll be here.

At one point, the head of HR helps her set up the phone on her desk, and they manage to forward my calls to her. No one can access me directly now, and it sets me on edge. It'll save time having Naomi field calls that I don't need to waste my time taking, but now she'll be privy to sensitive information I'm not ready to share.

At six o'clock, most of the office has emptied for the day, and I take the opportunity to make myself a coffee and a turkey sandwich in the kitchen. I eat at the long steel counter, reveling in the silence. My employees work hard, and I'm grateful to each of them, but my favorite time of day is once they've left, and I can move freely about the building without the scrutinizing looks of each person I pass.

Upon returning to my corner of the top floor, I find Naomi still at her desk, her tiny fingers rapidly striking the keys of her laptop.

"Naomi, you should go home for the day. There will be plenty of emails to send tomorrow."

She smiles, showing her many white teeth. They're slightly sharper than most human teeth I've seen, and I'm surprised I didn't notice this earlier. "Oh, it's okay," she says. "I don't mind working late. I'm a night owl anyway, so this is when I shine."

I hope this vigor for her new role wears off soon. The last thing I need is her hanging around until all hours of the night. There are other tasks I must see to, and she can't be here to witness them.

I pick up a snow globe from the corner of her desk and shake it. The white flakes swirl around the inside of the glass orb, falling atop the mountain peak, tall buildings, and the strange saucer-shaped structure that stands taller than the rest. "Seattle?" I ask, reading the text on the base of the snow globe. "This is where you're from?"

"Yeah," she says, her tone wistful. "I miss it." She lets out a sigh that makes me long to hear more, and I recoil in disgust at the unfamiliar emotion.

Her head jerks back in confusion, and I fumble with the snow globe, almost dropping it, before returning it to its home on her desk. "Uh, listen…" I begin. "Most of my waking hours are spent in this building, and I would never expect you to be here as late as I am, so I insist, go home for the day."

In Naomi's dark brown eyes, I notice flecks of gold close to her pupils. I also see a flicker of something I can't identify. Suspicion maybe? Though I can't imagine why.

"You got it, boss," she says, closing her laptop and tidying up her work area.

"I'll see you tomorrow."

This is not how I wanted this day to go, but I suppose I can tolerate her presence for the rest of the week.

She puts on her coat and hat and says, "Have a good night," as I head into my office.

"You as well."

I wait twelve minutes—more than enough time for Naomi to walk over to the elevators, ride down to the parking garage, and get in her vehicle—before I shut down my computer and lock up my office.

My ride on the elevator is short as I'm the only one in it, and I take it down to the basement level that sits beneath the parking garage. This floor is the reason I bought the building in the first place, and the most important work I do happens down here.

"Kyan," Andrei greets with a nod. This part of the basement is the only area that resembles a corporate office.

There is a cluster of three desks in the center of the room, one of which is currently occupied by Andrei. The lights are dim, as the brightness from the large computer monitors provides more than enough light to fill the room. There is a fake plant in the far corner, a ratty blue couch in the other corner, and a full-size fridge sits between two tables covered in snacks and soft drinks on the back wall.

"Andrei, any sightings today?" I ask. I hired him to take over monitoring reported UFO sightings across the country. For the first few years after I won the bid to take over the contract with the Pentagon, I monitored the sightings myself, clearing them from the database almost as soon as they were entered. Now, Andrei does this for me.

The Pentagon had no business giving me this contract, but it became immediately clear when I put in a bid that the potential of aliens entering Earth's atmosphere is at the bottom of their list of national security concerns.

It is, however, at the very top of mine. Now that my brothers and I are here, I need to know the minute someone sees something suspicious in the sky. It's not impossible that our handlers would follow us here, and it's likely other galactic beings are interested in harvesting Earth's resources. This way, I'll be one of the first to know if there's an enemy approaching.

He shakes his head. "Just one this morning coming out of Muskegon, Michigan, at nine twenty-seven central-standard time, but it's been cleared. The couple was high on mushrooms at the time, so it was easy to eliminate."

"Very good," I reply. "I need to check on the recruits. Keep it up."

"Yes, sir," I hear him say as I exit through the hidden side door and walk down a long utility hallway. I've added lights to it, but with the cement walls, dirty floor, and steel pipes running alongside me, it would take more than a few sconces to make the space bright.

At the end of the hall is a military grade, five-ton, blast-resistant door the color of fresh grass. I enter the nine-digit code on the keypad, and it opens for me slowly. The scents of blood and sweat grow stronger the wider the entrance becomes, and I can't help but smile as I watch the beasts before me roll across the padded floor, tearing fresh wounds into each other's thick hides. Already, I can tell their form is improving, as well as their stamina.

It seems my army is almost ready for battle.

CHAPTER 3

NAOMI

"*H*ow's your first week going?" Thea asks me as we step onto a crowded elevator.

Normally, I wouldn't leave at five o'clock sharp, like so many of Kyan's employees tend to do, but I have a meeting tonight and don't want to be late for it.

"Going well so far," I tell Thea with a smile shimmering with gratitude. It's a lie though. I've only had the job for four days, but it's awful, and I fucking hate it. It makes me feel like a twisted Freudian combination of Kyan's mother and his servant, and I'm one swipe of a Tide pen away from quitting. I even made a pro/con list last night to decide if being sent back to Xavier would be better or worse than another day of answering Kyan's phone.

The exercise bummed me out, so I gave up and drank a bag of weed-laced blood, then passed out on my couch while watching *Ugly Betty*.

"I hope Kyan hasn't been too tough on you," Thea adds, tugging the strap of her purse back onto her shoulder. A second later, it slips back down to her elbow.

It's a distinctly human behavior that vampires lose after being turned—the overall need to fidget and adjust and preen every moment of the day. I'm not sure why that changes, but vampires exist in perfect stillness, whereas humans seem to be on a lifelong quest to figure out what to do with their hands.

I spent weeks practicing this when I was a newborn vamp, and I sometimes have to remind myself to blink, or twirl my hair, or pick at my fingernails to avoid looking as at ease inside my body as all vampires are.

"No, not at all. He was cold at first," I tell her, "but I think I've already melted a few layers of that glacial exterior." It's not as blatant a lie as the first, but I'd put it near the top of the fib category. Kyan has softened a bit since the first day, that's true, but it's clear to me and anyone with eyes that he doesn't want me here.

He gets impatient when I don't give top clients the VIP treatment when they call, not that I was ever given a list, so I'm trying to flag them as VIPs based on Kyan's reactions. And he got really mad when his brother Mylo called to say that Kyan had an overdue book at the library called *How to Make Friends When You're Dead Inside: A Survival Guide for the Hopelessly Unpleasant*—a joke that I found hilarious. Kyan, on the other hand, did not.

"If you get a call from Mylo, Zev, Axil, or Luka, you tell them I'm in a meeting," Kyan shouted the moment I ended that call. "My brothers are clueless dipshits. Their calls are never important, and their jokes are unoriginal and lazy. Don't let them waste your time or mine. Understand?"

I gritted my teeth through an apology and spent the rest of that day reminiscing about my former life as the one of the top surgeons at Madison Park Hospital, and the respect I commanded in that role. No one ever raised their voice to me. They wouldn't dare. My patients adored me, my colleagues appreciated me, and my hands were never idle. My hands performed hundreds of life-saving procedures.

Now they copyedit Kyan's emails, carry his lattes from the kitchen to his office, and shred each piece of paper that gets handed to him once I scan it and send him a digital copy.

The elevator dings once we reach the parking garage, and Thea gives my arm a gentle nudge. "He's glad you're here, I promise you that. He might never say the words, but he's needed someone like you for a long time."

The genuine kindness in her words surprises me. I'm not used to receiving compliments anymore. Most of the time, my presence seems like a nuisance to those around me. If only I could be Thea's assistant for however long this ruse is supposed to go on.

We say our goodbyes, and I send a prayer to Lillith that my car will start. It does after a few tries, but instead of listening to the radio on my commute home, I try identifying a clanking sound the car makes whenever I press my foot on the gas.

I maneuver my dying station wagon into the employee parking lot of the Dunkin' Donuts on the edge of Sudbury and park next to Quincy's bright yellow Jeep before going inside through the back entrance.

Brown folding chairs are set up in a circle in the back room, and Quincy is pouring blood into red plastic cups.

"Hey, Quince," I say, hanging my stuff on the coat rack next to the door. "How many are we expecting tonight?"

"Uh, I think it'll be the four of us again," he replies in a proud tone. Our Sipper Support Group started with just the two of us venting about our shitty lives, but over the last month, Quincy has recruited two new members. We have a secret Facebook group with over a thousand, but with the members scattered across the globe, most can't attend the in-person gatherings.

We're lucky to have the meetings here. The only reason we can is because Quincy owns this location and works the graveyard shift seven days a week. He has two human employees that work the day shift, but once the sun goes down, the coffee and donut orders drop dramatically, and Quincy hosts events like this in the backroom to fill up the time.

He doesn't seem to realize it, but Quincy is like a hug in vampire form. The man has a way of bringing people together and making even the loneliest vampire misfits among us feel seen. I'm not sure where I'd be without him.

I found him on Facebook not long after I moved here. When I realized he lived so close by, I begged Elaine to let me meet him. She agreed, but only because she was sick of me tagging along on their hunts and begging Wyatt to fill a cup with their victim's blood just so I didn't have to suck it out of them. I brought down the vibe, so she was eager to get rid of me.

"Can you add three more THC bags to my weekly haul?" I ask him as I grab my cup and take a seat.

He snickers. "Bad day at the new gig?"

"Eh, let's call it a bad decade. The day, the job, the pressure from Elaine…it's just a nonstop loop of despair."

"Damn, maybe it should be your turn to share tonight."

"I went last week. I'm not going to hog the spotlight. Besides, I think it's Frat Boy's turn. He hasn't gone yet."

A few minutes later, Frat Boy shows up, followed by Betsy, our other new member. Betsy is a surly Cuban woman who was turned by her granddaughter last year on her seventy-third birthday, because her granddaughter couldn't bear the thought of losing her. It was a thoughtless and selfish move. When you're turned, you remain eternally frozen in the same physical condition you were in on that day, so Betsy's back is constantly sore, her hands are tight balls of arthritis, and she has a smoker's cough that sounds like a snowblower. The idea of living forever in her current state terrifies her.

"Would you like to share with the group, Cody?" Quincy asks Frat Boy once he and Betsy are seated.

Cody runs a hand through his wavy brown hair and drops his blank stare to the contents of his cup. "Hi, everyone. I'm Cody."

He waits for us to reply, but when we don't, Quincy leans over and says, "It's okay, Cody. You don't have to introduce yourself every meeting since our group is so small."

Cody lets out a nervous chuckle before continuing. "Right. Well, I was turned six years ago, during my junior year at Dartmouth. Beta Theta Pi was having this massive rager, and I was drunk off my ass." His laughter returns, but with the softness of being wrapped in a happy memory. "It was sick. I was dominating the beer pong table. I mean, people were fighting over who got to play with me next. It was unreal." He takes a sip of blood, and his mouth forms a grim line. "For some reason, I went outside. Probably to take a piss. I don't know. But somehow, I ended up in the woods at the end of Fraternity Row, and there was this total smoke show in a tight silver dress leaning against a tree."

"What's a smoke show?" Betsy asks, way louder than necessary in such a small circle.

"Somebody who's extremely attractive," I tell her.

She nods and gestures for Cody to continue.

"So she's standing there in the woods, eye-fucking the hell outta me, her tits practically falling out of her dress. What was I supposed to do? Reject her? This was the hottest chick I had ever laid eyes on." Cody looks at each of us expectantly. I guess he's hoping for some bro-y assurance that following a woman you've never met into the woods is a perfectly rational decision to make. His face falls slightly when the three of us remain silent. "Anyway, we start making out and everything seems cool. Then I woke up in a pile of leaves, my clothes soaked with blood."

"That's horrific, Cody," Quincy says. "I'm sorry that happened to you."

"Wait, so you don't know your maker?" I ask, unable to mask my curiosity. "You never got her name?"

He shakes his head while keeping his eyes on the floor.

When I hear stories about vampires who don't have a connection to the one who turned them, I'm always a little jealous. Waking up as a freshly turned vamp is traumatizing, of course. You don't fully understand what you are, or what, if anything, can kill you, and how to get enough fresh blood down your throat to make the excruciating burning sensation stop. Having your maker there to explain the basics is key to keeping you from losing your mind.

When I woke up to find Xavier, he seemed eager to guide me through that difficult transition, but only after he drained every drop of blood from the young mother and newborn baby he had just killed. I refused to partake and spent the morning silently begging for death.

Cody seems like one of the lucky ones.

"I don't know who I am anymore," he continues, wiping his palms on his threadbare dark-wash jeans. "My future was pretty bright, you know? I thought I'd graduate, get a job on Wall Street, marry a yoga teacher or some shit, have a few kids, and spend the weekends barbecuing with my Delta Chi brothers."

Quincy nods, his hands folded in his lap, looking much more like a therapist than the owner of a Dunkin' Donuts. "I assume you left school after you were turned?"

"Yeah, even without my maker to guide me, I knew I couldn't stay there. I was different in a way that I wouldn't be able to hide, so it just seemed easier to leave." Cody crosses his arms over his chest. "It's not fair, man. I don't even like the taste of blood, to be honest. I only drink it because I have to. But I'm not about to bathe in the spray of a torn artery just to eat my fucking dinner. The whole lifestyle is so messy and gross. I'd give anything to have my old life back, drinking beer every night and going to class hungover the next morning. There, at Dartmouth, I fit in."

"If it makes you feel any better, we don't fit in either," I tell him, surprising myself by offering support. When I first laid eyes on Cody, with his whole date-rape-sponsored-by-Abercrombie vibe, I thought I'd find his trauma a source of entertainment. How much can a guy with that much baked-in privilege actually be suffering? But his life was turned upside down in the matter of a second, just like ours, and there's still a big part of him that wishes he could go back to the way things were. I know that struggle intimately. It would be easier for him to fit in with his new brethren if he drained his victims, and the fact that he hasn't, despite his obvious loneliness, blows my mind.

The reason why he chooses to sip versus drain doesn't matter. We all have different motives for choosing this lifestyle. And it's nobody's business how we consume blood, frankly, but a large percentage of the vampire community sees us as a joke. A weaker generation of immortal beings who won't make it to our hundredth fangiversary unless we grow a pair and start sucking humans dry like our ancestors.

It's such a silly argument, and all it does is put a deeper wedge between a group of people who have to remain so hidden that humans are convinced we don't exist.

Isn't this how we evolve as a species? We question the way things have always been done, we find better ways to do it, and life becomes easier for us as a whole. Future generations of vamps won't have to hide in dark alleys or ransack blood drive vans to avoid starvation if we can find other sources of sustenance.

Quincy is attempting to do just that by developing a type of synthetic blood that takes most of the individual components of human blood, plus freeze-dried plasma, and multiplying them in a cold, sterile environment.

Before becoming Kyan's assistant, I'd spend a couple days a week working with Quincy on the different blood formulations. I remember only bits and pieces from my rotation in hematology in medical school, so when I help Quincy, I mostly record data and clean the beakers. But I am starting to understand how he tracks the samples and how he determines whether it's a success or failure, so it's less intimidating than it was in the beginning.

As the meeting comes to a close, Cody and Betsy pack up their weekly blood orders from Quincy and head out.

"How are the new samples doing?" I ask. "Any progress?"

"Too soon to tell. I think I'll test them next week."

I pause. "Is that safe? I mean, what if it's not viable blood? You can't die on me, Quince. The Sipper community needs your chemist brain to find an alternative."

He shoots me the same lopsided smile that appears whenever I compliment him. "If it isn't viable, it'll be like eating human food, and I'll spend an hour puking my guts out. I suffered a lot worse just to see if I could still ingest chicken nuggets."

My stomach growls, despite the mention of vomit. "I think I miss human food more than I miss my parents. Is that horrible?" I'd swap my left breast for a bowl of my grandmother's mapo tofu, or the Louisiana chicken pasta from The Cheesecake Factory because that shit was gold.

"Nah. We're already damned. We can miss whatever we want."

"For real."

"Any fun plans tonight?" He asks as he hands me my heavy blood-filled cooler.

"I bought some peanuts from the vending machine at work, so while I suck down drug blood and watch *Grace and Frankie*, hopefully Felix will be beside me getting a year's worth of protein. You?"

"I'm here until six in the morning, but when I get off, I think I'm gonna have the best day's sleep I've ever had. Check it out," he leads me over to the fridge in the break room and shows me a tray of vials filled with blood with a large purple M on each cap.

"It's my new melatonin infusion. We'll see how it goes. If you don't hear from me over the weekend, it means I'm still asleep."

"Ooh, put me down for a case if it works."

We bump fists and say our goodbyes as I leave.

When I make it home, I change into my pajamas and settle into the thick cushions of the couch as I turn my little TV on. On the table to my right is my stainless-steel water bottle covered in pink unicorns and filled to the brim with weed blood. To my left is Felix and the circle of peanut crumbs surrounding his feet. I've just wrapped myself up in my oversized Sherpa blanket when I hear a frantic rapping on my door. I know who it is before I even open it.

"Hi, Elaine."

Her posture is rigid, and her expression is impatient as she glares at me. "Intel. Have any yet?"

I chew on the inside of my cheek as I figure out what to say. "Well," I begin, willing the tremble in my voice to vanish, "now that I'm settling into the role, I can foc—"

Before I can finish, Elaine grabs the front of my shirt and yanks me forward, causing me to trip over my feet and land in the dirt just outside my trailer. My knees connect with the frozen ground, sending a sharp pain radiating up my spine. I hear Felix letting out a frightened caw as Elaine digs her long artificial nails into my scalp and pulls me up by my hair. I yelp in anguish as I fight against her grip, but she's so much stronger than I am, so it's no use. She finally lets go and tosses a clump of my hair at me.

I raise my hands in surrender as I take two steps back, tears freezing against my cheeks as they fall. "I promise I'll have something for you by the end of next week," I stammer. "Just a l-little more time…please."

"Do you think I got you this job so you can hang around the water cooler with your coworkers?" she shouts, adjusting the mink stole around her shoulders and smoothing out the skirt of the evergreen velvet dress beneath. It's a look befitting a night on the town in a big city during the Roaring Twenties and doesn't make any sense here, but Elaine doesn't care. She was turned in 1921 and hasn't changed her wardrobe since. "You bring me intel, and I let you keep this shitty roof over your head. That was the deal."

"Yeah, yeah, I know," I reply, my hands still shaking.

She takes a step toward me and raises her arm. Instinctively, I flinch and duck my head, expecting her large pointy rings to leave cuts across my cheek like they did last time she hit me. When the slap doesn't come, I open my eyes to find her fingering her hair, carefully brushing back the few strands that fell out of place while she was tearing my hair out. "You have until the end of day tomorrow to get me some information on this guy. Something I can use. Burton is getting impatient."

That's a tall order, considering I haven't even been there a full week, but if I can learn something about him, something that no one else in the office knows, maybe it'll be enough to get her off my back for a week or two.

"Fine. Tomorrow."

She flashes her fangs at me before turning on her heel and strutting back to the house like a model on a runway.

My hand goes to the bald spot on the back of my head, and I hiss in pain when my finger brushes against the raw, exposed flesh. It'll be healed by morning, but that doesn't make it any less painful right now. Slamming the door shut behind me, I grab an ice pack from the freezer and heave myself onto the couch next to Felix. He hops into my lap and pokes me with his beak until I stroke his head.

Tonight, I ice my scalp and relax with my crow. Tomorrow, I find a skeleton in Kyan's closet.

CHAPTER 4

KYAN

"I do not recommend more injection until fever breaks," Yvonne says as we hover over one of my recruits, Rex. In his polar bear form, he performed exceptionally well in the training exercises last night, but once the adrenaline wore off, he shifted back and immediately collapsed on the mat.

"No shit," I reply in a clipped tone as I watch beads of sweat run down his neck. "What's the half-life for the *wrathenol* at this point? Forty-eight hours?"

Wrathenol is a substance Yvonne created using my DNA mixed with sodium metabisulfite and saline. The goal of these injections is to see if my ability to breathe fire can be passed to a non-draxilio. It took her three years of research and testing to create the formula, and we've finally reached the point of being able to test it on the members of the pack.

"Not that long," she says. "We bring down to thirty."

Though Yvonne's accent is thicker than Mylo's collection of vintage encyclopedias, I'm now able to understand her, most of the time, without asking her to repeat herself. I don't have a clue where she's from, and the few times I've asked, she's given me different answers. What I do know is that she's a medical doctor whose license was suspended due to insurance fraud. Her background is in overseeing clinical trials, and I knew if I paid her enough, she'd be discreet about what I'm trying to achieve here.

"Give him a seventy-two-hour break. I don't just want the fever to break before we give him another. I want him rested and strong." I pat Rex on the arm. "Take it easy, Rex."

I hate seeing them suffer just to determine if the *wrathenol* is effective, but I have to remind myself that this is part of the process. They volunteered for this job, and I'm paying each of them handsomely to endure any and all side effects, but it still conjures memories of life inside the laboratory on Sufoi.

Yvonne nods and puts a second bottle of Gatorade on Rex's bedside table. "Yes, I keep in recovery."

We leave the dormitory, passing the shared kitchen where most of the men are eating breakfast, and head into the lab. I make sure it's empty before I pull out my phone. "I'm going to give you access to my financial accounts, as well as a document with specific instructions on what to do if I go missing."

"Missing?" Yvonne's makeup-smudged eyes widen in fear. "Why you go missing?"

"I'm not saying it's inevitable, but it could happen. There aren't many people I trust, and if the work we're doing here gets out, I'm bound to make some enemies. Powerful enemies who will steal our research and leave me for dead. There needs to be a protocol in place for you and Andrei to protect my assets and shut everything down within minutes."

"What about brothers?"

I let out a heavy sigh. It's not that I don't trust my brothers. Given what we've survived, there's no one else on this planet that I should trust more than those four idiots, but trust isn't what connects me and them at the moment. They're too distracted by their new mates and growing families to handle something this delicate, this time sensitive. It's no longer just the four of us. When it was, I could count on them in an emergency.

We grew up in a laboratory on Sufoi, the same lab in which we were genetically modified to become ruthless killers. Our only parental figures were the handlers charged with overseeing our modifications, our births, and our physical development until we were old enough to fight. They were cold, callous beings—always demanding more when we did something right and beating us senseless when we did something wrong. Sticking together was a necessity for me and my brothers in the lab. It ensured our survival.

I'm not a priority for them anymore though. Perhaps I never was. I'm the only one who didn't want to leave our home planet. Working as one of the king's assassins was a job I excelled at. The fury I was able to express with each kill brought me a sense of peace. It settled me.

My brothers have deep scars from our time on Sufoi. They would say I have them too, but I have yet to uncover them. Maybe I'm emotionally stronger than they are, or I have so much emotional damage that I'm beyond the place where help can reach. What I do know is that their kills still haunt them at night and mine don't. That feels like superior strength to me.

"You can alert them if I go missing, but they can't have access to this information," I tell Yvonne. "I'm dropping the file into our shared folder. If forty-eight hours go by, and you don't hear from me, you need to assume I've been kidnapped, okay? The code for this protocol is Key. Got it?"

She opens the shared folder on her laptop and scans the document. "Yes, code Key. I got."

My gaze drifts to the clock in the top right corner of her screen and I stifle a gasp. "Fuck, it's almost eight. The staff will start showing up soon. I need to get upstairs. Let me know if anything changes with our feverish recruit."

"Yes, yes," she says with a shooing motion.

I race down the utility hallway and slide into the secret elevator that opens directly into my private office bathroom. Then I scramble to splash my face with water and change into a fresh shirt, tie, and pants so it doesn't look like I've been here all fucking night.

When I step into my office, I find Naomi waiting for me, an impatient look on her face. "Where'd you come from? I was banging on the bathroom door for five minutes. Were you asleep in there?"

I knew it was a good idea to keep my bathroom locked. Thea found it peculiar, but it just saved my ass. "Did you knock?" I reply, feigning innocence. "I didn't hear you."

"The CEO from Langford House got here early and has been waiting for you in the conference room. I brought him and his assistant coffee. They barely acknowledged my existence. Are they assholes? They seem like it." Her foot starts tapping. I have no idea why she's so chatty this morning, but I find it irritating. "Are you prepped for the meeting? I went over the slides so many times, I think I have the presentation memorized at this point."

"Of course I'm prepped."

Her gaze narrows, as if she can see right through me, but I ignore it as I stride past her toward the conference room. Now is not the time to let a lowly assistant get inside my head and make me second guess whether I can handle my shit. I've been handling it on my own for years.

"Tom, good to see you." I shake his hand and give a quick nod to his assistant before I take my seat at the head of the long marble table. "Apologies for keeping you waiting. How was your flight?"

He chuckles as he strokes the length of his tie. "I didn't come from Manhattan to this backwater shithole to talk about turbulence and peanuts."

I'm surprised he didn't fly private on the fancy jet he purchased to overcompensate for his floppy dick, but whatever. Let him mock New Hampshire. What do I care?

"Certainly," I begin, gesturing for Naomi to fire up the pitch deck so I can begin my presentation. Once I deliver the overview, my VP of Sales will step in and take it the rest of the way, and I can hide out in my office until the workday ends. "Based on the rapid growth of Langford House over the last two years, you and your team need more than your basic email marketing software. We've been handling accounts like yours, with dozens of brands to oversee, for a long time, and you won't find another company out there with the same client retention as ours. When we promise something, we deliver. I know we can take the brands you own and implement a streamlined strategy that's easy for your staff to use and is so engaging, it'll jumpstart the growth you've established."

Tom scratches the neatly trimmed silver hair on his chin as he stares at me, looking bored. I continue going through the slides, but with each piece of data I share, he edges closer to falling asleep sitting up.

The heat kicks on, and warm air blasts us from the vents above. Out of the corner of my eye, I see the ends of Naomi's straight black hair lift off her shoulders and blow around her angular face. I wait for the scent of her to reach me, but it never does. It's then that I remember she has no detectable scent, and I find myself baffled by it all over again.

It doesn't make sense. Even Rex, a polar-bear shifter from northern Alaska, had the strong odor of a sweaty, feverish human as he tossed and turned in his bunk. Why does Naomi continue to smell of nothing?

I hear Tom mutter something quietly, but I can't take my focus off Naomi and her maddening lack of aroma. Why is she so odd?

She always carries that pink bottle in her hands, but I've yet to see her eat solid food. Could she be on a liquid diet of some kind? I suppose it's possible. I learned very quickly from Vanessa that the food trends of humans are often nonsensical and toxic, so I don't pay attention to the latest fads.

Tom continues to speak, his voice getting louder, but it isn't until Naomi gives me a strange, wide-eyed look that I snap out of my trance.

"My apologies, what was that?" I ask Tom.

He rolls his eyes and his assistant chuckles before he says, "Is this how you treat your top clients? Because if it is, I'm out." He gets to his feet, shaking his head in disgust. "You know, I've been talking to Markus at Excelsior Media Operations, and not only are his prices lower than yours, but he actually pays attention to the people he's trying to work with."

Fuck, I'm blowing this. My mind is fuzzy from lack of sleep, and I'm about to destroy the deal it's taken me over a year to set up. "Wait, Tom," I say, rushing to his side. "Allow me to explain."

Tom huffs a breath as he shoves his hands in his pockets, waiting for me to continue, but I've got nothing. My mouth falls open, and I silently urge a string of coherent words to come out, but they don't. Naomi rushes over with a jug of water and trips over Tom's foot, sending a big splash of water down my front.

"For fuck's sake," Tom says, staring at Naomi like she's a rodent about to run over his expensive shoe.

"Oh my god! I'm so sorry." She puts the jug on the credenza and heaves a pile of cloth napkins at me. "Please forgive me, Mr. Langford," she says to Tom, even though none of the water reached him. "This is my fault. The spill and, and the lack of respect you're feeling right now." Her small hand grips the sleeve of my shirt as she pulls me toward the door. "I accidentally deleted this very presentation yesterday, so Mr. Monroe was up all night working on it."

What's happening? Why is she lying?

"He had to start from scratch and wouldn't settle for less than perfection for you. Let me get another shirt for Mr. Monroe, and we'll be right back. Please don't leave."

Tom sighs heavily as he stomps back to his seat. Naomi continues dragging me to my office and doesn't say a word until my door is closed.

"Okay, you need to get your shit together," she scolds. "Where is your head today?" She looks around the room. "You have extra shirts here, right? Where do you keep them?"

I'm caught off guard by her tone and the ruse she created to get me out of that meeting when it was clear I was floundering. "How do you know I have extra shirts here?" It's not the first question I wanted to ask, but those are the only words that came out.

Naomi starts going through the file cabinets along the wall, shoving papers around and digging through each drawer. "Because you seem like one of those guys. Am I wrong?"

"No," I admit, slightly embarrassed that she has such a clear picture of me. I pride myself on maintaining an air of mystery. "The closet next to the bathroom. Second drawer down."

I unbutton the shirt I have on and peel the soaked fabric down my arms before tossing it to the floor. I'm lucky the water only hit my top half. Though it went through the undershirt I have on too. "Grab me an undershirt too, please. A white one," I tell her as I walk into the bathroom and remove my t-shirt. I splash water on my face in an attempt to wake myself the fuck up before I go back into that conference room. Tom's patience is gone, and I have one more shot to impress him.

Naomi gasps from behind me, and in the mirror, I watch her drop my shirts on the floor while her eyes remained locked on my bare chest, widening in innate approval as she takes me in. "I'm sorry, I, uh, didn't realize you were undressed in here. How inappropriate of me." She scrambles to pick up my shirts and tosses them at me before racing out of the bathroom with bright red cheeks. "Sorry!"

A smile tugs at my lips following her quick exit. The heated look in her eyes...I put it there. She was frazzled and flushed because of me. I don't know what to do with this information; I just know that it pleases me.

Perhaps that makes me a deviant, knowing my subordinate appreciates my body. It's entirely inappropriate for a professional setting, but I can't help the way I feel. The longing in her gaze coupled with the way she scolded me the moment we were alone, makes my cock ache with need. I can't let these thoughts continue though. She is my employee, and I'm her boss. We could never be anything more.

I finish getting dressed and find Naomi rubbing her temples as she leans on the edge of my desk. When I clear my throat, she straightens and rushes over. "I'm so sor—"

"What were you saying before you retrieved my spare shirt?" I ask, eager to remove the awkward tension between us. We don't have time to waste. "That I need to get my shit together?"

"Oh, yeah," she replies, biting into her bottom lip as if she regrets her words. I hope that's not the case. I wanted more of her fire. "Why are you letting that creepy bastard talk to you like that? He'd be lucky to sign with us. I saw the projections on your deck. Sure, they've had some impressive growth, but it's nothing compared to what it could be if he became our client. And Excelsior isn't even a competitor. The company is made up of three developers and an accountant. That's like saying a goldfish and a shark are competitors. It's bullshit. He should be grateful you're interested in working with him at all."

Her ardent support leaves me speechless. It's her first week here, how could she care so much this soon? Perhaps this is her nature, and whatever she does, she does it with every bone in her body, regardless of wage or title. It's an admirable quality, but I don't consider myself worthy of such devotion. Yet I can't deny the power of her praise. Suddenly, I'm greedy for it, but she can never know that. "Is that why you intentionally spilled the water on me?"

Naomi scrunches up her nose in a way that makes my stomach flip. "Was it that obvious?"

A chuckle escapes me as I nod. "Very."

Her cheeks turn a deep crimson as she lets out a low chuckle of her own. "Damn, I thought I nailed that."

She kept Tom from leaving and lifted my confidence. It's not the path I would've taken to get there, but it worked. "You did."

Naomi's gaze lifts to meet mine, and she offers me a shy smile. Does she never receive compliments from those around her? How could that be? She's a spectacular and clever human, better than most I've met, better than most who exist, I'm sure.

I run a hand through my hair, making sure it's still gelled back the way I like it, and gesture toward the door. "Shall we?"

Naomi leads the way back to the conference room, and I enter as if the previous portion of the meeting never occurred. Tom makes a joke about the spill, but I ignore it as I revisit the key data points from the deck that I know Tom cares about. He responds to arrogance, and that's what I give him. Members of my team present their portions of the deck, and we negotiate the terms of the contract. Tom comes in low, as expected, but we settle on a three-year deal without offering to lower the prices a single cent.

The rest of the day goes by painfully slowly. I expect the thrill of the deal to provide enough energy to get me through the afternoon, but after an hour of staring at the back of Naomi's head through the glass wall of my office, my eyelids grow heavy, and I want nothing more than to climb into bed until Monday.

My staff scuttles out of the office just before five o'clock, as is typical on a Friday, and once the last person exits the office, I head down to the basement to check on Rex.

"How is he?" I ask Yvonne once I enter the lab. "Improving, I hope."

"Yes, yes, much improvement," she says, carefully pouring a lime-green liquid into a beaker. "He begs to train, but I tell him no. Must wait."

"He wants to train? So soon? That's a good sign."

She nods. "Yes, half-life getting shorter."

"I'll go see him."

I find Rex sitting on his bed sideways, reading a book of poetry. His face brightens when he sees me. "Hey, boss," he drops the book in his lap and holds his arms out. "My fever is gone, and I'm feeling fantastic. Can I get back out there?"

I pull a chair over to the bed and pat him on the leg as I sit down. "I'm afraid not. I need you to take it easy for another day. I want to be sure the *wrathenol* has left your system, and you won't have further setbacks. Are you okay with that?"

His face falls. "Of course. It's your call. I'm just eager to hone my skills. I want to make sure I'm in top form for when the day comes."

Rex recently turned twenty-five, and he has the stamina of a spry young male, with the tenacity to match. He reminds me of a much, much younger version of myself, when we were first appointed to serve as the king's assassins. I had to be dragged from battle and felt too much time passed from one to the next. My body wanted nothing more than to fight until my combatants lay limp beside me. It was what I was made to do.

"I know, and you will be. Your muscles can't grow without rest. Give them what they need. The day will come soon enough."

"Yes, sir."

I change into a loose pair of shorts and a t-shirt in the locker room and meet the rest of the men in the large training room with mats covering the floor. I lead them through a series of sparring exercises while Yvonne sits off to the side taking notes on her tablet. Once the exercises are over and we're dripping with sweat, she leads the men to the side of the room, giving *wrathenol* injections to two of them.

"Once your bodies fully adjust to the *wrathenol*, there's no limit to what you can do, or the ways you can destroy the enemy who stands before you," I explain, stepping into the middle of the room, where I have the most room to shift into my draxilio. "Particularly with the addition of your fire. It doesn't matter what kind of animal you can shift into, or the physical limitations of being in that other form. Jaguar shifters, polar bears, werewolves, and snakes—you will all have the ability to unleash a ball of fire from the depths of your throat onto your target, and you'll be able to control the shape and mass of your flames using just your mind. Allow me to demonstrate."

My chest grows warm as I picture my draxilio and let him come forth. He is a dark, twisted creature of few words, and I've been able to restrict him to the deepest corners of my mind, but when I let him out, he cherishes the freedom.

We've developed a sort of understanding and trust between us since we first landed on this planet. I'm seldom interrupted by his thoughts, so long as I accept the parts of myself that long to kill. I spent years denying it, knowing my vicious nature has no place here. But the more I rejected this part of me, and him, the louder his voice became. He would scream at me through the night to flee, to find a victim and snuff the life out of them. I ignored him, much to my own detriment.

It wasn't until I found my true purpose here on Earth that I finally found peace inside my own head. Creating this space, assembling this crew, and giving them the tools to fight against the most evil creatures this land has to offer has settled my draxilio. He knows we are working toward something grand, and now he lets me sleep.

One by one, my bones begin to snap with the shift, my fingernails growing into sharp claws, and my skin tightening and expanding into blue scales. My horns almost brush the top of the ceiling, so I duck once the shift is complete and lumber over to the training dummies set up on the far wall.

My draxilio, now the dominant occupant of the body we share, purrs with delight. For the first target, I release a standard ball of fire. This takes very little effort, as it's the easiest to form. The target instantly becomes engulfed, but the nonflammable materials used quickly reduce the flame to a low flicker until it dies. For the second target, I take a deep inhale, and a shallow, low exhale, which forms a thin, straight line of fire. This is ideal for blocking an opponent's approach or burning several opponents using a single breath. The third and final target will be the recipient of my favorite technique. A deep inhale followed by a series of short exhales creates smaller balls of fire that can be shot from the mouth by creating a tight O shape with my lips and this has the same effect as bullets. One shot might not kill the opponent, but with enough of them, and fired to the right places on the body, it will stop their heart.

I explain all of this to my crew upon shifting back into my flightless form, and I'm met with a round of applause. The men hoot and holler their excitement to someday mimic my actions here, and pride surges within me at the thought of seeing that progression.

After we go through a few more exercises, carefully measuring the vitals of those on *wrathenol*, I change back into my business attire and make my way down the utility hallway and through the hidden door into the empty front office. Andrei's shift monitoring reported UFO sightings is long over, and I assume he's retired to the small, one-bedroom apartment I had built for him on the other side of the office.

Before I reach the door that leads to the parking garage, I hear a strange clinking sound. Puzzled, I slow my steps, trying to find the source. It's an uneven rustling of metal against metal, and I worry that rats have burrowed their way into my walls, creating a colony that will soon breach my private basement quarters. Then I see the subtle movement of the door handle as it moves up and down.

Someone is trying to break in. But why? And who? None of my employees even know I own the space down here.

Rage shoots through my veins as I watch the locked handle's stunted jiggle. This invasion is unacceptable and will not end well for the person on the other side. Wrapping my fingers around the handle, I yank it open, prepared to obliterate the criminal in a number of twisted ways, but what I find leaves me shocked and utterly confused.

"Naomi? What are you doing here?"

CHAPTER 5

NAOMI

"Oh! Oh, Kyan. Hello," I stammer as blood rushes to my cheeks in embarrassment. How long can I stall until a plausible excuse for why I'm snooping around the parking garage pops into my head? "I, uh, I..." *Think, damn it. Think!*

Although, the very fact that he's on the other side of this door tells me there's something extremely important he's hiding, and if I want to keep my life quiet and boring and free of Xavier, I need to figure out what that is.

"It's a funny story, actually," I continue, still without a clue of what to say in order to save my ass. "My, um, my car wouldn't start, so I called my um, my roommates..." I almost said cell mates. Yikes. "But then I remembered they're out of town for the night, so I thought maybe there were some tools in this utility closet to help me get the car running. I don't have much experience with car repair, but I figured there would be jumper cables lying around in here." I suppose that's a good enough cover, and maybe if I really lean into the utility closet thing, I can take a peek. "Do you see any around here?" I ask, craning my neck around him to look into the drab, beige space with a few desks and minimal other furniture. Kyan immediately blocks my view by stepping forward and closing the door behind him.

Then he crosses his arms over the wide expanse of his chest and stares at me expectantly. "Should I still be waiting for the funny part of the story? Or has it passed me by?"

"Touché," I say with a grin. "It wasn't as funny as I thought it was."

"This is not a utility closet, I'm afraid," he says, hurriedly pulling a set of brass keys from his pocket and locking the handle. "Even if it were, I don't think jumper cables are a staple found in most utility closets."

"If it's not a utility closet, what is it?"

Kyan clears his throat and starts walking toward his car. "What's that?" he replies over his shoulder. He's deliberately avoiding my question.

I jog to catch up with him. "If it's not a closet, what is it?"

"Just some empty offices I'm looking to rent out," he mutters in a nonchalant tone. "Is this your car over here?" He points to the hideous station wagon in the corner spot that looks like it's begging to be driven off a cliff.

"Yep," I say with a sigh as we move further away from the secret I'm desperate to uncover, "that's the one." An idea wiggles its way to the front of my brain, and I have to hide my smile. "You know, if you need help renting out those offices, I have experience." What am I, a realtor now? I don't have experience in commercial rentals, but I also don't have experience in being an assistant, so whatever. I'm sitting on a heaping pile of lies at this point.

Kyan sticks out his hand, and I place my car keys in his palm. Rather than respond to my offer, he remains silent as he opens the door and gets in behind the wheel. It emits a pitiful wheezing sound from the engine as Kyan starts it up and quickly spits out a plume of smoke before it craps out. Hesitantly, my boss climbs out of the car and waves the smoke away before popping the hood. His brow furrows as he looks around, then throws up his hands. "I have no idea what I'm looking at. Apologies, Naomi. This isn't my area of expertise."

I can't help but chuckle at his refreshing honesty. He approached the situation like a typical guy but, knowing he's clueless about cars, didn't even bother poking around before admitting defeat.

"I will take you home," he says, gesturing for me to follow. "My car is this way."

"That's kind of you, but totally unnecessary. I can call an Uber."

He grunts in a dismissive way. "Nonsense. Come with me."

Kyan drives a sleek dark gray Mercedes SUV, and an appreciative moan escapes me when I settle into the heated leather seat. "This is gorgeous."

He smirks. "Yes, it is."

After a few moments of surprisingly comfortable silence, he pulls up Spotify on the large digital screen between us and turns on a playlist called 'lo-fi chill.' "Where do you live?" he asks, opening the Maps app.

"On the northeastern border of Sudbury. A stone's throw away from Loudon."

His mouth drops open. "Sudbury? That's where I live. How is it possible that we haven't run into each other around town?"

"I don't get out much," I reply with a shy chuckle. If only he knew it's because I'm not allowed to mingle with the living. "You know that part of town with the power plant and the abandoned textile mill?"

He nods without taking his eyes off the road.

"That's where I live. It's not the prettiest."

"Pretty isn't a word I'd use to describe any part of Sudbury."

"No?" I ask, surprised. "Do you prefer the hustle and bustle of city life?"

His mouth forms a grim line. "No. Manchester is also a dump, in my opinion."

Huh. "Then what's your ideal place? Where would you settle down if you could? If nothing were keeping you here."

I watch his gaze go unfocused as he ponders this, and his jaw tightens. "I don't think such a place exists for me."

That can't be true. If I weren't a danger to society, I'd return to Seattle in a heartbeat. I miss the cold weather, the incredible food, the proximity to Puget Sound, and most of all, my family. I'd give anything to go back to that life.

"There's gotta be some place. Maybe you've only seen it in photos, but a place that has all the beauty and tranquility that you could never find here. Where would that be?"

He lets out a weary sigh. "My mind requires more than a tranquil setting to soften its harsh edges."

Sheesh. Forget small talk. What am I supposed to say to that?

Instead of prodding him with additional fun get-to-know-you questions that he'll no doubt put a dark, dreary spin on, I lean my head against the window and watch the sleet fall from the sky.

I have to figure out what I'm going to tell Elaine. Kyan has given me nothing that she'll find useful or interesting. He's hiding something behind that door, but the door itself isn't enough to give her. I've tried so hard all damn day to get him to crack, and the most I got was an eyeful of his swirling chest tattoos and his twelve-pack abs. I'm so fucked. Luckily, she and the guys went down to UNH to hunt frat boys for the night, so I won't have to face her until tomorrow, but when that moment comes, it's going to be brutal. I don't even want to think about how much hair she's going to rip out of my scalp.

Kyan pulls off the highway, and I notice the tension in his neck and jaw as he navigates the slick back roads to Sudbury. Is this just who he is, or is he going through a tough time? I can't tell.

I guide him toward my section of town, and as we're pulling into the driveway, I decide to give it one last shot. "Thanks for the ride. If you're not busy, want to come in for a bit?" I say, more nervous than I thought I'd be. "I baked some mango weed cupcakes that need to get eaten, and you look like you could use a break from reality."

I expect him to decline my invitation, even mock me, perhaps, for the recreational drug use. Instead, he offers me a brilliant smile, and says, "You know what, Naomi? That sounds delightful."

"Oh, o-okay. Great," I stammer, racing around the car with my bag and blood bottle in hand. "Give me a sec? I wasn't expecting guests, so I just need to tidy a bit."

I hear Kyan say, "Uh, sure," as I hustle inside.

It's not like I'm a messy person, per se, but I'm also not what most would consider clean. Most nights, I clean up Felix's pile of crumbs off the couch, toss the empty blood bags into the trash, and put my dirty laundry in the hamper. Last night, however, I got so high after Elaine attacked me that I left shit on every surface.

Once my underwear is in the hamper and safely out of sight and I refill my bottle with THC-laced blood, I open the front door and invite Kyan in.

As soon as he steps inside, he looks completely out of place. He has to duck his head to avoid smacking it on the ceiling, and his broad shoulders take up half the width of my trailer. "This is where you live?" he asks, scanning the scene. I can tell he's trying not to sound judgmental, but he's failing. "I thought we'd be going into the house. Is that not yours?"

"No, that's where my roommates live. This little piece of paradise is all mine."

One of his eyebrows lifts. "How can you have roommates who don't live under the same roof?"

I take a long pull from my bottle and feel the weed settling into my bloodstream. Shrugging, I reply, "I don't make the rules, boss." Eager to shift the conversation away from Elaine and her cronies, I pull the tray of cupcakes from the pantry and take the tin foil off. "Care for a treat?"

It doesn't matter that I can't eat human food, I still love to bake. Before I was turned, I got pretty good at it, and now, when I'm stressed, baking eases my mind. Usually, I'll drop off my goodies at Dunkin' Donuts for Quincy's human employees to take home. It'll be nice to see someone enjoy my treats for once.

Kyan's eyes light up like a little boy's, and he takes two. When he sees me re-cover the cupcakes, he asks with a full mouth, "Aren't you going to have one?"

I shake my head. "Not just yet," I lie. "Enjoy them. I'm going to change real quick."

There's no way I can truly relax until this business casual outfit is off my body and my hair is tied into a low pony. I pull shut the curtains that separate my bedroom from the rest of the trailer and make quick work of getting into my teal sweatpants and black hoodie. Once my hair is off my face, I rejoin Kyan in the kitchen/dining/living room area and find him pulling a third and fourth cupcake from the tin.

"Aren't they yummy?" I ask with a proud grin, wishing I could partake. "My mom taught me how to make mango sago from an old family recipe, so I spent years figuring out how to get the texture just right, like rice pudding. Once I nailed that, boom. Mango cupcakes with a buttercream frosting and gooey mango center."

"This is exquisite. I've never tasted anything like it." His eyes are pinched shut, and he lets out a groan as he chews. It's a low and gravelly sound that makes me clench my thighs together.

My emotions are warring within me as my head grows fuzzy from the weed. I'm jealous he has the ability to eat human food, and I'm moderately turned on by the sight of him eating. Having no idea what to do with any of those feelings, I drink more weed blood.

Time starts to slow way down, and at some point, I turn on old episodes of *Veep*. Kyan laughs the loudest when Selina exhibits disgust or animosity toward others, which is most of the show, so he seems to be having a good time.

I discreetly refill my bottle behind the open fridge door and grab Kyan his fifth cupcake on my way back to the couch. He doesn't seem to notice my lack of interest in them, which is a relief. In fact, I think he's glad he gets them all to himself. Once I'm seated next to him, a loud tapping sound against the kitchen window makes Kyan jump, and he glares at Felix with wide eyes as I let him in.

"Don't be scared," I say, stroking the back of the crow's head. "This is Felix. He's one of the best friends I've got here."

"What about your roommates?" Kyan asks, watching Felix intently, as if readying himself to be pecked to death by the little guy.

"Ugh, they hate me," I tell him, grabbing a handful of peanuts from the jar and putting them on the couch cushion between us. As Felix eats, I continue rambling. "Well, Elaine hates me. Mike tolerates me, at best. It depends on Elaine's mood. He tends to follow her lead." I tuck my feet beneath me on the couch and take another sip. "Then there's Wyatt, the third member of our cell. He's the nicest, but that's because we used to hook up occasionally."

A flicker of rage darkens Kyan's eyes at the mention of Wyatt but passes quickly as a look of confusion takes its place. "Your cell?"

"Yeah, that's what it's called when a small group of vampires live together."

I don't realize the words have left my mouth until I watch the way Kyan's face changes. It happens in slow motion. At least, that's how it looks to me, but that has to be the drugs. His head jerks back in disbelief, then there's a furrow of his brow, and finally, his brows shoot up as the words settle in. "Did you say...*vampires?*"

My mouth falls open as I sit there, trying to figure out how to respond. At some point, I decide that my brain feels like it's bending itself into a pretzel, and I prefer the aftermath of the truth to spending another minute in a state of panic. "Uh-huh," is all I can muster. Then I start laughing. It begins as a soft giggle and quickly spirals into a maniacal cackle that shakes my entire body.

"Is this funny to you?" Kyan shouts as he gets to his feet. "Some kind of sick joke?"

I have no idea why he's so offended by my admission, or why he doesn't think this is as funny as I do, because, from where I'm sitting, this shit is hilarious. I'm getting high with my gorgeous, wealthy boss inside a trailer that's one storm away from collapsing in on itself while a crow eats peanuts on the couch, and he just realized that I'm technically dead. How is he *not* laughing?

"You know what? I'm done with this," he says, pulling his jacket on in a huff. "Goodnight, Naomi."

"No, wait!" I call out, my mouth still forming a smile as his palpable anger registers in my brain. "It's okay, Kyan. Really. I wasn't planning on telling you that tonight, but I don't know. It just came out, and now you know."

His hand stills on the doorknob. "You're telling me the truth?" He turns, the muscles in his jaw flexing in a way that has me mesmerized. "You're a vampire?"

Shit. What if he fires me because of this? I didn't disclose it in my new-hire forms. If I get fired before I learn what he's keeping in that basement, Elaine is going to skewer me. "Yeah, but, it's not like it's a big deal," I say, playing it off as if I was just asked if I had a religious upbringing. "It doesn't impact me as much as you'd think."

He grunts in disappointment, and my breath lodges in my throat.

Maybe if I make him see we aren't so different, he won't fire me. "You're not human either. Both of us have to hide. We have that in common."

His shoulders tense, but I barely register the movement before his hot breath fans my cheek, and his hand is wrapped around my throat. "What the fuck did you say?"

CHAPTER 6

KYAN

This has to be a hallucination. A drug-induced delirium that's causing me to see and hear things that aren't there. Why else would there be a crow in here watching TV? None of this is real, and Naomi has no idea what I truly am.

The beat of my heart is loud and chaotic as I look down at Naomi. There is such intense fear in her eyes. Fear that I created. I hate myself for that. As my grip around her long, delicate neck loosens, Naomi brings her arm over mine and drives her elbow into my forearm, causing me to let go completely. Her movements are much faster than I anticipated, and her shape becomes a blur as she breaks free. I stumble backward, but not before Naomi sends her fist into my crotch.

Searing pain shoots through my body as I double over and fall to my knees. This is a greater pain than I have ever experienced, and on more than one occasion, my scales were slowly burned off my body during battles on Sufoi. I would trade this pain for that in an instant if I could.

How did that tiny vampire best me? It doesn't make sense.

"N-not a hallu…hallucination," I groan as I press my forehead against the cool linoleum floor. I wait for Naomi and her mystical undead strength to land another blow, but instead, she places an ice pack on the floor next to my head.

"For your balls," she says, "or the tip. I don't know which part took the brunt of my punch."

I whimper as I take the ice pack in hand and slowly inch backward and wiggle myself into a seated position against the wall next to the couch. Pressing the ice against my cock instantly provides relief, and I sit there with my eyes half-open as I wait for the pain to fade. Naomi takes a seat at the small round table beside the fridge and places her chin in her hands as she watches me. There's no malice in her gaze, however. If anything, there's remorse, which I find odd.

"Sorry about that," she says, confirming my suspicions. "It's crazy because I'm not even that strong of a vampire yet, since I'm so young. But the elbow thing is a self-defense move I learned before I was turned, and the superhuman speed certainly helped."

"Tell me," I mutter through gritted teeth. There's an endless list of questions I wish to ask, but those two words are all I can get out at the moment.

"About what?" she replies. "How I know you're not human?"

I nod.

"Easy. You don't smell human, and I have no desire to kill you or suck your blood. I've only felt that way around other vampires, and I knew you weren't one of us. But it was also obvious you weren't one of them."

"Obvious?" How the fuck was it obvious? I'm insulted. My brothers and I have spent more than a decade trying to blend in among the pale, flannel-covered beings of central New Hampshire, and Naomi could detect my otherness the moment we met?

"Yeah," she says with a chuckle. "Well, obvious to me."

I grunt in discomfort as I adjust the ice pack and shift my position against the wall. "Explain."

"Just little things," she begins. "Your stillness, for one.

Humans are always scratching or stretching or shifting their bodies. They can't remain still for more than a handful of seconds, but you can. I've seen it. And whenever I notice you being unnaturally still, it's a reminder that I need to move more so that I don't stand out. It's a skill I'm still working on."

I suppose stillness is not such a drastic tell. Luckily, humans are such self-absorbed creatures that I doubt any of them would notice me being still for too long. They are far more concerned with how they are perceived by others than they are with what others are doing.

"What else?"

"Um, lemme think." She drums her fingers against her cheek as she takes a sip from her bottle. I've never seen her without that bottle in hand, come to think of it. She brings it into meetings, she drinks from it on video calls, and it's always on her desk. A bottle that surely has blood in it, I now realize. "Oh! You don't sneeze in the sunlight. That's how I knew you weren't a vampire."

"What?" It's such a bizarre observation, I'm not sure where to begin. "You sneeze in the sunlight?"

"Yeah. It's a mild allergy. Some of us have it worse than others, but none have died from exposure to sunlight in over a century. That's one of the many aspects of our lifestyle that fiction authors continuously get wrong. Haven't you noticed that I wear that big hat into the office on sunny days?"

"I've seen your hat, yes, but I thought nothing of you wearing it into work." Why would that be something I would notice or care about? It's a hat, not a shield of armor, although, I suppose that's what it is for her. Now that she mentions it, I have seen people sneeze in the daylight upon looking at the sun. I thought it was an innocent human quirk. "You're telling me that everyone who sneezes because of the sun is a vampire?"

"Yep." She laughs, then lowers her voice to a conspiratorial whisper, "We're everywhere."

I suck in a breath as a nagging thought pops into my head. "Wait, is that why you have no scent?"

She nods. "We don't sweat. Our hearts don't beat. Physically, we're frozen in time and will forever look the way we did when we were turned. My hair will never grow longer than this, and I'll never get my period again, or form wrinkles. We're technically dead, but still alive. It's weird."

"Your lack of scent did baffle me."

"Does it bother you?"

"Not at all. I appreciate it, actually."

"I get that. Humans are so foul, aren't they?"

"Yes!" I shout in agreement, relieved that someone finally understands. "Why do they have such strong odors? And why do they add even more artificial scents to cover their natural ones? It doesn't work. It just creates multiple layers of rank."

"Oh my god, I know. Like Beverly from accounting? How awful is her perfume?"

Beverly is precisely who I was picturing when I mentioned artificial scents. No one smells worse than Beverly. "I'd prefer a decaying corpse beneath the hot sun to her perfume. Does she have a faulty nasal passage? How can she not know how offensive it is?"

Naomi throws back her head and laughs. "It's so bad. Or what about Jeremy, Thea's assistant? There's the pine-scented deodorant that he must put all over his body, and the beachy cologne he clearly pours on himself every morning."

"He has worked for Thea for six years, and not once has she mentioned it to me. I don't understand it. I wouldn't be able to breathe."

"I appreciate the effort in trying to smell good," Naomi adds. "But, bro, that is too much. This is an office, not a club in Miami."

"Then there are the rare good-smelling humans like Clyde, the maintenance supervisor. He always smells like apple cider. I believe he makes it himself."

"Really?" Her eyes light up at that. "I haven't met Clyde yet. I'll have to track him down just to get a whiff."

She offers me the last mango cupcake, and it's then that I realize my high is gone. I'm not looking to return to the state of awe that held me firmly in its grasp before, though it was quite fun, but my stomach is reminding me that I haven't had dinner, and nothing sounds more appetizing than another one of her cupcakes.

"Mm," I groan in pleasure upon my first bite. The burst of tangy fruit on my tongue is a welcome distraction from the throbbing pain of my bruised cock, and I have to urge myself to take smaller bites to make it last.

I now realize this is why I've never seen her eat. Because she doesn't.

"So what are you, boss?" Naomi asks, a sly expression on her face. "I showed you mine…" She opens her mouth, and I watch as her teeth lengthen into sharp points. Then, not even a heartbeat later, she retracts her fangs and offers me a shy smile.

Should I tell her? She already knows I'm not human, but she isn't either, and if she were to reveal the truth of my kind, I'd have the same leverage over her. "I come from a planet called Sufoi. Quite far from here and well beyond your galaxy."

"Ooh, an alien?" Her eyes sparkle with excitement as she chews on the inside of her cheek. "I was kind of hoping I'd get to see the first female president before the discovery of aliens, but, eh, I'll take it."

"Yes, I am what you would call an alien, but I'm also able to shift forms."

She smacks her palm on the table. "A shifter? No fucking way! That's so cool. What can you shift into?"

This is not the reaction any of my brothers' mates had. With Naomi, there's not even a hint of fear. She seems curious and excited to learn more about my other form. Not that I see Naomi as a potential mate, of course. That kind of bond with another is not meant for me. Though I suppose she is the closest woman in my life. It used to be Thea, but in just a week's time, I've grown to like Naomi more than I thought possible. I...trust her, somewhat. Not entirely, as that would be foolish, and I am no fool.

I think she's becoming my friend. There's no one else I can speak to like this. Not even my brothers.

"Where I'm from, we are called draxilios," I tell her, "but you'd call me a dragon."

Her mouth falls open in a silent shriek. "A dragon? As in a flying, fireball-spitting, nemesis-destroying dragon?"

I don't know why she added that third term, but my draxilio purrs happily upon hearing it. "Indeed."

"That's so handy. You must fly everywhere. Why do you even own a car when you can fly?"

"Because I don't fly everywhere. In draxilio form, we have the ability to cloak ourselves as soon as our feet leave the ground, to ensure no one can see us from below, but in order to cloak, we first need to shift, and it's hard to do that without someone seeing us."

"Us? So your brothers are dragon shifters too?"

Fuck. I shouldn't have said *us*. The focus needs to be on me. Only me.

"That's a dumb question," she says, shaking her head. "They're your brothers, so obviously they're the same species."

I decide to ignore her comment and hope a change of subject helps her forget she ever brought it up. "Tell me more about your life as a vampire. How long has it been since you were turned? What else do authors get wrong about your kind?"

She proceeds to tell me about her previous life in Seattle as a doctor who guided babies on their journey from womb to world and how much she loved that responsibility; no matter how heavy it hung on her shoulders. She was proud to deliver critical care to people during such a precious, life-changing moment. Her face lights up as she recalls a night when a woman in labor was driven to the hospital by her husband, and the birth was so quick that, with the help of Naomi and her team, she delivered a set of healthy twins on the sidewalk just outside the hospital doors.

Her mood turns somber, however, when she tells me about her maker, Xavier, and how he tore her away from a life she loved and used violence and psychological torture to break her spirit. But her spirit could not be broken. Despite what she had become, she still felt a deep sense of duty to protect humans from harm. It meant denying her new instincts, but she did so in order to keep those around her safe. And to this day, eight years later, she still refuses to feed the way her peers do.

Her willpower is impressive. The only source of sustenance vampires have is blood, so knowing she rejects the primary method of securing it in order to find a more humane alternative leaves me speechless, especially when she tells me how much stronger a newly changed vampire's thirst for blood is. I've never encountered a more selfless act than what Naomi has done and continues to do each day she walks this Earth.

"I was so lucky to find Quincy and others like us. Before that, I felt so alone. Like such a freak. The Sippers, as we like to call ourselves."

She tells me about Quincy's secret meetings, held in the back of the Dunkin' Donuts location he owns, and the other Sippers she's met there.

"Without them, I'd probably turn into the monster Xavier wanted me to become," she says, her voice shaking a bit when she says his name. "It would take time, but that would be my fate."

I crack my knuckles instinctively as she continues sharing memories of her maker. He is a vile creature that I would be honored to personally destroy. Perhaps, if we are friends long enough, she'll tell me where he is. "Why you?" I ask. "Why did he choose you?"

"There were a few doctors in the area that went missing around that time," she says, her voice growing hoarse with emotion. "Xavier never explicitly told me he did it, and I was too afraid to ask, but I heard him talking on the phone one day, and he said something about needing more medical staff to secure our immortality."

"You are immortal? Why would he need to turn more doctors if nothing can kill you?"

"Well, we're mostly immortal," she corrects. "A stake through the heart is the only thing that can kill us, but the Sippers movement is growing. I didn't know it at the time, but that trend was already a thing, and old-school vampires like Xavier like to spout off about Sippers creating a generation of weaker vampires who won't live as long because they don't know how to suck and who are destined to become slaves to the humans, yada, yada, yada."

"Mm. You disagree with this."

"Yeah," she exclaims, loudly enough to wake Felix from his peanut-induced stupor to caw at us. "Vampires like Xavier see the world as Darwinian, so if our main method of survival is hunting humans for blood, then those of us who refuse to do so won't survive. We were easy to ignore when there were only a few of us. Sippers back in the day would be mocked or ostracized from their cells, and nobody paid much attention. But now they see that our numbers are growing, probably because we don't need to hunt the way we used to and because of the Internet. There are other ways to access blood without hypnotizing humans into a non-consensual act, or worse, murder. And if we keep killing off our main food source, how the fuck do any of them expect us to remain immortal? Their argument makes no sense."

I haven't seen Naomi this worked up except when she spilled the water on me in the middle of this morning's meeting. It's an intoxicating sight to behold. Her cheeks pinken, and she gestures with her hands more frequently to make her point. It must be a habit from her human days, as she explained earlier that stillness is more instinctual for vampires.

She's no ordinary vampire though. Naomi sparkles like the rarest of gems, and I find myself humbled to catch even a flicker of her light.

I don't know how or why she came into my life, but I like that she's here. Though that doesn't explain why such a brilliant woman would settle for a job as my assistant. When I ask her about it, she shrugs, gazing off in the distance, and says, "I needed something to occupy my time, and it's not like I can go back into practicing medicine."

"Why not?"

The look she gives me indicates the answer should be obvious. "Too risky. I'd worry that my true nature would take over the moment I saw fresh blood, and I'd be a danger to everyone around me."

"But you seem so composed in the presence of humans at the office, and that was a job you worked so hard to get."

"Compared to most vampires my age, I have exceptional control over my thirst. I was turned just eight years ago, and technically, it's illegal to let vampires have consistent access to humans before they turn twenty. Most can't be trusted."

"Illegal?" I ask, confused. "According to what laws?"

"Vampires have their own legal system," she tells me. "There were too many rogue vampires making their own vampire armies, and it became a huge, bloody mess. A lot of people died, and it took a lot of hypnotizing to make the surviving humans forget it ever happened. The oldest vampires from across the globe came together and founded the International Vampire Administration, the IVA, and drew up the first set of laws our kind was expected to follow."

How fascinating. An entire species that the people of Earth are certain does not exist, has existed for centuries, and they even live by their own justice system.

"That's why every vampire has to be registered with the IVA within thirty days of being turned. There are monthly dues that makers are responsible for paying. It's a whole thing."

I prop my head up on the back of the couch with a pillow as I let out a yawn.

"Oh, Lillith, I'm boring the boss," she says with a lilting giggle. "How embarrassing. Go ahead and fire me. No hard feelings."

"You think I'm going to fire the best baby doctor the city of Seattle has ever seen?" I reply, chuckling along with her. Her smile is infectious, and I don't feel compelled to smile very often. "Do you think I'm an idiot?"

Her hand finds my forearm, and she gives me a soft squeeze as the sweet sound of her laughter fills the trailer. My skin prickles with awareness at her touch. Her skin is cold, which I never noticed before learning of her vampiric state, but my arm feels like it's on fire beneath her hand. If she feels the same, she doesn't let it show, and I have to stifle a groan the moment she pulls her hand away.

"You are not boring me, Naomi," I promise her. The couch is surprisingly comfortable, and I feel like it's sucking me deep into the cushions. "It's been a long week, but I'm eager to learn more. Tell me more."

"I feel like you know me better than I know myself at this point."

"Nonsense. Tell me about the other lies the fiction authors perpetuate about your kind."

"Well, let's see," she says, scrunching her nose as she tallies them up in her head. "Garlic reeks but can't hurt us. Some vampires have the power of hypnosis but not all. Elaine can do it. Oh, we do have to be invited in, unless it's a location we frequent. Then it's just the initial invitation that's required. Um, the sun can't kill us, nor does it make our skin sparkle like diamonds."

Why does that sound familiar? "Is that from…"

"*Twilight*. Yeah. We can run super fast like they can, but we can't climb trees like spider monkeys or whatever."

My eyelids grow heavy as she continues, and I curse myself for this overwhelming exhaustion. I don't want to miss any of what Naomi is willing to share with me.

"If you tear my head off and set me on fire, I'll survive," she adds with a smirk. "We don't turn into bats, and we can't fly. Holy water and silver can't hurt us, but we do tend to stay away from churches. Even when I just walk by one, I get this eerie feeling. It's like a wave of darkness trying to push me away."

The sound of her voice lulls me into the most restful slumber I've had in ages, and I don't realize I've fallen asleep until my eyes flutter open, and I find myself stretched out on her flimsy couch with my shoes off and a blanket covering me. She must've done that.

I'm relieved to discover my dick free of pain, and my high has faded entirely. The curtains that separate Naomi's bedroom from the rest of the trailer are closed, and I strain to listen for a snore or even deep breathing. It's faint, but I do hear a soft snore coming from her. The clock on my phone reads three thirty-two, and as quietly as possible, I shove my feet into my shoes and tiptoe out of the trailer toward my car.

My smile doesn't fade on my drive home. It lingers, just like the sound of her laughter in my head. I still hear it, and an unfamiliar warmth spreads through my chest as I recall our conversation and the way she made sure I was comfortable when I slept. As delightful as the evening was, however, I doubt it would have remained so when she discovered her boss on her couch in the light of day. It's best to end on a high note and make sure this smile fades before the weekend is over. Otherwise, my employees will suspect there's something wrong with me.

CHAPTER 7

NAOMI

A thumbs-up. That's all Elaine sent me after sharing that Kyan and his brothers are alien dragon shifters. Seriously, a thumbs-up? I wasn't expecting praise or a hug—a hug from Elaine would likely be awkward and too tight—but that was a tasty morsel of intel I gave her, and her response is lackluster at best.

I keep opening the text chain between us as I settle in at my desk on Monday morning and fire up my laptop. Still just the emoji. Though I suppose that's better than her usual all-caps replies threatening to evict me or call Xavier.

My eyes dart to the hallway past the kitchen, waiting for Kyan to arrive. We haven't spoken since Friday night, just before he passed out on my couch. When I woke up on Saturday morning, he was gone, which I understood. No matter how much fun you have with someone, having them in your space or you in theirs the next morning is always awkward. I don't need my new boss to see my bed head and dimpled ass hanging out of my booty shorts.

He was a much better hang than I expected though. Around the office, he's gruff and intimidating. The receptionists refer to him as Crankenstein on the staff group chat. But get the man high on weed cupcakes, and he's a blast. He was so easy to talk to, and seeing him with such a relaxed smile the whole night gave me a tummy full of butterflies. It was impossible to look away from that strong jaw, full lips, and his brilliantly white teeth. He might even be the most beautiful man on Earth when he smiles, and it gives me a massive ego boost knowing not everyone gets to see him like that.

If our circumstances were different, and I didn't need to dig up his secrets and share them with Elaine, Kyan and I would probably become friends. Good friends, even.

My computer dings as the group chat window lights up. "Crankenstein has entered the building."

The elevator doors open a minute later, and out he comes, the crease between his brows deepening as he surveys the floor, his stride long and emanating confidence. I watch as those he passes sit up straighter, their fingers suddenly flying across their keyboards as if immersed in writing the most important email of their lives. As soon as he rounds the corner, I find myself smoothing out my hair and unable to hide the smile that tugs at the corners of my mouth.

He nods at me as he reaches my desk. "Naomi."

I hold out the treat I made him on a paper towel. "Banana nut muffin, boss?"

Kyan stops and looks down at the muffin, turns to scan the office, then looks back at the muffin. "No, thank you. I already ate."

I feel my shoulders sag at the rejection as his office door closes behind him. *What the fuck was that?* Why did he just speak to me like we didn't spend hours watching *Veep* and feeding Felix peanuts on my couch?

Does he feel weird now, like we took things too far? I suppose it did cross the typical boundary between assistant and boss, but it's not like we made out or anything. We just got high together.

Maybe he regrets it. Or maybe me taking off his shoes and covering him with a blanket was too intimate. But it's not like I could leave him on my couch, passed out with his fancy shoes all laced up. I wanted him to be comfortable. Well, as comfortable as a seven-foot-tall alien dragon shifter could be on a love seat from IKEA.

If that's how he feels, then I won't offer him any more drug-filled baked goods. In fact, I won't offer him regular baked goods either, if he's not going to appreciate them. I'm not sure what I expected him to do when he walked in this morning, but it wasn't this.

It's not like it matters anyway. I'm not his friend; I'm his employee. An employee who needs to find a way into that basement. I'll just focus on that.

My inbox starts filling up with forwarded emails from Kyan, saying things like, "Follow up on this," and, "Please confirm this call." All business.

It isn't until after lunch that he comes out of his office.

"Naomi," he says, his throaty voice sending a shiver down my spine.

He's going to apologize for being cold this morning, I tell myself.

"Did you see that email from the CFO of Vernon Press?"

My dead heart sinks. "Uh, no. Let me check." I scroll through my inbox, frantically searching for it.

Kyan sighs. "He's saying the revised contract we sent over still has the same issues as the last version. Can you make sure he gets the correct one? I want that deal to go through by the end of the day."

"Of course," I mutter, trying to ignore the way his nearness is flustering me. "I'll send it over right now."

"Thanks."

He leaves for lunch after that, and for the rest of the day, our only conversations take place over email.

Tuesday is pretty much the same, apart from offering him a muffin when he arrives. I'm not doing that again. By late afternoon on Wednesday, I've (mostly) let go of my frustration with his mood swings and have decided to keep our interactions brief and professional going forward. Any doubt I had about sharing his secret with Elaine begins to fade.

On Thursday night, I visit Quincy during his shift at DD, hoping to get some insight on how to proceed with my mission. "He has the keys to that door. I'm not sure anyone else does, but when I tried peeking inside, he was quick to close it and lock it up tight. How the fuck am I supposed to find a way in?"

Someone barks an order through the drive-through intercom, and he rushes to fill it before returning to the back room.

"Need a refill?" he asks when he sees my empty cup.

"Nah, I'm good for the night."

"Have you tried installing cameras around the exits?"

It didn't occur to me, mostly because it seems like a terrible idea. "Won't he notice new cameras around the outside of the building?"

"Not if you get the right cameras," Quincy says, taking his phone out of his pocket and pulling up a shady-looking website. "These are the size of a dime. They're weatherproof, with an adhesive backing, so you can stick them anywhere."

"Jesus, they're so small."

"Crazy, right?"

"Have you used them before? Do they actually work?"

He opens an app on his phone. "Yeah, I have them here and at home." Swiping through the different screens, I can see the entire drive-through lane that circles the building, and a view of the street. The footage from around the outside of his house is slightly different, but most of those cameras seem to be installed on tree stumps and high ledges, making them even more discreet.

"Wow, the footage is so clear. Where did you find these?"

"My man Jay. We go way back. He used to own a pawn shop in Boston, but now he and his wife own a weed bakery in Colorado. This dude can find anything you want."

Envy slices through my middle when I envision this man, Jay, who I've never met, and his loving wife. They probably have a cute house with a view of a mountain in the distance, a child or two running barefoot down the hall, while the two of them discuss menu ideas for their bakery over a cup of coffee.

I miss being able to eat human food. The best part about baking is tasting the finished product, and I can't do that anymore. If my mom were still in my life, she'd be thrilled I can no longer eat my favorite things, though she'd still wear that look of disappointment upon seeing that I haven't gotten any smaller.

In my head, I can still hear her voice when I would reach for dessert. She'd make a tsk noise and say, "xiao pang pang" which is Mandarin for little fatty. Yet when I didn't finish eating what was on my plate, she'd tell me to eat more. My grandparents on her side were the same way. It was exhausting to grow up in this body around them. But regardless of how often Mom fat-shamed me, she did love my cakes.

I'm a fantastic baker. It's why I still make muffins and cupcakes that I don't even get to enjoy. Seeing other people enjoy my treats is still nice. It's just not the same.

"Yoohoo, Naomi," Quincy says, snapping his fingers in my face.

Was I spacing out for that long? I didn't even hear him talking. "What?"

He laughs as rolls his eyes. "Do you want me to order these cameras or not?"

"Oh. Oh yeah. Definitely. How soon can they get here?"

"Jay never charges me for shipping, and it looks like," he pauses as he reaches the checkout screen, "they'll be delivered by Saturday. That work?"

"Hell yeah." That's perfect. The building will be empty, and I can set them up once it gets dark. "Will you help me install them?"

"Sure, as long as we get it done before seven," he says. "I have a shift that night."

That'll be easy. The sun goes down around five this time of year, so that'll give us plenty of time. "I promise I won't keep you too late." I start to wonder when Quincy last took a day off. "You work too hard," I say, elbowing him in the ribs.

He lifts the brim of his orange visor and runs a hand through his tight black curls. "Money, money, money, sis. That's what it's all about. I'm not taking a day off until I have the funds to open my lab."

I'm not sure when he started saving to open his own laboratory, but he's got a poster on the wall of a savings thermometer that's a quarter filled in with red marker, and the number at the top is three hundred thousand. Once he reaches his goal, he'll buy a place with enough room and the proper equipment to develop synthetic blood. I have no doubt he'll achieve that, once he has the funds to do so, and the world will be forever changed.

"Hey, I just remembered I get my first paycheck next Friday. Put me down for five hundred a month, okay?"

His eyes widen in disbelief. "You fucking with me?"

I pull my coat on and grab my blood bottle off the table. "Not even a little. Count me in as your first investor, you mad scientist."

Quincy lifts his blood bottle toward me. "Cheers to you, then. I'll make sure to name a whole-ass wing after you."

"Ooh, I like that." I raise mine and clink it against his. "Gan bei."

"Gan bei."

I run home through the woods brimming with excitement, knowing the cameras will get here soon and the footage will hopefully provide some guidance on how to get into Kyan's secret basement. As soon as I settle into bed, I send Elaine a text letting her know about the next phase of my plan.

> Elaine: 👍

Ugh. This bitch.

Felix flies from the couch to the windowsill next to my bed, and I open it to let him out. "Night, buddy. See you tomorrow."

He caws back before he launches into the night sky.

CHAPTER 8

KYAN

*N*aomi has been distant with me as of late. I can't blame her for it. Her clipped tone and shortened email responses began the day I denied her muffin offering. It wasn't personal; I merely felt it was important to establish a boundary between us, given that I'm her superior. It was foolish of me to partake in the weed cupcakes, despite my mouth salivating even now at the memory. But we were sharing personal details about ourselves, in her home, while our inhibitions were lowered because of the drugs, and we were steps away from her bed. Upon reflection, it felt wrong. I should've told her as much, but it felt easier to keep the past in the past and not call attention to it.

Two weeks have passed since then, and it seems she's carrying a grudge. When I ask for a coffee from the kitchen, it's either cold, or she forgets to add sugar. Considering she prepared my coffee precisely the way I like it during her first week, this seems intentional.

It's not just the coffee, either. I noticed her station wagon in the garage, still in the same spot, and offered to drive her home one night. She said she'd rather run home. When I pointed out that it was raining heavily and a thunderstorm was expected to roll in, she said, "Yep. Still prefer to run."

I know she runs fast due to her vampire speed, but that felt petty.

The quality of her work has not suffered because of this, which is a pleasant surprise. In fact, the clients are getting used to interacting with her, and her rapport with them is nothing short of stellar.

The boundary I set feels more like an impenetrable wall than a line in the sand, and I'm not sure how to fix it.

I like Naomi. She seems to understand me better than most. Plus, she's brilliant and kind. If she weren't my assistant, I might even describe her as breathtakingly beautiful, with a laugh that could melt entire glaciers. She *is* my assistant, however, and such observations are improper.

It's probably for the best. She sees me as an asshole, and she's right. I'm not built for camaraderie of any kind. I was genetically modified to be a heartless, highly skilled assassin. It's the only thing I've ever been good at. A change of planet doesn't mean I'll become someone else. I may not be able to use my skills on this planet, but my personality remains the same.

"Where have you been?" Mylo asks when I enter the house and kick off my shoes by the door.

"At work. Where else would I be?"

"Of course," he says with a sneer. "Your big important job in the tall building where you have meetings and sign contracts." He crosses his arms over his chest, thankfully hiding a particularly hideous sweater with big birds scattered all over it. "Did you get my text?"

I brush past him on my way to the fridge and down half a bottle of water before I decide to respond. "You know I don't read your texts. They're filled with insults."

"Not all of them."

I narrow my gaze. "Too many of them."

"Agree to disagree."

The house is abnormally quiet given how many people tend to be hanging out here since my brothers started collecting mates. "Where is everyone?"

"At Vanessa's," he says. "Harper and Luka are in town with the boys. Ryan too. Checking on the baby. I don't know where Zev is. Luka said he went to get tacos for lunch, but we haven't seen him since."

Why am I not surprised that Mylo appears so glib about Zev's disappearance? If it isn't within the pages of a book or related to his precious library, he doesn't take it seriously. "Has anyone called him? Do we know he's alive and well?"

He scoffs at my questions. "Calm down. I'm sure he's fine. He's a big boy."

That may be true, but Zev is still the youngest among us, and when I look at him, I see the bone-deep scars of abuse he endured from our handlers. His different-colored eyes hold pain and fear. He needs protecting, no matter how many centuries old he gets.

"If you don't care that our brother could be lying lifeless in a shallow grave, then neither will I."

Mylo laughs. It's the coarse, arrogant laugh I only hear when we bicker. "You think a draxilio with the ability to communicate with machines is going to be bested by a human and tossed into a shallow grave? Even an entire army couldn't take him down. I'd bet on Samantha's life that he'll outlive us all."

I've grown tired of my brother, but more than anything, I'm just tired. Throwing my laptop bag over my shoulder, I head for the stairs. "I'll be sure to let your mate know that you're making wagers with her life. She'll love that. Goodnight, Mylo."

"Wait a minute," he calls out. "We haven't had a meeting in a while. I know it's been hard to get everyone in the same room lately…"

Because everyone but me is happily mated, moving out, and building families of their own. Even Zev has found his match, which is not something I thought I'd ever see. "And?"

"Have you been exposing yourself to your assigned form of media? Reality TV? What have you learned lately?"

These meetings. I find them abhorrent, and not only because I have the worst assignment. "Why must we continue this charade?" I ask with a sigh. "I understand why we needed them in the beginning. We were new to this planet and needed to learn more about humans and their culture. It was a good idea, brother. It was." I don't like giving Mylo praise, but in this instance, I suppose he deserves it. "Now, however, it seems these meetings are a waste of time. Besides, I learn from the humans I've hired. The ones I'm surrounded by most of my waking hours. The rest of you have public-facing jobs or mates to ask should a puzzling aspect of life occur."

Mylo's mouth forms a hard line. He's disappointed in my response. That's nothing new. Out of the five of us, Mylo and I are the most likely to come to blows. I continue climbing the steps to my wing of the house, eager to end this day. As I reach the top, I call down, "All reality TV shows are aggressively boring, with one exception: *Survivor*. That's what I've learned. Oh, and one more thing. Value."

He jerks his head back, puzzled. "Value? What the f..." Then his eyes widen in dismay. "Is that today's Wordle?"

I laugh as I walk down the hall to my room.

"I had two more guesses left!" he shouts. "Fuck you, Kyan."

"Eh, fuck you too."

I get an hour of restful slumber before the tossing and turning begins. It continues long enough to force me out of bed, and that's when I call Yvonne. She answers after one ring.

"Hi, Yvonne. Glad you're awake." It's no surprise she's still awake. Her main form of sustenance is energy drinks. "Gather the recruits and meet me at the western corner of Nottingcook Forest in Bow." Adrenaline pumps through my blood as I picture how the rest of my night will unfold. It won't be restful, but it will be deeply satisfying. "I'm bringing the recruits their first live target."

※ ※ ※

I arrive before Yvonne and the guys, which gives me time to shift back into my flightless form just outside the tree line on the edge of Nottingcook Forest and heave the unconscious body of the target over my shoulder. Once I head deeper into the woods and find a suitable clearing, I toss him to the ground and prop him up against a tree.

"Kyan," Yvonne says as she approaches, the recruits trailing close behind her. Though, with her accent, it sounds more like "kay-yawn." She chuckles as her gaze drops to the man with the bag over his head. "This is it?"

"Yes. This is tonight's target."

"Did you knock him out on purpose?" Rex asks. Doubt flashes across his face as he runs his fingers through his unruly beard. "I thought we were going to hunt. This doesn't seem like much of a challenge."

I kick the man lightly in the hip, and he lets out a muffled groan. "We won't begin until he awakens, I assure you. And no, I did nothing to this man apart from binding his hands and covering his mouth and eyes. The moment I unmasked before him and he saw my horns and blue skin, he fainted."

Julian, the Eastern Diamondback rattlesnake shifter, clears his throat, and in his surprisingly quiet, smooth voice, asks, "Why him? Do we get to learn anything about our targets beforehand?"

"Certainly. I didn't form this pack to engage in senseless killing," I begin. "Our primary objective in our work together is to deliver justice to those who have not been held accountable for their crimes. The system in which we are expected to coexist with humans is irreparably broken, allowing politicians, those who hold wealth or status, members of law enforcement, and religious and community leaders to receive minimal punishments, or more frequently, no punishment at all, for the ways they abuse their power and harm others. Our targets will not be limited to those in positions of power. Unfortunately, even the common criminal is able to avoid a prison sentence, so long as he is male and has skin the color of snow."

"With respect, boss," Owen, the jaguar shifter, says, "there are only four of us, and shit like this happens all over the world. Are we expected to take out every shady motherfucker who gets away with abuse? We're shifters, not superheroes."

A collective chuckle spreads throughout the group, rousing our target enough for him to make panicked moans from beneath the tape I used to cover his mouth. I take the opportunity to remove the bag from his head and lift the blindfold from his eyes.

"I'd like you all to meet Elias Billington III."

Elias's eyes widen in horror as he takes in the group of large, burly men in front of him.

"Elias here has quite the storied past." I turn to our target. "Don't you, Elias?"

I pull my phone out of my pocket to refer to the rap sheet I made when I started researching him.

"He has been a Catholic priest for over thirty years and has been accused of sexual abuse by twelve young boys across three states. The church apparently conducted their own investigations following each accusation and determined that instead of laicizing him, they would instead transfer him to a different parish. The boys he hurt, and their respective families, were given no justice." A steady growl fills the air as I scroll further down the page. "That's not all. Elias's niece came out when she was fifteen, and he immediately had her sent to a conversion camp.

The day after she returned home from said camp, she unalived herself."

Elias whimpers as the growls spread through the group, and he looks up at me with desperation etched on his horrible face.

I step toward the recruits. "The system in place to protect the most vulnerable among us from this kind of abuse allowed this monster to continue his insidious behavior without even a slap on the wrist."

"Sick fuck," Derek, the werewolf, says through gritted teeth.

"I realize you aren't superheroes," I tell them. "And I certainly have no plans to eradicate all sources of evil from the entire planet. That's not possible. What we can do, though, is use the unique abilities we possess to improve the lives of people around us. Particularly those who have suffered at the hands of unchecked abusers. I believe the proper term for us would be vigilantes." I point to Elias. "This man is still a priest. What's to stop him from hurting another child? Nothing."

Owen rubs a hand down his face. "Look, I get what you're saying, and obviously this dude deserves to die."

Elias moans in protest.

"But we don't even have fucking rights," Owen continues. "Like, we have to walk around all fucking day as if the best parts of ourselves don't exist, because of what humans will do to us if they find out. Why should we be risking our asses to make life safer for them?"

It's a fair question, and one I've asked myself many times, especially after we first landed. My brothers were eager to immerse themselves in the culture in order to find their mates, and almost immediately we discovered how awful these beings are to each other. I haven't lost my pessimism, but I've accepted that humans will be in my life whether I like it or not.

"Unless you're living in closed societies with only other shifters, you will end up with at least one human you care about, and this kind of abuse is so widespread, that one person is likely to have survived some form of it, especially if that human is a woman, and even more so if that form of abuse is sexual assault."

"You have a mate you're trying to avenge or something?" Rex asks.

"No. No, that's not it," I say with a sardonic laugh. "I don't have a mate. My brothers do though. All four of them. Well, my brother Zev is still trying to woo his mate, which I'm sure will happen soon. I care about these women. I do. My brothers deserve the happiness they've found and the comfort of knowing their mates will never know that kind of pain again.

"There is a cop in our town who has been terrorizing our family," I continue, rage heating my blood as I picture Burton's face. "He abuses his power and protects men like this, and the residents of Sudbury have no recourse. I want his reign of terror to end.

"But don't mistake my motives as wholesome and selfless. I'm not a good man. I was made in a lab. My handlers, they didn't want to *train* a killer. They wanted to build one from scratch. My genetics were altered in such a way that nothing soothes the monster inside me quite like extinguishing a life. What most humans get from taking a bath or reading a book, I get from seeing someone take their last breath."

Julian crosses his arms. "Your brothers weren't modified in a lab?"

"They were, but we were given different dominant traits. Different desires." I lean my shoulder against the tree Elias is leaning against as I recall the struggle to make peace with this dark hunger. "I used to envy their ability to adapt, to become better, softer, for this world and the women they love. I'm not sure why they were able to change, and I can't. I tried denying my true nature after we first arrived. The more I rejected that part of myself, the louder the beast inside my head became.

"Eventually...I don't know. I realized it wasn't about willpower at all." I run a hand through my hair, frustrated by how fresh that ache in my chest feels. The disappointment of realizing I can't change the way I thought I could. "A shark can't sprout wings and fly, no matter how much time he spends watching birds soar above the surface of the water."

"I don't know, man," Owen says. "Who needs wings when you're the baddest motherfucker in the sea?"

Their laughter echoes through the trees, reminding me of why we're here.

"Enough sharing. We have a task to accomplish before the sun rises."

I grab Elias by the forearms and yank him up into a standing position. He sags against the tree, but still remains upright. "Elias, there is a stream about three hundred feet in that direction," I say, gesturing where to go. "If you can make it to the stream, we'll let you live."

He looks in the direction I'm pointing, then holds up his hands, a plea for me to remove the duct tape binding his wrists together.

"Oh, no, no. There's nothing I can do about that, I'm afraid, but your feet are unbound, so you should be able to run without much difficulty. I'll even offer you this," I say, lowering my voice to a whisper as I take in his round shape and short, stumpy legs. "We'll give you a head start of...eh, two minutes."

Tears pour from his eyes as he shakes his head. His fate is clear to him now. His freedom, his choices, his power, they have all been taken away, and there's nothing he can do about it. It's a breathtaking sight.

I pull out my phone and open the timer app.

"You shouldn't waste time crying," I caution him as I give him a pat on the shoulder. "Focus on running."

He starts hyperventilating. Poor old pedophile. He'll probably collapse before he gets fifty feet.

"Annnnnd go!" I shout.

He stumbles, tripping over a fallen branch immediately. After four and a half seconds, he gets to his feet and starts to run.

"Now, who would like to take the lead on this mission?" I ask the recruits. "Any volunteers?"

Rex steps forward. "If I catch him, I get to end him?"

I nod. "Correct. You'll get the *wrathenol* injection, shift, and the rest of the pack will offer support. They'll shift and follow and help you corner the target for the final blow, if needed. But that blow belongs to you."

He surveys the others, seeking approval. Their nods satisfy him. "Yeah, I'll do it."

"And is there anyone you're seeking justice for tonight, Rex?" I pause. "You don't have to share if you don't want to."

Rex drops his chin to this chest. "My brother, Ritchie. I don't want to get into it, really, but Ritchie's no longer with us, and maybe if a man like Elias, a teacher, were held accountable for his actions, I'd still have my brother."

I press my fist over my heart. "For Ritchie."

In unison, they reply, "For Ritchie."

Yvonne gives Rex his injection, and the recruits undress before they shift into their other forms. He waits for my signal that Elias's head start has come to an end and takes off at incredible speed toward the stream. The rest follow on his heels, and it doesn't take long for Rex to catch up with Elias.

As their celebratory roars and howls reach my ears, a smile tugs at my lips, and my draxilio purrs inside my head. This. This is what I was made for.

CHAPTER 9

NAOMI

I can't put it off any longer. Every pair of underwear is dirty, and going commando at work is just not something I'm comfortable with. Steeling my spine, I haul my hamper into my arms and trudge up the narrow stone path toward the house. If I had planned better, I would've done my laundry while Elaine, Mike, and Wyatt were playing bingo at the nursing home.

It's the only group activity of theirs that doesn't end in bloodshed, primarily because they don't like the taste of "old blood."

Wyatt once compared it to hot cow piss. I didn't ask how he knew that.

"Knock, knock." I say the words as I slowly open the door.

"Ah, Naomi," Elaine calls from the living room in a cheerful tone that instantly puts me on edge. "How are you?"

How am I? She has never, not once, asked me that question. What the hell is going on? "Uh, fine. Thanks." I lift the hamper up to my chest. "Just doing some laundry."

Elaine's eyebrows lift, and her mouth tightens around the corners. It takes a second, but it's clear what she wants.

"How are *you?*"

"We are having a fabulous night. Yeah," she replies, bouncing in place.

"Come, Naomi," Mike says from the couch. "You must hear of our brilliant dinner plans."

I drop the hamper in the hallway and let Elaine drag me by the arm into the living room. All three of them look like they've just won the lottery, and part of me wishes their dinner was sprawled out on the floor with several deep holes in their neck, like it usually is, because whatever they have planned must be worse.

Mike opens his mouth to speak, but then waves a hand at Wyatt. "Wyatt, you tell her."

"One of the geezers at bingo started telling me about these food delivery applications that are available on phones."

Yikes. This is painful.

"He showed me how to set up an account on Elaine's phone," Wyatt continues, his face flushed with excitement. "So we ordered a pizza..." He starts laughing so hard he can't speak.

"A buffalo chicken pizza, of all things," Elaine adds, also very amused. "Can you imagine?"

I can, but sure. Whatever.

Wyatt's face is beet red as he tries to calm himself. "The delivery person is going to show up here, thinking he's dropping off our meal, when really," another burst of laughter, "he'll be the meal."

Mike holds up Elaine's phone. "Behold, we can follow his journey in real time. He shall arrive in twelve minutes."

I'm still waiting for the punchline because that can't be it. "So, to be clear, you're going to drain him when he arrives? Or you're just going to hypnotize him to feed and let him go?"

"Why would we let him go?" Mike asks. "He's showing up at a house full of vampires. We can't be expected to show restraint."

Do they truly not understand? "What happens when he

doesn't make it home at the end of his shift and the app shows his last known location was this house?"

Elaine looks at me like I've just asked her to explain quantum physics.

"What do you mean?" She stomps her kitten-heeled feet across the creaky floor and grabs her phone from Mike. "They can see us in here like we can see them?"

"Yes."

This spectacular moron holds my fate in her hands. It's so unfair.

"Wyatt, did the old man with the suspenders tell you about this?"

Wyatt pouts as he plops down on the couch next to Mike. "No. Don't you think I would've remembered that?"

They start bickering like children, giving me the chance to slowly back out of the room and grab my hamper. After I've started the wash, I creep upstairs to find them still yelling at each other.

"I can't cancel the order!" Mike yells at Wyatt as he glares at the phone. Wyatt tries stealing the phone, but Mike continues batting his hands away. "This dunderhead keeps saying a lack of hunger isn't an acceptable condition for a refund."

"Give me the phone," Elaine demands, holding her hand out. "I told you we needed to consult a young person first. This whole night has been a complete wash."

I have no interest in being present when they come up with a plan B, so I wait until Elaine's back is turned, and slip out the front door, hoping this scheme is over by the time I need to move my clothes into the dryer.

When I get back inside my trailer, I find Felix hopping up and down on the kitchen counter. He looks delighted to see me, or he's just hungry and wants me to open the cabinet above his head that contains his peanut stash. I choose to pretend he's happy to see me. "Okay, okay. Hold your horses." I pour out the remnants of the jar, which is only about five peanuts, and he actually tilts his head at me, as if to say, is that really all you've got?

"I'll get more tomorrow. I promise."

My phone beeps from the nightstand, and I discover a text from Kyan.

> Kyan: Can I see you? I need your help.

He needs my help? On a weeknight? That seems odd, but I'd be lying if I said I wasn't a little intrigued by the request.

Admittedly, I think I'm developing a bit of a crush on him. Maybe more than a bit. It's stupid and dangerous and can only end badly for me, but I can't deny it anymore.

Spending every day with him at the office and watching for him on the cameras Quincy and I installed certainly isn't helping. I've developed this Pavlovian response since I started watching the footage, and now whenever he shows up on my screen, I can practically feel my pupils dilating.

I haven't learned anything from the footage that seems worth passing along to Elaine. Other than the few times I've seen Kyan coming and going from that same locked door, no one else goes in or out. There was the night earlier this week when a white cargo van drove through the lot around midnight, seemingly from a lower parking level than I knew existed and returned just after four in the morning. There was a blonde woman driving, but I couldn't see anything inside the van. It seemed like a lousy lead to pursue.

Watching him through the security cameras clearly isn't getting me anywhere, so maybe the best way forward is to actually spend time with him. After all, I wouldn't have found out he's a shifter if we didn't get high together. I could also try breaking the lock on the door, but that can happen later.

> Sure. Can you fly or walk here though? I don't want my cell mates to see your car in the driveway.

Kyan: Why not?

Because they're working with a cop who hates you and wants to destroy you and your family.

Because Elaine is an asshole and will probably barge in on us.

Because they're currently expecting a pizza guy to arrive whom they plan to eat.

About a million reasons come to mind, but none that I can tell him.

> Because they're nosy, and I don't want to deal with their questions.

Kyan: Fair. I'll fly.

I wonder what it would take to convince him to take me for a ride.

Kyan: Be there in ten.

My stomach flutters with anticipation.

> Oh wait! Can you bring peanuts? Asking for a crow.

Kyan: Which one of you is the owner and which one is the pet? It seems like he's calling the shots.

I giggle as I read. He's not wrong.

> Rude. I like to think of us as equals.

> Kyan: The wild bird in your house has developed a taste for gourmet peanuts.

This is the playful version of Kyan I was expecting at work after the night we got high.

> What can I say? We're a pair of bougie bitches.

My breath stops as the three dots appear then disappear. I expect a sarcastic response. More silly banter. An amused grin tugs at my lips at the thought of him overthinking what to say next.

> Kyan: I'll be there soon. Thanks for this, by the way. I really appreciate it.

It's not the response I thought I'd get. This is way more heartfelt. Genuine. I wonder what's going on inside his head.

Several minutes pass before I hear a soft knock at my bedroom window. I gesture for Kyan to come around to the front door. When I let him in, his hair is more disheveled than it was earlier at work, and there are dark circles under his eyes. Despite the slightly unkempt appearance, he still looks like he's too beautiful for this world.

"You didn't have to sneak up to my window like a teenage boy," I tell him when he removes his jacket and drapes it across the back of the chair in the kitchen.

"Well, you said you preferred to keep me hidden from your cell mates," he replies as he brushes a lock of hair off his forehead. How does an alien dragon end up with such soft looking hair? I need to ask what products he uses. "I'm just trying to stay on your good side."

I have to pat the spot on the couch next to me before Kyan takes a seat. Why is he so shy all of a sudden?

"What's going on? You said you needed my help. Is everything okay?"

He clears his throat. "Yes, fine. I just...I've had trouble sleeping lately, and when I thought back to the last time I slept well, it was the night I was here."

Oh my god, is he about to request a slumber party? I couldn't say yes to that, right? No. No. That would be wrong. Even though I think I'd really like to say yes.

"I wondered if you had any of those special baked goods on hand?"

Wow, buzzkill. "Ah, so I'm your assistant *and* your drug dealer now? Is that how it is?"

He smiles and the gleam of those perfect teeth wipes away my disappointment. "I apologize if this puts you in a tough position. Please feel free to say no if you're uncomfortable."

I feign annoyance as I get up and grab the glazed lemon loaf from the cabinet. "Made this a few days ago. It's all yours." Why did I make it? I like baking, but mostly because I was hoping for this exact situation to arise.

"Mm," he groans as he takes a deep whiff of the sweet bread. "This smells heavenly." Then he looks over his shoulder and asks, "And this has the weed, yes?" which makes me really feel like a drug dealer.

I nod. "It does. You'll sleep very well on it."

"Thank you, Naomi."

The silence that sits between us stretches on, and I'm not sure what to do. "Is that it, then?"

He looks surprised by my question. "Oh, am I interrupting your evening plans? I can go." Kyan gets to his feet and grabs his jacket off the chair. He pauses to look at the bulge in his coat pocket. "I almost forgot." After pulling a can of peanuts out, he hands them to me.

"Well, no. You're not interrupting," I say, taking the peanuts and pouring some on the countertop for Felix. "My plans are limited to laundry. If you want to stay…stay."

He holds my gaze, one side of his soft mouth curving upward. "I'd like that."

It doesn't take long for Kyan to devour the entire lemon loaf, and within an hour, he's high off his ass. Felix keeps flying across the length of the trailer and landing on Kyan's shoulder or head, and he giggles gleefully like a child at a petting zoo. Knowing how entertained he is by my crow buddy, I sneak over to the house to put my clothes in the dryer. There's an unfamiliar car parked out front, which I assume is the delivery guy's, and my suspicions are confirmed when I walk in and find a trail of blood from the living room to Elaine's bedroom down the hall.

I hope their idiotic plan gets them in all kinds of trouble when this guy is reported missing.

When I make it back to the trailer, I stumble at the sight of my boss. Between when I went to the house and now, his skin turned a rich shade of cerulean, and he has thick black horns jutting out of his head just behind his hairline.

Kyan doesn't notice my reaction as he stares in wonder at the watermark on my ceiling. "Naomi, have you ever noticed how much that spot looks like a donkey on roller skates?"

"Whoa, what the hell happened here?" I lean over him and put my hands on either side of his face. He's beautiful. Absolutely mesmerizing. "Is this what you really look like?"

He reaches up and strokes the tip of his left horn before nodding. "The weed must have caused me to unmask." Shame fills his gaze, and I watch as the blue starts to fade.

"No, no! What are you doing? Don't make it go away."

At my request, the blue returns. My eyes trail over his face and neck as I notice little parts of him that shimmer or fade into a lighter blue just above the neckline of his shirt. What does the rest of him look like? Saliva fills my mouth at the thought.

"You like it?" he asks, his voice quiet and uncertain. It's not a version of his voice I thought existed since he only ever projects arrogance. But he's so vulnerable in this state. It makes me think I'm one of the lucky few who's gotten to see him this way.

"How could I not? Your skin…" I stammer, trying to find the right words. "It's gorgeous. I've never seen a color like this. So much depth." My gaze lifts. "And these horns are insane." They're so wide, and the way they curl back reminds me of an ibex. I reach up to lightly touch the sharp point of one, marveling at how easily he could impale someone by just tipping his head back. "It's hard to believe you're real, even though you're sitting right in front of me."

I notice in that moment that I'm practically in his lap. I'm not sure how it happened, but the discovery leaves me frazzled and somewhat embarrassed. "Uh, let's go for a walk," I say, straightening to my full height and tugging on the bottom hem of my t-shirt just to give my hands something G-rated to do.

Kyan looks dazed enough to not have noticed my intimate lean. "A walk? Okay."

I take him down the narrow dirt trail through the woods until we end up at the abandoned bridge. The ground is soft from the recent rain, but not so muddy that boots are required. Wind whips through my hair, and I find myself glad to be a vampire, if only in the sense that cold weather no longer affects me. The coats and gloves and hats are just accessories to blend in during winter. We lean over the guardrail and watch the angry ripples of the river below.

"Do you come out here often?"

"Yeah, it's a good place to think. It's also a good place to not think," I amend. "When I'm depressed, I can watch the movement of the water and let my thoughts fade away."

He sighs, a contented, relaxed sound. "It is quite peaceful."

I chuckle as I look over at him. His fists are stacked on top of each other against the rail, with his pointy chin resting on the top one. Slowly, his blinks turn into fully closed eyes, and I wonder if he could fall asleep in this position.

They pop open suddenly, and he grabs his phone from his back pocket. I try to avert my eyes, but I can't help but notice it's a text from someone named Yvonne.

Is he seeing someone? I suppose it's none of my business. Who is she though?

"Is there somewhere you need to be?" The words come out before I can stop them. I wasn't able to read the text, so for all I know, Yvonne is mated to one of his brothers. But the petty, jealous part of me is desperate to find out who this person is and why she's texting him so late.

"Nope," he says after reading the text and returning the phone to his pocket.

My chin lifts at the knowledge that he left her on read while he's here with me. I kind of hate myself for feeling that way, but I can't deny it.

"You look tired," I tell him, nudging his arm. "Let's head back."

As he goes to turn, he steps on a large rock and stumbles a bit. Reflexively, I rush to his side, and he leans into me as his arm drapes across my shoulders. "Easy there, boss."

He makes an adorable sound that resembles "whoa," but jumbled, and brushes his knuckle against the tip of my nose. "Where would I be without you?"

Oh brother, this man is as high as a damn kite. Should he fly home in this state? What if he gets dizzy in midair and crashes into a tree?

By the time we make it back to the trailer, I decide it's best he stays here. I practically had to carry him back, and since he's about two feet taller than me and, I would guess, an additional buck-fifty in pure muscle, it was a struggle despite my strength. There's no way he's launching himself into the sky.

I get him over to the bed, and he flops onto his back with his eyes already closed. Carefully, I remove his shoes and drape a throw blanket on top of him before climbing in on my side. Using two of my supremely fluffy pillows, I create a barrier between us, so there's no funny business. Not that I expect him to ravish me in the middle of the night. I just don't want to end up with the same weird tension we had after last time.

Not long after I drift off, I hear Felix let out a few soft caws, alerting me to the fact that I forgot to open the window for him, but I'm too comfortable to get up, so I turn onto my other side and hope he finds a comfy spot on the couch or windowsill to hang out until morning.

"Mm."

A soft rumble against my ear rouses me. It must be morning, because I can feel the sun peeking through the blinds and shining on my face. A tickle forms inside the tip of my nose—a clear sign I'm about to sneeze—but I burrow deeper beneath the blankets, refusing to get up just yet. I'm so comfortable in a way I haven't felt in a long time. When did this ancient bed get so comfortable?

When a large hand flattens against my upper back, I become extremely confused. My eyes fly open, and I realize my cheek is pressed against Kyan's bare blue chest, and his arms are wrapped tightly around me.

I have to stifle a gasp so as not to wake him, but inside I'm screaming. The pillows that separated us are on the floor, along with Kyan's button-up shirt and undershirt. How did we get here? Am I responsible for this? Did my body seek him out while I was asleep? My gaze lands on the folded edge of something gray…and…shit, it's his pants. Is he…naked under the blankets?

I shouldn't look. I really, really shouldn't.

As I go to lift the blanket for a peek, he awakens, and immediately wears the same frantic expression I'm sure I'm wearing.

"Naomi?" he stammers, rubbing a hand down his face as he looks around the room, then beneath the sheets. "What, um…?"

"Yeah, yeah, I know," I interrupt because I know what he's thinking. "But I'm certain nothing happened. You were high, but I wasn't, and I'd sure as shit remember if something happened between us."

This is awful. I can see the panic etched deep into his angular features, and I cover my face with my hands as I envision how much worse things will be than they were last time. He'll give me the cold shoulder, or not talk to me at all. Eventually the work will suffer, and it'll be so awkward between us that he'll fire me, and I'll never see him again. Now that I know what it's like to be in his arms, I can't let that happen. I don't want to lose him.

Why did I bring him over to the bed? I should've left him on the couch. "Shit. I'm sorry. I'm so sorry."

"Naomi," he says in a soft voice.

"I don't know how…" If he's trying to calm me down, it won't work. I've fucked everything up, and if Elaine is awake and comes over here before he leaves, I don't even want to think ab—

"Naomi, come here."

His hand is warm as it caresses my back. I feel him reach for me, wrapping his long fingers around my wrist and prying it away from my face.

When I turn to face him, his smile is warm, and there's longing in his eyes.

"Don't apologize," he says, crooking a finger under my chin. "I don't care how it happened, and I don't want you to think of this as a mistake, because it wasn't for me."

I don't realize my breaths are rapid and shallow until I struggle to talk. "Are you sure?"

I want him to be sure. We shouldn't do this. It's a terrible idea to go down this path, and I think we both know it. But fuck, I want to more than anything.

He nods. "I'm sure." Then he leans back in bed and opens his arms. "I want more."

My body reacts before my mind can stop me. I sink into the warmth of his embrace and sigh as I drop my head to his chest. He runs a hand down my back, and I'm surprised to find his touch so comforting. There's no trace of Crankenstein in the way he holds me, like a hurricane could knock down the walls around us, and I'd still be perfectly safe. My eyelids get heavy as the steady beat of his heart thumps beneath my ear, and the rest of the world fades away.

CHAPTER 10

KYAN

Zev seems to have successfully wooed Charlie. Not officially, I've been told, but they're married, and Charlie and her daughter, Nia, are moving into our house, so it seems official enough. My brothers and I are even assembling furniture for Nia's new room. It's a confusing situation, but I haven't bothered to press Zev for more details because I can't get Naomi out of my head.

I have no recollection of how our bodies became entwined a few nights ago, but what I'm sure of is that I have never had a better night's sleep in my three hundred years. When I woke up and realized what had happened, I knew how I was supposed to feel: ashamed, apologetic, and fearful that I had crossed a line that could never be uncrossed. However, none of those feelings were present. I felt whole, at ease, and hungry. The desperation for Naomi to press her soft, supple body against mine for even one more second was maddening.

But then she did. She tucked herself against me and laid her head on my chest. I expected my draxilio to purr the way he does when I kill. That steady purr of approval is the closest thing I have to experiencing deep, unwavering happiness, and I assumed the only way to reach that feeling was to continue giving the beast what it wants. I was wrong. When Naomi let go of her fear that we'd made a mistake and let me hold her, it was almost as if the beast inside me stilled. He didn't know what to make of the tenderness of the moment. Truthfully, neither did I.

I experienced sex and other forms of physical intimacy with human women after we landed here. That stopped after Luka's eyes turned red while having sex with Harper, almost ending their relationship.

But the sex I had was absent of tenderness. It was cold. Transactional.

Nothing happened with Naomi beyond snuggling in her bed, but it felt like the most significant nothing I will ever experience.

After my draxilio's initial shock faded, what took its place was a serene concession. It was new. It pleased him. And the only thing he was sure of was that he wanted more of it.

More, he groaned inside my head as Naomi placed her hand on my stomach. *More,* he repeated when she let me stroke her silky hair.

I didn't argue. More is all I want too.

Clearly, I'm failing at hiding my happiness, because my brothers won't shut up about how weird they think I'm acting. Zev even had the nerve to suggest I may have found a human mate. They don't seem to find humans and their many odors as repulsive as I do, because they give me odd looks whenever I point it out.

"Very well, you shall be alone forever," Axil mutters with a dismissive wave. "It happened for each of us, but I'm sure it won't happen for you."

The focused attention on my marital status agitates me enough that I tell them to fuck off as I stomp out of Nia's new room and slam the door closed once I reach mine. I have no idea what will happen with me and Naomi in the future, and frankly, I don't want to think about it right now.

I've only just had my first cuddle. Why must I already consider whether she's my mate? She's a vampire, and I am draxilio. Is it even possible for us to be mates?

More, my draxilio pleads.

Not now, I send back. *We'll get more later.* I hope.

Eventually, Zev asks us to leave, as he, Charlie, and Nia are having a family date. I'm irritated that I'm being asked to leave my own house, considering I'm the only one that still lives here, but he is still in the process of making Charlie his mate officially, so I relent and follow Axil to his and Vanessa's house.

Vanessa isn't feeling well, which has been a common occurrence lately, so she remains in their bedroom while Luka and his two sons, Hudson and Cooper, gather in the living room. Axil brings a tray of toast and ginger ale to their bedroom and returns several minutes later to say he's going to lay down with his mate and asks if we can go to the grocery store to buy the foods Vanessa has been craving.

Luka wholeheartedly accepts this request and volunteers the four of us to go.

"I will drive," he says as we get to our feet.

"No. I'll drive." If I'm to be part of this adventure, we're taking my car.

"Why?"

"Because your car is older and has a strange smell."

"I have two boys," he replies. "What do you expect it to smell like?"

I can't pinpoint exactly what the smell is; I just know it's unpleasant. "My car is also nicer. We're taking mine."

He rolls his eyes but puts his keys back on the front table by the door.

The boys sit in back, and Luka starts fiddling with my Spotify radio stations once we pull out of the driveway. I smack his hand away and return it to my favorite instrumental hits.

"How can you listen to this?" Luka asks, disgusted.

Cooper chimes in from the backseat. "It's boring, Uncle Kyan." My poor nephews. I pity them for being forced to endure the grating racket of Luka's nineties rock bands.

"It calms me," I tell them. "It allows me to decide how I'm feeling, rather than a singer telling me how to feel with their lyrics."

"You think The Beatles are forcing you to feel a certain way with their songs?"

Ugh, here we go again with The Beatles. It's not that I dislike them; I just don't revere them the way Luka does, and he has always seen my lacking mania as a personal flaw.

I let out a heavy exhale, which tries my brother's patience even more.

"Then how do you justify..." Luka trails off as he scrolls through my playlists, "this."

He switches it to Dolly Parton's greatest hits, wearing a smug expression that I'm tempted to slap. The boys start laughing as Dolly reaches the chorus of "9 to 5."

"What is this?" Hudson asks. In the rearview mirror, I see his scrunched-up face and shake my head.

"Dolly Parton doesn't tell anyone how to feel. Her lyrics either tell a story or reflect part of her soul," I explain. "And if she weren't aging at the rate of an average human, I'd suspect that she came from the stars, just like we did."

"Oh yeah?" Luka asks through a deep, mocking chuckle. "Why is that?"

"Because she's the only good one on a planet of almost eight billion people. This has been proven on multiple occasions." I turn on the cool air, as this subject is making me heated. "If you have only one truly good human for every eight billion, then something is off. Either she isn't one of them, or the species is evolving too slowly and is ultimately doomed."

I watch as Hudson considers this, then begins bobbing his head to the music.

"And there is no chance that Dolly is evil and exceptionally skilled at hiding it?" Luka posits. "Lots of humans have that ability."

Given what I know about Dolly, I confidently reply, "No. No chance."

As we go through Axil's grocery list, I notice Hudson and Cooper sneakily adding bags of chips and frozen pizzas in the deep corners of the cart. Luka sees it but does nothing. When Cooper puts in a bottle of ginger ale for Vanessa, he tucks a candy bar behind it.

"I didn't realize we were shopping for the apocalypse."

Luka looks amused. "It is fine. They work hard in school and never get into trouble. They may eat whatever they wish."

"Why are you the only one among us still refusing to use contractions?" I ask.

He scoffs. "It is not proper. I like the way I speak."

That may have been true on Sufoi, where anyone combining words was seen as a lazy pauper, but that rule doesn't apply here. "I admit, I was resistant at first, but since I've made this change to my speech, my employees don't give me as many odd looks."

An aisle over, I hear two women talking.

"Did you hear about that missing priest?" one asks. "Apparently, he had been accused of sexual abuse by several minors, and the church has been trying to cover it up."

"Seriously?" the other replies, aghast. "That's terrible. Can you imagine? I'd scratch his eyes out if he did that to my kid."

"I know. I hope they never find him."

I can't suppress the smile that stretches across my face. The work we're doing matters.

When Hudson passes me, I grab his shoulder and whisper, "Get me a bag of Starbursts. I think Charlie has been getting into my stash. Make sure it has the orange ones on the front or I don't want it."

My nephew looks at me like I'm an idiot. "They all have the orange ones."

I don't pay attention to the latest candy trends. How am I supposed to know?

Then Luka utters six words that leave me stunned, with my mouth hanging open in the cereal aisle.

"We have missed you, you know," he says, looking at his two boys walking in front of us. "You seem so busy lately. Is everything okay?"

"Of course," I tell him. "Work has been busy. I'm fine."

"My kids want to see more of their uncle. Right, boys?"

Cooper looks over his shoulder and nods.

When Hudson returns with my candy, he asks, "Do you have the day off today, Uncle Kyan?" He looks at Luka, his expression seeking approval. When Luka nods, Hudson asks, "We're going to a movie later. Wanna come?"

Hudson has always been my favorite of Luka's sons. Harper has told me repeatedly I shouldn't have a favorite, but I don't give a shit. It's the truth, and I can't deny it. He has the strong moral compass of his father and the endless curiosity of his mother. That combination is what makes a man unstoppable in what he's able to accomplish, and the older he gets, the clearer his potential becomes.

Since they've made so many recent trips up here from their home in Salem to follow the progress of Vanessa's growing fetus, Hudson has seemed eager to spend more time with me. It crushes me to deny him that, but I simply have too much going on to spend hours in a theater when I could be tending to the many tasks I've put off at the office, working with the recruits in the basement, or, possibly, enjoying the feel of Naomi's magnificent breasts pressing into my side.

"I'm sorry, Hudson. I won't be able to make it to the movie," I tell him. "But maybe in a few days we can go for a flight up to the Canadian border and back. Would you like that?"

"That is too far," Luka says in a stern tone.

Hudson rolls his eyes. "Dad, come on. It's not that far."

Hudson is right. Luka is far too protective. His son is sixteen. He needs to start learning how to exist on his own.

"A flight to the border and back would take less than an hour," I note.

Luka shakes his head. "Harper would be worried sick the whole time. I cannot allow it."

"Then you should come with us, Dad."

My brother crosses his arms as he sighs heavily. Eventually, he gives in. "Okay, but no stopping. We go to the border and right back."

Cooper's eyes light up. "Can I come too?"

"No," Luka says immediately. "You stay at Axil's and look after your mother."

My phone vibrates.

> Thea: Friendly reminder that we have an interested buyer coming to meet with us on Tuesday to discuss his proposal. I just sent you our conversation dating back to last March when he first reached out. Take a look and let me know what you think. I have a good feeling about him.

I'm skeptical about anyone who promises a bottomless bucket of gold in exchange for full control of my company, but Thea mentions this guy every chance she gets, so I'll hear him out, despite having no intention of selling.

> On my way to the office soon. I'll send my thoughts upon review.

We finish shopping, pay for our items, and head back to Axil's. I pull Hudson aside and offer him five dollars to bring the Starburst to my house next door, open it, and take out the orange ones, leaving them in a pile on the nightstand in my bedroom. He nods eagerly and races out the side door. Then I quickly slip out the front and start driving to the office before Luka can scold me for working too much.

Upon reviewing Thea's email, I see she's not only forwarded their correspondence over the last several months but also provided links to this man's social media profiles, as well as articles highlighting his string of recent acquisitions. He's a smart investor; the proof of that is clear in the consistent success rate of the companies he buys. I'm not certain this is the right move for us though.

Even if he bought a forty-nine percent stake in the company, I would still have to listen to his opinions on hiring policies, staffing changes, budget projections, and sales strategies. I barely have the patience to tolerate that from Thea right now, and she doesn't even have an ownership stake.

My COO cares about the future of this company, and despite reaching revenue goals year after year, I can tell we're nearing the ceiling unless we get a large cash infusion to really transform the products and services we offer. I have more than enough money to provide said infusion, but Monroe Media Solutions has never been my passion. It's always been a cover for the business I conduct in the basement, and it's the only way I was able to buy the building. This building is zoned for offices not a covert UFO monitoring operation...and definitely not a training facility and dormitory for shifters to practice fighting.

Ultimately, I humor Thea and send her some vague but positive notes on the potential buyer we're going to be meeting with before I take the elevator to the basement.

Andrei tells me about the various sightings he's seen over the last twenty-four hours, but all of them have been cleared.

"Nothing concerning," he vows. "There weren't even two that had matching descriptions."

"Good work," I tell him before opening the hidden door to the hallway.

Julian greets me and tells me that Yvonne is sleeping, and they're all trying to be quiet so as not to disturb her.

I pat him on the shoulder and whisper, "I'm glad to hear that. She needs to get more sleep."

"Yeah, she's a machine." He pauses, looking nervous. "Can I talk to you for a sec?"

I nod at Rex and Owen as I pass them in the kitchen. Rex is busy mopping the floors while Owen is working on prepping meals for the rest of the pack.

"Where's Derek?" I ask as Julian leads me to the room they share.

"He's cleaning the training room."

A proud grin tugs at my lips. I made it clear to them when they were hired that part of their job was to keep this place clean and feed themselves. They needed to split the chores evenly and take turns. Groceries and household cleaning items would be delivered weekly, but everything else was up to them.

Derek, the youngest of the pack who had never previously lived on his own, asked why Yvonne wasn't going to be cooking and cleaning for them, to which I replied, "Because that's not her fucking job."

I was worried that she'd feel pressure from them to participate in these chores despite my warning, but they've left her alone in that regard. From what I've heard, they include her in their meal preparation. They often include Andrei as well, even though his work is completely separate from theirs.

"What is it?" I ask as I sit on the edge of Derek's bed across from Julian.

He scratches his cheek, then rubs his hands against his thighs, as if physically trying to psyche himself up for whatever he's about to say. "It's not that I'm ungrateful for the opportunity you've given me, sir."

My teeth clench. He wants to leave. I feared this would happen after the first live target was destroyed. Training together in sparring drills and scorching dummies is not the same as killing a real person, and I knew at least one of them would struggle with the reality of what's expected here.

"It's just, I grew up in the South."

I'm not following.

"My mom took me to church every week, and what we did to that priest..." He trails off, cracking his knuckles over and over as if unsure what to do with his hands. "It's hard for me to reconcile my upbringing with my role here. I know that man deserved what he got, but I'm not sure if I'll be able to handle it when it's my turn to lead the chase, you know?"

"I understand." As I consider how to respond, I remember something from his intake form. "May I ask, Julian, where is your mother now?"

His mouth twitches. "She passed when I was fifteen."

"I'm sorry to hear that," I tell him. I wish I could offer him something to indicate I understand his pain, but never having had a mother, condolences are all I can offer.

"Yeah. Car accident. Drunk driver." He scoffs. "This college girl hit her. Didn't have a scratch on her when she was pulled from the wreckage. Why does it always happen like that?"

Does it? I have no knowledge about drunk driving accidents,

only that they seem wasteful and completely avoidable. "It shouldn't," I reply. "That should never happen."

He shrugs, trying to fight back the emotion that fills his eyes.

"You went into foster care after that, correct?"

Julian nods, staying quiet. I would guess it's a subject he's reluctant to delve into.

"Well," I begin, "this isn't a prison, Julian. I hired you for a six-month trial period, during which you would live on-site and allow us to monitor your health while on the *wrathenol*. Nowhere in the contract does it state that you're required to kill anyone. I won't make you do that if you don't feel comfortable with it. The contract expires in two months' time, and at that point, all of you are free to live on your own. You'll still get injections before assignments we take, but the need for constant monitoring will cease. If you decide not to renew, you're obviously free to go."

"So I don't have to participate in taking out the targets?"

"No. You don't even have to be present for them."

He jerks back. "Really?"

"Really."

"What's the catch?"

His question makes me laugh. "You're letting us inject you with my DNA. That's the catch. We had no idea what it would do to you guys when we started this experiment. It could've hurt you, or worse. I hoped we'd reach the place we're in now, with minimal reactions, quick recoveries, and the ability to breathe fire, but I'm not forcing anyone to become a killer. The first one always sticks with you, and for some, it gets easier after that," I explain, picturing Axil, who didn't like what we did on Sufoi, but could handle the mental weight of it. Then Zev pops into my head—brilliant, sensitive Zev. "And for some, it's a rain cloud above your head that follows you wherever you go.

"What I want," I continue, "are the right people in this pack to help me achieve my goal. My list of targets is quite long, and the more news I watch, the longer it gets. But I don't want to be the reason for any additional pain in your life. You've been through enough already."

Julian purses his lips as he ponders this.

"Think it over. I will respect whatever decision you make."

We bump fists, and I get up to leave.

"Would it be possible to get a copy of that target list?" he asks. "I think if I had time to learn about their past crimes, it wouldn't be so difficult for me when it's my turn."

This is a pleasant surprise. I thought I would have an email from him in the morning letting me know he has no plans to renew the contract and would like to opt out of the chases. Showing them the target list wasn't part of my plan. It seemed optimal for them to learn about a target's past immediately before the chase began, to keep the feelings of rage fresh and right on the surface, but if it would help them prepare, I'm happy to provide it.

"Are you sure?"

It takes him a minute, but finally he nods.

"Certainly. I'll give Yvonne approval to provide all of you with access." When I reach the door, I pause to face him. "I don't know how much you and the other recruits have shared about your pasts, but it might be beneficial to discuss them."

If I were in his place, I'd be a closed book. Vulnerability usually only leads to pain, but they have more in common than they may realize. Every one of them came from a tragic situation that left them isolated and alone.

"Yeah?"

"There's a reason you're all here together."

CHAPTER 11

NAOMI

"We shouldn't be doing this," I tell Quincy as he uses his blow torch to melt the lock on the door to Kyan's secret lair. "What if he has cameras installed too?"

Quincy pauses to lift his mask. "Well, then his cameras would've caught us installing our cameras, and you probably would've heard about it by now."

"Fair point."

It still feels wrong. Ever since we cuddled, I've been plagued with guilt about my role in this bullshit scheme. For what, so Elaine can continue murdering ex-cons? If Burton was the one to arrest them, they probably weren't even guilty of the crimes they were charged with. Why am I doing this? Am I as evil as she is?

The melted remains of the lock fall to the cement floor with a clatter.

"Ah, got it."

I take another look around the parking garage, making sure there's no one around. "Okay, let's make this fast."

Quincy tosses the broken lock in the trash bin by the door, and I step ahead of him to whip it open. What we find inside is...an office. A plain-looking office with three desks in it. One desk has large double monitors, a keyboard, and a mug filled with pens. There are no posters on the walls. There's a water cooler next to a fake plant, a table covered in snacks, and a blue couch that looks like it spent months on the side of the road with a free sign on it. But that's it. There's nothing else here. No dimly lit corridors, chains on the walls, Batmobile-like cars, or young children sewing clothes together in poorly ventilated rooms—nothing I expected to find in Kyan's basement.

I swallow the lump in my throat. "You've got to be kidding me."

Is this really all there is? Offices that he's trying to rent out, just like he said.

"Maybe there's more to it," Quincy notes as we step inside.

Before I reach the desk, I hear a flush coming from the door directly behind it, and a white guy wearing a heather gray hoodie and black track pants steps out. He's wearing headphones, but I can hear the death metal blasting into his ears from where I stand.

When he notices us, he looks alarmed and pulls his headphones down around his neck. "Who are you?"

"Uh…" I mutter. Shit, why can't I think of something? I thought I'd get this door open and find prisoners in horrific conditions, not a thin white guy who looks like he plays video games for a living.

My disappointment consumes me. Thinking I'd find something awful behind his door is the main reason I haven't abandoned this scheme. No matter how much closer I've gotten to Kyan, in the back of my mind, I was sure his attractive qualities would be obliterated when I finally got inside this room. Then I wouldn't feel any remorse for reporting my findings to Elaine, who would then tell Officer Burton, leading to Kyan's arrest. But it's just a boring office.

"We're with maintenance," Quincy says, taking the lead.

Thank Lillith he's here. "Someone called us about a heating issue."

I doubt he's going to buy it. I'm wearing a peacoat over a bright green cable-knit sweater, skinny black chinos, and black oxfords. Nothing about my appearance shouts *maintenance worker*.

Headphones Guy shakes his head. "There's no heating issue."

"Hm, maybe we got the wrong office," I add, looking at Quincy as if I'm truly confused by this turn of events.

Headphones narrows his gaze as he grabs his phone off his desk. "Who called you?"

In the few seconds Quincy and I exchange a worried glance, Headphones calls our bluff.

"No one is supposed to enter these rooms. I need to check with my boss before I let you in here. One moment."

Before he can make the call, I use my speed to race to his side, snatching the phone from his hand and slamming it on the corner of the desk, creating several spiderweb cracks on the screen. I regret it immediately.

"What the fuck?" Headphones shouts.

Quincy grabs Headphones by the shoulders and forces him to meet Quincy's gaze. Then he softens his voice as he says, "You broke your phone. It's okay, you dropped it. These things happen."

He can glamour people? Why didn't I know about this?

"No one entered this office while you were here," Quincy continues. "The lock was destroyed, but you have no idea how that happened, isn't that right?"

Headphones nods, looking dazed. "Right. I have no idea."

"We're going to leave now, and you never saw us."

"I never saw you."

"When you hear the door close, you'll snap out of this, and you'll be overcome with frustration that you broke your phone."

"Yes, I broke my phone."

Quincy pats him on the arm and backs up toward the doorway. I slip out first, so as not to get in his way and break the trance early. I don't breathe or speak until we're back in the parking garage and a safe distance from the door. Then I turn to Quincy with an accusing glare. "You can glamour people? Since when?"

He smirks. "For a long time, but it's a power I don't like to use. It feels icky."

"Quincy, you could just walk into a bank and demand they give you enough cash for your lab. Why haven't you done that?"

"That would be a prime example of ick, Naomi. Nah, I don't want to do it like that."

Such a saint. Well, as much as an immortal vampire could be. "How does one get the power to glamour?" I ask, realizing that I've never wondered this before. "Only some vampires seem to have it."

We make it to my dead station wagon, and Quincy leans against the side. "It's like getting into a country club. You need three vampires to sponsor you before you're accepted."

"So this was a power you sought out? I thought you didn't like to use it."

He gazes at something off in the distance with a haunted expression. "My maker was involved with the mob, so I got into some dark shit when I was first turned."

Wow, Quincy just got a thousand times more interesting. "I can't believe we've never talked about this." When we've discussed our pasts in previous conversations, he kept his story vague. The only thing I knew was that he ended up with a large group of vampires, but there was never any mention of the mob. "Now I want to hear everything."

He chuckles. "That was another life. I'm not that guy anymore."

The sound of a car meets my ears, and I spot Kyan's headlights about to turn toward us. "Hide!"

Quincy ducks behind my car as I attempt a confident, unbothered stride toward Kyan.

His face lights up when he sees me, and he hurries to park in the spot closest to the elevator. Out of the corner of my eye, I see Quincy scurry to the other side of my car and duck down. Relief washes over me knowing Kyan won't be able to spot him from here.

"Naomi," Kyan says in a husky rasp as he climbs out of his car, looking dapper as ever. "I wasn't expecting to see you here." He pulls me into his arms, and I breathe in his subtle but glorious scent: fresh laundry and sandalwood, which I assume are from the dryer sheets he uses and his deodorant, respectively. It's not overpowering, but still manly and clean. If my heart could still thump wildly inside my chest, it would.

When he lets go, his brow is furrowed. "Why are you here on a weekend? You realize I don't pay you overtime, yes?"

"Oh, I, um, I thought I left my favorite sweater in my car," I lie. "But it's not in there, so it must be under my bed or something."

He sighs as he glances at my car, and I cross my fingers and toes that Quincy doesn't move from his hiding place. "It might be time to say goodbye to that heap of metal. Let me have it towed for you." A wholesome level of hope brightens his eyes. "Then I could drive you every day."

It probably wouldn't be the best idea in terms of optics, but I would much rather ride in his beautiful car than run to and from Sudbury, especially with winter quickly approaching. Plus, more time with him is exactly what I want.

"Yeah, I'd like that."

"Do you have time to come upstairs with me? It won't take long; I just need to review a contract that a client just signed."

"Sure," I reply, hoping he doesn't decide to check in with Headphones Guy for any reason before we leave. As far as I know, when you glamour a human to forget your face, it sticks, but what if seeing me again so soon jogs his memory? I can't have that. We need to get in and out of this building as fast as possible. "Then do you want to come back to my place?" I ask, hoping my tone sounds seductive.

The early afternoon sun casts a warm glow into the garage, landing perfectly on Kyan's sharp cheekbones as he smiles. "I'd like that."

My entire body flushes as I continue gawking at him. Only an alien could contain that much beauty in one large, chiseled package.

The silence is heavy in the elevator as it takes us to the top. At one point, he adjusts the computer bag on his shoulder and his knuckles brush against mine. I freeze in place, desperate to reach for his hand but too nervous to make the move, like I'm back in high school.

Once we reach the top floor, we shift into work mode. I fire up my computer and start checking emails as he goes into his office and gets settled. At one point, he calls me into his office with a deep holler instead of the usual DM over the staff chat window. I don't mind this way. Hearing his low rumble as he says my name leaves me clenching my thighs. Hardly appropriate during actual business hours though.

"You rang, boss?" I ask, leaning against the door frame.

"Did you see that Thea has me double booked for Wednesday at three? What is all this shit?"

I come around the desk and lean over his shoulder as I look at the calendar. "Oh, she must've made a mistake. Here, let me take a look." He moves his hands out of the way, and I take over on the keyboard, opening the meeting invites to see the notes. "Hm. There isn't even a subject listed in here."

"Why did she mark it as urgent?" he asks.

I open the second meeting invite and find the notes in the tiny box labeled 'additional information.' "Ah, see?" I point to the notes she left. "It looks like it's a prep meeting for an upcoming demo with a prospect. She put the notes in the wrong section, and sometimes when you put them in here, it creates a duplicate invite. A glitch in the system or something." I delete the empty duplicate, pleased I was able to provide some insight.

I go to head back to my desk, but Kyan grabs my wrist, spinning me around until my hands are on his wide, muscular shoulders, and I'm standing between his long legs. He's so tall I don't even have to look down. Even with him seated, we're at eye level, and his eyes are heavy lidded and swirling with heat.

He closes the distance between us so fast I barely register what's happening before his lips are pressed against mine. The kiss is soft, at first, much more tender than I'd expect from a Crankenstein like Kyan. But then his lips move against mine as he nips at my bottom lip, and his big hands get lost in my hair, gripping the back of my head like he'll never let me go.

I moan into him as I trace his bottom lip with my tongue, and he lets me in, sending a lightning bolt straight to my core as he explores the depths of my mouth.

I've never been kissed like this before.

His chest vibrates with a deep rumble as his hand travels down my back and his fingers squeeze my left cheek. I whimper as my legs start to buckle, but he's there, holding me securely in his muscled arms. The kiss turns frantic and hungry as we paw at each other, and he lifts me onto his desk, pushing my knees apart so he can fit between them. The shift in position exacerbates our height difference, but he doesn't seem to mind as he bends down to drink from my lips once again.

Suddenly, he breaks the kiss and presses his forehead against mine. "Tell me you want this like I do," he says, panting.

His hands gently cup my cheeks as he waits for my answer. I'm surprised to see uncertainty in his expression. My arrogant boss actually looks nervous that I might reject him. I nod as I grip the collar of his crisp white button-up and pull him closer, wanting him everywhere. He growls at that, low and deep, and the walls of my pussy clench around nothing.

I feel him reach for the hem of my sweater, and I lift my arms as he tugs it over my head. He sucks in a breath at the sight of me in my lacy purple bralette.

For a fraction of a second, I grow self-conscious because my breasts are pretty small. I've never needed an overly supportive bra because my tits just don't bounce around that much. But when Kyan traces the line of where the fabric meets my skin, I shiver, and when he dips his chin and sucks my nipple through the thin fabric, the room fades away. I arch against him, feeding him more of my breast as he uses his hand to squeeze and pinch the other.

"Oh god," I moan, my nails biting into the magnificently carved marble that is his bicep.

He stops and shoots me a heated, predatory glance as his mouth hovers just above my nipple. "God isn't here, sweetheart. But I am, and I'm going to make you come until you cry."

Fucking hell. I almost come right then and there.

I expect him to continue his oral assault on my breasts, but he straightens to his full height, and the cool air against the wet fabric provides such a delicious sensation that I'm practically writhing on the edge of his desk.

With deft fingers, he unbuttons my pants and shoves his hand inside. I let out a gasp as he slips a finger in easily. He adds a second as his mouth covers mine, trapping my muffled cries.

"Tell me what you like," he whispers against my lips. "I want to learn your body."

I feel like it should be obvious that I love everything he's doing, given the obscene wet sounds filling the room as he thrusts his thick fingers inside me, but I love his eagerness to get it right.

His palm presses against my clit, but the touch is too direct. It feels good, so good it borders on painful. It's not what I need. "The s-sides," I say through short, rapid breaths. "Rub the sides of my clit."

Kyan follows my directions, pulling his fingers out and focusing entirely on the swollen nub. His touch is relentless as it circles and flicks and brushes my clit from side to side. Need begins to build at the base of my spine, slowly pushing me higher and higher.

"Yes," I cry out. "Like that."

My whole body trembles as I buck against his hand. When he dips his head and bites my nipple, I explode, my arms and legs quaking in ecstasy. That doesn't stop him though. His hands and mouth continue to work my body as I come down, drawing out my orgasm as long as possible.

His kisses are light as they run along the length of my neck, and I know if he wasn't holding me up, I'd collapse in a puddle all over his keyboard. When he pulls out, I ache at the loss of his touch. Holding up his glistening fingers, his gaze locks onto mine, and he licks them clean, groaning at the taste of me. The sight is so obscene and hot, I swear I fall a little bit in love with him.

"I wondered what this would be like," he says with a smirk. "Your taste. With no scent, I worried I wouldn't be able to taste you either. I've never been happier to be wrong. Mm." He sucks on his fingers once more. "Even better than your cupcakes."

Something buzzes, and Kyan pulls his phone out of his pocket.

The name Yvonne is all I see. Another text from the mystery woman. My stomach drops.

He mumbles a curse, and I can already tell I'm about to get mad.

"Who's that?" I ask, trying but failing to mask my annoyance.

"Work."

"Work?" I repeat. "Who is it, Thea?" I know it isn't, but he needs to climb his way out of this hole, because whoever the fuck Yvonne is just ruined a perfect moment.

"No, it's..." he starts. "It's a little side hustle I'm working on."

Side hustle? Is he referring to Headphones in the basement? Or is Yvonne actually booty call number two? "Tell me about it."

"I will. Another time." He puts his phone back in his pocket and pulls me in for another deep, toe-curling kiss. Then he presses his forehead to mine. "The last thing I want to do right now is leave you. I promise you that."

"Agreed," I say with a pout. "You didn't even get a turn."

Another kiss, but this is more of a smacking peck. "Watching you unravel like that was more than enough, Naomi. I've never seen a more beautiful sight."

Well, I can hardly stay mad now.

He lets go and straightens his clothes. "I can drive you home first, if you'd like."

"No, it's okay," I tell him. "I'll run or take an Uber."

"Pick you up on Monday? Around nine?"

I nod as I pull my sweater back on. "See you then."

There's clearly still something that he's hiding, but what? And now that my body is addicted to his touch, do I even want to know what it is?

CHAPTER 12

KYAN

My brothers are stupid and reckless. I'm inclined to tie them together and set my flame upon their heads until nothing remains but a pile of bone shards.

After a sleepless night with the pack in Nottingcook Forest, during which Owen eagerly volunteered to destroy a target with a long history of gross vehicular manslaughter while intoxicated, I came home to a quiet, dark house, and was able to get forty minutes of sleep before my world turned upside down.

Two tornadoes touched down in our front yard, one a dark gray color, and the other bright red. Except they weren't tornadoes. Instead, they were other alien dragon shifters who reside in Europe—Italy and Scotland, to be exact—and decided to pay us, their "cousins," a visit after the bouncy dark-haired one felt Mylo's presence in Italy while he was on honeymoon with Sam. They tracked Mylo back here and wanted to make an official introduction.

Were they invited? No. Did they alert us to their travel plans ahead of time? No. Yet Mylo is acting as if their presence in our town is somehow a good thing, and we should become allies with them. My idiot brother even exchanged numbers with them.

What bothers me most, apart from the dark-haired one—Dante, I think his name is—acting as if we'd be lucky to have them in our corner, is that I had no prior knowledge that other aliens existed on this planet.

This is the primary function of Andrei's job. I hired him to secure a contract with the U.S. government to monitor any suspicious activity that could be considered UFOs. The contract was easier to get than I anticipated. "The government doesn't want to waste their manpower on this shit," Andrei explained to me at the time. "Most of the higher-ups don't believe they exist, so they're inclined to make reported sightings disappear as soon as possible. There's already a public perception that the government knows they're real and is hiding evidence. The sooner they can jump on a sighting and chalk it up to a civilian's overactive imagination or a bad trip, the happier they are."

The only way Dante and his brother—*tikanos*, as he called them, from Planet Nocturna Tora—could've sidestepped this monitoring system is if they were here before us. That doesn't sit well with me either.

And now Charlie has learned that her husband, Zev, is not a human man, like she thought, and is instead a dragon from another planet with strange European cousins. Charlie left the house moments ago, needing time to process this discovery.

This is a multi-layered mess, involving too many people, and I am far too tired to remain composed. Charlie and Zev are not officially mated yet, and not only is she now aware of what we are, but Zev just let her leave, prioritizing her emotions over the danger she could be putting us in.

"Should we be worried that she knows the truth about us, and we let her drive away?" I ask, irritated that I'm the only one considering this.

"What would you have me do?" Zev snaps. "Lock her in the basement until she agrees to solidify the bond?"

He doesn't have to be such a child about it. "Very well. What we should be talking about are those sneaky fucking *tikanos*, Dante and Ronan," I add. "Don't call them, Mylo."

"Why not?" Mylo asks. "They don't seem like a threat. If they wanted to attack us for trespassing, they would have." Although he likely means they had the opportunity to react while he and Sam were in Italy, I am not convinced. The moment Mylo felt their presence, he and Sam left the country.

"It would be good to have an ally outside the U.S.," Luka notes. "They can alert us to other outsiders who arrive. We need to do more to track that anyway."

Fools. All of them. If they bothered to ask what I do for a living rather than mercilessly mock me for how much time I spend away from the house, they would know I have that covered and require no assistance from those European pricks.

I scoff at Luka's suggestion. "We don't need them for that. In fact, we don't need them for anything."

"Oh, are you saying you have the ability to track aliens entering Earth's atmosphere all by yourself?" Axil asks with a smirk.

If my right hand had not so recently been responsible for the look of sheer ecstasy on Naomi's face as I made her come in my office, I'd use it to knock a few teeth out of Axil's mouth. But I need to keep that hand in top form for my little vampire. He doesn't realize how lucky he is.

"What if I am?"

Axil, Luka, and Mylo start laughing hysterically. "Is that how you spend your days in your high-rise corporate office?" Luka asks. "Making spreadsheets and hacking into Area 51?"

My patience has reached its limit, and if I don't leave, someone is getting pummeled. Letting out a steady growl, I march out of the room, flipping one of the counter stools in the kitchen as I pass. One of the legs breaks in three places.

"You're paying for a new one," Mylo shouts.

What does he care? It's not his stool. "You don't even live here anymore!"

* * *

When the work week begins, I'm still fuming over the visit from Dante and Ronan and at my brothers for being so quick to trust these new aliens, but at least Charlie and Zev have resolved their conflict. All it took was my willingness to let Zev electrocute me with a laptop, and Charlie felt she could count on Zev to protect her and Nia. They're a strange pair, and I don't understand their bond, but as long as my brother is happy, I suppose that's what matters.

My face healed quickly, but it wasn't pleasant feeling my skin sizzle against the top of that MacBook. I hope he keeps that in mind the next time he feels inclined to give me shit about my job.

I slow my car to a stop a few feet past Naomi's driveway. She texted me late last night requesting I stay on the road, to avoid being seen by her cell mates. Every part of me comes alive, buzzing at the knowledge that Naomi will be within reach in mere minutes. My hands don't seem to know what to do when they're not on her skin. Not that I've spent much time touching her thus far, but I know I need more.

Yes, more.

One moment inside her hot, wet cunt, and my draxilio has become Mr. Chatty. He won't shut up.

Soon, I send back, trying to calm him.

Perhaps I've been lonely, and that simple fact can explain this new, insatiable need, but I don't think that's it. I run hot. Hotter than the average human, due to my inner flame. Naomi runs cold. I expected her to be unpleasantly cold, like hugging an iceberg, but it's not like that. Holding her is akin to pressing a cold beverage to a sweaty forehead on a hot afternoon. There's relief in her icy touch that reaches the center of my marrow.

"Hi there," she says when she climbs into the passenger seat. Her hair is swept up in a twist, making her elegant neck look longer than usual, with little pieces of it falling around her face. Large sunglasses cover her eyes, and her plush, perfect lips are the color of cherry blossoms. The wide brim of her hat takes up the majority of her side of the car.

"Wow." I'm instantly vexed at the distance it puts between us. "Is it supposed to be sunny out today?" I ask, looking at the cloudy sky above.

"It is," she notes, "but not yet." Then she knocks the hat off her head and pulls me in using my tie.

The brush of her lips catches me off guard, but I have no problem with it, and I quickly melt into her. Recalling her first day as my assistant, I thought she was kind, but meek. Since then, she has continued to surprise me, and this, right here, is the best part. She takes charge, and it's exactly what I crave. Would she be willing to take this dynamic further? I have yet to find a woman who's interested in playing that role, but it seems Naomi might be open to it.

Before long, our tongues are swirling around each other, and a jolt of electricity shoots to my throbbing cock at the sound of her breathy moan. I picture her eager lips wrapped around me, sucking hard, struggling to fit me in, her tongue tracing my ridges, and my hips buck in my seat. My need for her sets my skin on fire, and my draxilio rumbles in approval deep inside my chest.

When she pulls away, her lips are swollen from my kiss and more of her hair has escaped her twist. Then she begins to sneeze. The sound reminds me of a cartoon mouse being tickled, and it's the most adorable noise I've ever heard. The cloud cover seems to have disappeared, and a bright beam of sunlight shines directly on her face. I laugh as four more rapid sneezes burst from her, and she frantically puts her hat back on.

"I told you," she mutters, slightly out of breath from the sneezing fit. "Ugh, that sucked."

"I respectfully disagree. It very much did not suck."

She pokes me with her elbow. "Oh, you find my allergic reaction funny, do you?"

"Only because I know it's not dangerous. Also because it's cute."

"Cute?" She shakes her head. "Absolutely not."

I wonder how mad she would be if I hid that hat on the next sunny day, just so I can watch her sneeze.

"How was the rest of your weekend?" she asks when I merge onto 93 south.

"Irritating."

She pauses, as if waiting for my reply. When I don't elaborate, she asks, "What happened?"

"I won't bore you. My brothers are dipshits, and I didn't get enough sleep. Let's leave it at that."

"Sounds like you need more of Naomi's special treats."

My stomach growls in response and she laughs.

"How about my mom's famous almond cookies?"

"Almond is the flavor? That sounds dull. No offense to your mother, of course."

"It's okay. I get it, but you're wrong. It's a subtle flavor compared to the mango cupcakes, but they're equally delicious, with a crumbly texture and the right amount of crisp, topped off with a sliced almond. You'll love them. I promise."

"I trust you." The words are out of my mouth before I can stop them. Do I trust her? Not entirely. Trust isn't something that comes easily for me. Though I suppose when it comes to desserts, I do trust her.

We make it to the office ten minutes late, but I don't care. No one is going to reprimand the CEO for being tardy.

"Ah, there you are," Thea says when I exit the elevator. Spoke too soon. Her gaze shifts between me and Naomi and a crease forms between her eyes. "You…arrived at the same time? That's some convenient timing."

"No, we drove here together," I reply, looking down at Naomi. She tucks a lock of hair behind her ear as her cheeks redden.

"Huh." Thea's expression is unreadable. "Well, it's certainly great for the environment. Kyan, we should prep for that meeting I emailed you about."

"Sure," I say. "Let me get settled and figure out where to squeeze it in. Probably late afternoon."

"Okay, sounds good."

"She's onto us," Naomi whispers once Thea is out of earshot. "We're so fucked."

"No, I don't think so," I say, replaying the interaction in my head. "If she is, she'll ask me about it later. Don't worry."

It's impossible to concentrate on work when I can stare through my glass wall at Naomi's plush backside all day. The back of her chair blocks most of it—blasted thing—but she gets up to do something once an hour, and my breath catches at the full view. She catches me each time and gives me a knowing, heated smirk. It makes me long for five o'clock, when everyone will leave and I can have her all to myself.

I don't get the chance to meet with Thea until the very end of the day, but luckily, when I do, she doesn't mention the moment with Naomi. Her sole focus is on the meeting with the buyer. After referring to the notes I made in my reply as "non-definitive and unhelpful," she tells me more about his background. I promise not to phone it in when the buyer comes to the office, and she seems satisfied with that. She leaves for the day shortly afterward, and as I lean against Naomi's desk, we realize in the same moment that we have the floor to ourselves.

My heart doesn't even have time to beat before Naomi's lips are on mine and my skin heats where her hands are pressed against my chest. It's as if my body is in stasis, and her very touch gives me life.

"I've wanted to do this all day," she moans against my mouth. "It's so hard to stay away from you when you look this good in a tie."

"You like my ties?" I ask. It seems like an additional barrier to remove and nothing more, but I'll wear them every day if she wants me to.

"Mm." Her fangs extend in her mouth, and she brushes the sharp points against my bottom lip.

My cock jumps at the sensation. Suddenly my head fills with images of Naomi leaving bite marks all over my chest, blood dripping down my stomach, and her licking my wounds clean as my blood paints her lips and chin the deepest shade of crimson.

She wraps the end of my tie around her wrist, pulling me flush against her. "I *love* your ties."

I don't hear the ding of the elevator until the flinty, high-pitched voice of my COO reaches my ears. "Would you believe I forgot my ke–"

Naomi must hear her before I do, because she shoves at my chest, putting a foot between us.

"Oh. Hey, guys," Thea says, her tone confused.

"Kyan," Naomi says, giving me an exasperated look. "How do you keep spilling food on your ties? And where did I put that Tide pen?" She looks around and starts digging through her desk drawers.

Thea clears her throat and awkwardly waves her keys at us. "Anyway…see you both tomorrow."

Both of us wait for the elevator doors to close, and then wait about ten seconds more before taking a breath.

Shit. Keeping this secret is going to be much harder than I thought.

CHAPTER 13

NAOMI

Nothing gets me energized for a workday like a big cup of blood in the morning, and on those sluggish, meh days when I'm tempted to climb back under the covers, I treat myself to some AB negative. It's the tastiest blood of all, likely because it's the rarest type. Quincy thinks he could switch the stickers with a bag of O positive, and I wouldn't know the difference, but I don't believe him. It's more savory, somehow. It's also the most expensive, so I only bust it out in dire circumstances. Today is one of those days, because Kyan has turned me into a cat in heat. I can't keep my hands off him, which is extremely inconvenient because he's always busy and most of the time we spend together is at the office, where I'm expected to keep my hands to myself.

It's not fair, and since I haven't had the opportunity to get him naked and blow his mind, I stayed up until dawn with my hands all over myself. Now I'm tired and cranky and horny, and that's a problematic combination that only AB negative can solve.

I pour myself a heaping mugful in my oversized goth unicorn mug and scroll through Instagram as I try to wake up.

"Bleh!" I squeak in horror after taking a sip. No. No, no, no. This isn't right. I check the blood bag to make sure it's AB negative and not expired. My stomach drops when I see the blank checkbox next to the word "Suppressant."

I call Quincy immediately. He sounds groggy when he answers, as if I woke him up.

"Quince, I-I think you sold me the wrong bag of AB negative. Or... or... this one was missed in your final quality check."

Silence. And then, "Why? What happened?"

"The bag I'm looking at right now...the suppressant box isn't checked."

"Fuck," he mutters quietly. "Okay. Naomi, you're gonna be fine. It's not a big deal. I'm coming to your place right now with two free replacement bags. You just need to lie low for twelve hours and it'll wear off. Call in sick. Don't leave the trailer, okay?"

"Call in sick?" I reply. "Kyan knows I'm a vampire. That won't make any sense to him."

"So? It's not like he's going to fire you for playing hooky because he knows you can't get sick."

"I'm not worried about that. What if he calls my bluff and wants to come over to see what's really wrong?"

He sighs, then softens his tone to one filled with empathy. "I know you haven't been through this yet, but I have. Plenty of times. It's not as bad as you think."

"But..." My breaths start coming out short and fast. "It's not how I want to be. I'm trying to be better. *We're* trying to be better. It feels like it'd be too primal, too much like *them*."

"I know. I get it."

I take a step toward my bed and the room tilts. "Oh fuck. I think I'm having a panic attack. Is that possible? I thought that was a human problem I left behind." Kyan is probably getting ready for work at this very moment. He'll be on his way over soon. "I can't let him see me, Quincy. How do I keep him from coming here?"

"All right, hang up with me and text him. Tell him you can't come to work today and you can't go into details, but you'll be there tomorrow. I'm on my way now with the replacement bags."

"Okay," I tell him, trying to focus on the lightning-shaped crack in the wall next to the fridge as I steady my breathing. "I'll do that."

> Hey boss! Sooo I'm really sorry for the short notice, but I can't make it into work today. I still get sick time, right? 😅

Legally, he can't take that away from me just because I'm a vampire, can he? Ugh, I'm sure he can. It's not like I'd be able to dispute it with the truth. *Okay, keep it vague, but don't lie. A lie will worry him, and he'll come over. Don't worry him.*

> I'm feeling under the weather, so I'll be using one of those for the day. No biggie. I'll give you the details tomorrow, which is when I'll return to work, bright and early.

Then I remember what today is.

> Oh, and good luck at the meeting with the buyer. Knock 'em dead!

Quincy shows up at my door right after I hit send. "You text him?" he asks as he hands me the bags.

I nod. "Hopefully he buys it."

"Just chill. Everything will be cool by tomorrow."

Then I feel it. The flicker. Soon to be an inferno. "Okay, you need to bounce before shit gets weird. Thanks for the free bags. I'll talk to you later."

He rushes out the door, giving me a supportive thumbs-up, and I can only hope he's right.

My phone rings, and my jaw clenches when I see that it's Kyan.

"What's wrong?" he asks as soon as I pick up. His voice is thick with concern and, somehow, an entire octave lower than his normal voice. My clit throbs at the sound. "Did something happen between you and Elaine?"

"No, nothing like that."

I have no idea what to tell him, so I sit there on the edge of my bed with my mouth hanging open. Then I catch my reflection in the mirror on my dresser and I start wondering how big Kyan's dick is and how wide I'll have to open my mouth to fit him all in.

"So then, what?"

There's clearly no way around this, and he's not going to buy the sick thing, so I might as well be honest. He must have weird bodily shit happen to him that humans wouldn't understand, right?

"It's silly, really," I begin, trying to laugh it off as casually as I can. "Um, so vampires are an extremely passionate breed." Ugh, already off to a terrible start. "Sex is very much built into our biology. We sort of, uh, need to have a lot of it. A lot more than humans, and especially when we drink blood."

Kyan listens intently, but I can't see his face, so I have no concept of how he's processing this information. I just know that I'm more embarrassed trying to explain it than I've ever been about anything. It's worse than when my period seeped through my pants on my very first date. Another core memory directly tied to blood, I now realize.

"Okay…" he finally says.

"Part of the motivation to maintain the Sipper lifestyle is to not be driven by primal instincts. We don't want our thirst to hold us hostage, you know? We want to live normal lives. As normal as possible."

He sighs. "Naomi, I'm not following."

Clearly, he's getting impatient and even more confused because I'm doing a shit job and *oh my god*. The walls of my pussy contract, and the long blue vibrator next to my pillow catches my eye. Losing control and running out of time, I blurt, "This morning I drank blood that didn't have a libido suppressant. My friend Quincy gets the blood for me. He's a chemist who owns a Dunkin' Donuts, by the way. Good guy. Anyway, he usually adds the suppressant into my bags, but he forgot, and now I want to fuck everything that moves, so I need to remain in isolation until this blood leaves my system, which should be in twelve hours."

Kyan goes quiet.

I really wish he FaceTimed me, so I could get an idea of what's going on in his head, because this silence feels like a knife through my intestines. Then I'd also get to see those full lips of his, and that chiseled jaw line. Images of his bare, blue chest and black tattoos fill my mind, and I have to swallow a groan that threatens to escape me.

Eventually, he says, "Okay, wait. You're telling me that when vampires drink blood that doesn't have a libido suppressant added to it, they need to have sex?" There's no judgment in his voice like I expected. He sounds curious.

"Yes."

"And you drank some of this blood today."

"Uh-huh."

"Why wouldn't you want that?" he asks.

I don't understand the question. "What do you mean?"

"Why would any vampire actively avoid that sensation? The need to fuck every time you feed."

"It sounds hot when you put it like that," I tell him. His train of thought makes sense. At first, hearing it sounds like a fun existence, but it gets old after a couple days. I need him to understand the reality of it. "How many meals do you typically eat in a day?"

"At least three. Sometimes four. It depends on how busy I am."

"Okay. What about snacks?"

"I love snacks."

"Who doesn't? How many of those do you have?"

"Um," he starts, and I can picture him twisting his mouth to the side, making a face like he's not impressed. "Probably three."

"Okay. And what about beverages?"

"Oh, I don't know. A lot."

"Right." Time to bring it home. "Imagine whenever you ate a meal, had a snack, drank a coffee, had a sip of water—anytime you consumed anything, you had the overwhelming desire to fuck the closest person to you. So overwhelming that willpower isn't an option. It's gone. You don't have a choice in it because this is how you're designed."

I pause. "Would you want to live like that?"

"No." He chuckles, the sound a mix of nervousness and mild disgust. "No, that sounds exhausting and inconvenient."

"Exactly!" I reply, sitting down on the edge of the bed. "Ahh," I mutter, embarrassed. I'm so horned up that even sitting down is too much friction. I'm already teetering over the edge. At this rate, I'll come just sitting still.

"I don't under— h-how? How do vampires get anything done?"

Typical Kyan. His mind goes straight to productivity, and I find that completely adorable. Such a boss. "Most of them don't," I tell him. "It's another reason Sippers get teased. They think we're prudes because we don't want to spend at least ten hours a day fucking other vampires who happen to be close by."

"Wow." He says the word a few more times, still in awe.

"What did you do before you had access to the blood with the suppressant?"

"I'd limit myself to one drink a day," I explain, wincing at how awful that was. "It was hard. My throat would get scratchy and so dry it hurt. I'd try to make sure my one meal was big enough to keep me full for as long as possible, then I'd lock myself in my trailer with a few rechargeable vibrators and swap them out whenever one died."

"Are you…in pain?"

"No, I'm fine. I promise." I don't want him to worry. He has such an important day ahead of him and this is just a sucky part of what I am. "Go to work. Crush that meeting. If there's anything I can do from here to help, let me know."

"Okay."

He sounds genuinely sad that he won't see me today, which makes me want to straddle his face. Who knew Crankenstein had such big feelings?

"Good luck," I tell him.

We end the call and I get back in bed, ready to spend the day too turned on to function. Instead of reaching for my vibrator, I scroll through the latest smutty romance on my Kindle app.

About an hour later, I'm deep in the latest Sarah Jaeger novel, and the two main characters are just about to tear each other's clothes off when there's a loud, angry knock at my door.

It better not be Elaine. I'm so not in the mood for her bullshit.

Steeling my spine, I open it to find Kyan holding what looks like a plastic container filled with chicken soup.

"Kyan, what are you doing here?" Holy Lillith, he looks good. His light brown hair is mussed, and he's wearing a light gray button-up with a dark gray and maroon checkered tie. The black dress pants he's wearing are tailored to perfection. They're tight enough for me to get a glimpse of the impressively long and thick cock pressed against his thigh, but only if I really look, which I am. They're not so tight that it's obscene. And his tie is loose, as if he's been tugging on it all morning.

I don't understand why he brought soup, and I don't care.

My pussy aches at the sight of him.

"You shouldn't be here," I mutter through shallow breaths, taking a step back. If I get a whiff of that sandalwood deodorant he wears, I won't be responsible for my actions.

He lifts the soup in front of me as he steps inside my trailer. Uh oh.

"I brought soup."

"I can see that." But why?

His gaze darts between my mouth and the soup, and he looks distinctly uncomfortable. "You took a sick day. When humans are sick, they eat soup."

Okay, now he's starting to sound like he's concussed.

"Right, but I'm not human."

He looks at the soup for a long moment. "Fine. Fuck the soup," he says, then tosses it aside. The container's top flies off when it hits the floor, sending a pile of noodles and beige broth all over my kitchen.

I throw up my hands. "Kyan, what the he—"

His kiss is bruising and hungry. I lean into it, at first, but remember my current state and jerk away.

"No, Kyan. We can't."

Chest heaving, he steps closer, trying to remove the distance I just created. "Why not? You need this, and I want to give it to you."

Ooh boy, do I want him to give it to me. I want it more than anything, but not like this.

Across the room, my phone lights up with a text I can't read, but I do notice the time. "Because you should be at the office, getting ready for your big meeting. Stop worrying about me."

"I went, and I was fucking miserable there without you," he

says. His pupils are blown out, and I can see the curve of his spectacular pecs through his shirt. If I had a working heart, those words would stop it from beating.

I want him to unmask for me and remove all the barriers between our bodies. Then I want to hold onto his horns and ride him until I black out. But should I? He might want this now, but won't he regret missing the meeting once our bodies are sated? I don't want to be the reason this meeting goes poorly or why Thea is mad. She already suspects something's amiss. It's obvious.

"That might be one of the most romantic things I've ever heard, but we really shouldn't. I'm serious."

He lowers his head, still holding my gaze, but now he's looking at me through those long eyelashes of his. I hear a low rumble start deep in his chest as he takes a predatory step in my direction. I back up, trying to summon restraint but also desperate to be caught by him.

"Kyan," I say, warning clear in my tone. "I'm not myself right now. I can't control my impulses. You really should leave." My resolve is weakening. He can tell. The subtle tremor in my voice lights a fire in his eyes.

"Are you conscious?"

Is he kidding? "Yeah."

He takes another step. "Do you want this?"

I swallow. "Y-yeah."

"Will you regret it tomorrow?"

"I mean…"

"Tell me the truth, Naomi." He's got me. He knows it.

I shake my head.

There's less than an inch between us. His breath is warm and minty as it fans my face.

He strokes a finger across my cheek. "Do you consent to this?"

I nod.

A muscle in his jaw ticks, and I want to trace the movement with my tongue. "I need to hear it."

In a trembling whisper, "Yes."

For what feels like a long time, his gray eyes dart between mine, back and forth. Back and forth, as if he's waiting for me to take it back. When I don't, he cups my face in his hands and crushes his lips to mine.

We become a frenzy of hands and mouths, never getting quite close enough to satisfy our crippling need for one another. At one point, he pulls away, and I whimper at the loss of his soft, perfect mouth.

"I need to tell you something," he says, panting heavily. "Before we do this."

Oh no. Please don't ruin the moment. *Whatever it is, I'm cool with it. Tell me later,* I want to say. I settle on, "Okay."

"I like," he begins, then pauses, looking more vulnerable than I've ever seen him, "to be dominated."

Did I...? Did he really just say that? I'm not dreaming, am I?

"You do?" I ask, needing to confirm it was a real sentence that came out of his mouth and not my horny brain feeding me my most recent fantasy as an illusion.

He nods. "I don't want control. Not in the bedroom. I have it pretty much everywhere else, but here, like this, I want to be controlled."

Never have I felt so relieved and so excited at the same moment. I giggle as I tug him down by his collar and give him a big, smacking kiss. "Today's your lucky day, boss man, because *in here,* I like to be in control."

He sucks in a breath as his nostrils flare. "You do?"

"Mm hm."

The smile he wears is boyish and endearing as I tug him by the tie toward the bed. When the backs of my thighs bump against the edge, I undo the knot and place it gently on the comforter. "I have plans for this."

He resumes the kiss, growling whenever our lips part to remove an article of clothing. At some point, I'm able to move his large frame around until his back is to the bed, and I gently push at his chest. I can see the blurred shape of his dick in my periphery, and my throat has already started to dry up at the sheer size, but I don't want to ruin the surprise. He needs to be in his natural state before I take it all in. Not some disguise in order to be accepted by the masses. Right now, I need the real Kyan.

"Unmask for me."

Slowly, black horns appear to grow out of his hairline, and his skin fades from a pasty white shade to shimmering shades of blue. I don't let my eyes travel all the way down until the unmasking is complete.

I refuse to rush this moment, as I study the sweeping black tattoos that cover his shoulders and curl around his arms. There are solid lines, both thick and thin, and dotted sections that overlap the former with incredible precision. My fangs extend as I move down his chest and reach the peaks and valleys of his many abs—I count ten, and they become even more prominent with each panting breath he takes.

That entrancing V outlining his hips takes my eyes all the way down to the main event and…wow. There have been many sleepless nights trying to complete the image of a naked Kyan in my head, and somehow, the reality is even better.

It's about as long as my forearm, with a fat mushroom head and more than one protruding vein that I plan to trace with my tongue. It rests against his stomach, twitching every now and then. Ridges cover his length, and saliva fills my mouth at the sight of them spiraling around him to the very bottom. They're a darker shade of blue than the rest of him, and the heavy balls that hang between his legs are a matching shade.

What I'm most excited about, however, is the row of eight silver barbells that run along the underside. "A Jacob's ladder?"

He nods.

My boss has a Jacob's ladder. I feel like I just won the penis lottery.

"When did you get this? Why did you get this?"

"Naomi." His voice is a breathy rasp. He doesn't answer my questions, and the information doesn't matter anyway. The expression that he wears can only be described as aching hunger, and I can't wait anymore.

"Do you want a safe word?" I ask, eager to ensure his comfort as we proceed.

It comes to him in an instant. He shoots me a playful smirk. "Soup."

A laugh escapes me. "Soup it is."

Grabbing the tie from the edge of the bed, I crawl up the length of Kyan's seemingly mile-long frame, until I'm straddling his rib cage. "Give me your hands."

He does as he's told, and lifts them above his head, wrists crossed. I keep the tie loose enough that it's not cutting off circulation, but tight enough that he can't slip out and grab me.

"Keep them above or behind your head. You don't touch me until I say you can, and you don't get to come until I allow it. Got it?"

He grunts in agreement, but that's not good enough.

"I need to hear it."

His Adam's apple bobs up and down as he swallows. "Yes."

I scoot backward until my core hovers just above his thighs, and I notice the smooth patch of blue skin where pubes would normally be. He arches into my touch as I wrap my hand around him, his girth making it impossible for my fingers to meet. I lock my gaze onto his as I flatten my tongue and run it along the underside of his cock, moaning as I cross each ridge and barbell, my pussy gushing at the different textures and sensations. When I reach the tip, I lap the pre-come away as it starts to roll down the sides like a melting ice cream cone.

Kyan throws his head back against my headboard with his eyes pinched shut as I move down to his balls. I lick and suck and kiss my way around them as they lay heavy and hot against my tongue.

"Fuck," he says through gritted teeth. "Your mouth."

I don't know if it's a request or a compliment, but I take it as the former.

"That was the plan."

The sounds that fill my trailer are his loud panting breaths and the wet suction of my mouth as I take him in deep. I'd choke before fitting all of him inside, so I go as far down as my gag reflex allows. I swear he grows hotter and bigger by the second, and soon I'm trying to relax my jaw to accommodate him. A strangled moan makes its way up my throat, and he growls in response as he looks down at me.

"Your lips," he whimpers, "I never want them to leave my cock. You look so beautiful like this."

My eyes sting with tears as spit dribbles down my chin, so I can't imagine I look that ravishing, but whatever. He likes the show I'm putting on, and I like the salty taste of his skin. Nothing else matters but our shared pleasure.

Then I change the pace. I go faster, sucking deeper as I stroke him. His hips buck, and my eyes widen when he hits the back of my throat. When I feel his hand grip the back of my head, I go still and release him.

He sucks in a startled breath as his gaze turns anguished.

"No touching," I remind him. "Not yet."

Nodding his apology, he lifts his bound hands above his head and rests them against the headboard.

As I continue lapping at his pierced shaft, I lightly dig my nails into the skin of his chest and drag them down to his hips. His entire body trembles, and knowing I, a plump doctor from Seattle who never had satisfying sex as a human, possess that much control over this humongous alien dragon's pleasure makes me feel like a wanton sex goddess.

I never felt like I had any control in my past relationships—not emotionally and certainly not physically. Or even that I was good at sex. The only thing I was good at was my work, and since becoming a vampire, I don't even have that. Sex got better after I was turned, but this element was still lacking. Wyatt didn't know what to do with me when I tried dominating him, and instead of asking for it directly, I decided to stop sleeping with him altogether, because I was more bored than attracted to him anyway.

But Kyan is giving me a gift right now. A gift I didn't realize would feel so therapeutic until now. I can use him however I wish, and he trusts me enough to let me take the lead. It's humbling.

I kiss a trail along the V, over his hips, and I take time to worship each rippling ab as I crawl up his body. His cock brushes against my folds, and I moan when the top barbell bumps against my clit.

"Go slow," Kyan cautions me as I guide his fat length into my opening, one agonizing centimeter at a time. "I don't want to hurt you."

When I can't hide my wince, Kyan lifts his head in alarm.

"No, it's okay," I say, trying to reassure him. "Just give me a second." There's no way we're stopping here. I finally have the one I want exactly how I want him. His monster dick can stretch my pussy until it snaps for all that I care.

Once the pain dissipates, I take more of him until I'm fully seated. Then I lean back, bracing one hand on his thigh and dropping the other between the swollen lips of my pussy.

The sound that tumbles from his lips is pained as his gaze

lands on my clit and the circle I'm drawing around it with my finger.

His hands flex as they press against the knotted tie. I can tell he's losing control and wants to touch me, but I'm not done having my fun yet.

"Kyan," I warn. "You can look, but don't touch."

When I start moving my hips, my tender, submissive boss turns positively feral.

CHAPTER 14

KYAN

Naomi's small, pert breasts bounce as she rides my cock. The walls of her cunt grip me like a vise as she slides up and down, soft moans escaping her lips as she brings herself closer to release. Her round tummy jiggles with each movement, and I become entranced by the melodic dance of her skin. I want to do more. I want to be solely responsible for making her come, but my hands are literally tied above my head, and I won't disobey her orders. If I do that, she might stop moving, and if that happens, I fear my heart will stop.

She's perfect, my little vampire.

She's giving me exactly what I crave. What my draxilio craves.

We know what we are—two beasts sharing one body, capable of toppling entire towns with a single breath. There's nothing in the galaxy that can best us, no matter which form we take.

It's precisely why I don't want or need control during sexual encounters. One flex, and the tie knotted around my wrists will snap into multiple scraps of fabric. If I wanted to dominate Naomi, I easily could. What gets me hard is seeing how effectively she can control me. Following her commands and letting her use my body for her own pleasure has me teetering on the edge of release already, though neither one of us has come yet.

I won't come until she does. That would be unforgivable. I doubt she'll even let me.

The thought of her keeping me from coming until she decides I can has me thrusting up into her welcoming heat, trying to carve a path inside her cunt that no cock but my own could follow. She's *mine*, and I'm going to make sure I fuck her so hard she'll never want anyone to sate her needs but me.

Mate? my draxilio purrs in question.

No, I send back. *There is no mate for us.*

But Naomi and I don't need a mate bond to be with each other like this. We're immortal beings, mostly. Who needs the exchange of pretty words and promises for the future when our future is endless? I don't know what will become of us ten, fifty, or hundreds of years from now. We may spend the next decade naked and wrapped in each other's arms, then decide to go our separate ways.

The only goal I currently have is to cover every inch of her voluptuous body with my mouth. If she'll allow me to paint her skin with my seed, even better. Whatever comes after that, I don't care.

She reaches for my hands and pulls them close to her mouth. When I look up, I notice her fangs are extended. "When I come, I'll get the urge to bite you. Is that okay?"

She could tell me she needs to chop off a limb in order to come, and my response would be the same. "Of course."

Her body jerks, and her walls close in all around me as she shatters, her teeth sinking into the thickest part of my forearm. The way her cunt squeezes me combined with the sharp pinch of her bite tests my resolve, practically summoning my release as my orgasm builds at the base of my spine. I don't want to disappoint her, but she feels too good. So warm and slick. It's divine. I won't be able to last.

"Naomi," I groan through gritted teeth, "I can't hold on much longer."

"You can. I know you can," she replies, panting, as she licks the wound before releasing my hands and collapsing atop my chest.

I slow my thrusts and change the rhythm as she comes back to herself. Her black hair fans my chest, the ends tickling my nipples in a way that I was not expecting to enjoy as much as I am.

When she lifts her head, her lips are still stained with my blood, and her entire body radiates a commanding, confident aura that leaves me breathless. Such an unsuspecting power that she possesses. It makes me proud to be…whatever I am to her, even if I'm nothing more than the dick she likes to ride. That would be enough.

Her thick thighs continue to twitch as she crawls up my body, leaving a trail of her warm nectar in her wake. She reaches for the knot at my wrists and my heart leaps.

"I'm going to untie you." Before she loosens the knot, she stills. "Once your hands are free, you may touch me."

I nod, my mouth suddenly dry. "Then what?" *Tell me what to do, please. Then tell me I did I good job.*

Her response is unwavering and immediate. "Then I want you to lick my pussy until I scream for you to stop."

I waste no time. Clutching the soft globes of her ass, I lift her and switch our positions. She squeaks in surprise at how easily I toss her onto the mattress. As if her weight could ever hinder my movement. I'm made of muscle and fire, and she's lighter than air. Then I wrap my hands around her ankles and pull until her ass hangs off the edge of the bed. Kneeling on the floor, I press my hands against her inner thighs, spreading her wide. Her pretty pink flesh glistens with her juices, and I run a finger along her seam, gathering enough to taste.

She watches me with rapt attention as I lick it off, showing off the many shapes my tongue can make as I swirl it around my fingertips.

"Fuck." Her taste is unlike anything in this world. It's salty and tangy, and also distinctly feminine. So quintessentially Naomi. Somehow more perfect than perfect, beyond a place even words can reach.

"Ooh," she moans as I lean in and lick the length of her seam, stopping at the top to spread her swollen pussy lips and clamp down on her clit with my lips. Her back arches, and she rolls her hips against my mouth, crying out, "Yes, Kyan. Like that. So good."

My chest puffs at her praise as I continue devouring her. If she calls me her good boy, I might have to abandon my previous thinking and ask her to marry me.

A steady purr fills my head. *More.*

This is more, I send back, puzzled and slightly annoyed by the plea. *This is the most. What more do you want?*

More, he repeats, and I decide to ignore him.

Naomi threads her fingers through my hair and grips the back of my head, pressing my nose against her clit as I fuck her with my tongue. "Mm. So fucking good."

Getting closer, but what will send her over the edge?

Out of the corner of my gaze, I see her head pop up. Our eyes meet and don't stray as she palms her breasts, pausing to pluck at her hardened nipples. "Stroke yourself for me."

I do as I'm told, happy to find my dick still coated with her release. My sac tightens against my body as I begin jerking myself off.

She reaches for my other hand and pulls it to her mouth. "Still okay?" Asking for another bite.

How much blood does a draxilio even need? I'm sure I could survive with a lot less. She can have it. "Still okay."

"What a good boy," she whispers, her gaze heavy lidded as her fangs graze the underside of my wrist. "So good for me."

The taste of her, the sight, and now the praise—it all becomes too much. I'm close. Too close. And she hasn't screamed at me to stop yet.

Just then, I figure out how to send her toppling over the edge. I twist my head sideways, and alternate sucking hard on her clit and grazing the edges of my teeth against the sides. This sends her into a frenzy. Her legs kick up by my ears as she fucks my face, and I increase the speed and pressure of my hand. I want her to come first, but I'm desperate to be close behind.

She unravels seconds later, her thighs clamping the sides of my head as she cries out. I assume she bites me, but I don't even feel it. More of her decadent juices flood my tongue as she shouts, "Come for me."

I explode. Blackness seeps into the corners of my vision as my come shoots all over my stomach and chest. Naomi's hands are on me a moment later, guiding me onto my back atop the mattress.

When my vision clears, and I feel like I can breathe once more, I find her cleaning my front with a wet washcloth. Her touch is gentle. Giving. It deepens my need for her.

I don't know how much time passes, but eventually she lies down next to me, throwing a blanket over both of us as the tips of her small fingers trace along my nose and cheeks. My eyes remain closed as she does this, and I wonder when I last felt this content. This seen.

When my eyes flutter open, I find her staring at me with a shy smile. "How was that?"

She has to ask? I feel higher now than I did on her mango cupcakes. I turn to my side to face her. "The best."

"The best?" she repeats with a laugh.

"Better than anything else would be the best, yes?"

The look she gives me is skeptical, but she doesn't press further. She leans in and brushes her lips against mine in a kiss that's so light, I hardly feel it. Then she wiggles her way into my arms and tucks her cheek against my chest.

I stroke along her spine, loving the feel of her smooth skin.

"Thanks for coming today," she says in a quiet voice. "I didn't know I needed you, but you came."

"I always will." I wonder, briefly, if the response carries too much emotion, too much promise. But no. It doesn't matter how things evolve between us. I'll show up when she needs me.

"Are you sure it's not a big deal that you missed that meeting today?" she asks. "With the buyer?"

"No. I have no plans to sell the company anyway."

"Won't Thea be mad?"

"So what if she is? I'm her boss. She isn't mine." Then guilt creeps in, and I wonder if Naomi is right. "Perhaps I'll make it up to her. Do you think one thousand dollars in cash would be sufficient?"

"Seriously?"

I can give her more. "Two thousand?"

Naomi's eyebrow quirks up. "Didn't realize it was that easy." She holds out her hand. "I'll take ten thousand, please."

"The cash is for people who are mad at me. Are you mad at me, Naomi?"

She purses her lips. "I can get there. Yeah."

A comfortable silence settles over us as we lay together. At one point, she drapes her leg over me, and her knee gently brushes against my cock, rousing it once more. I shift closer to her, wrapping my hand around her calf as a way to keep her flush against me. Then my fingers drift down to her slim ankle and continue to caress as I make my way back up to the glorious line that separates her ass from the top of her thigh.

My hips move of their own accord, seeking the friction of her body. As I go to tease her nipple between my fingers, a soft snore reaches my ears.

Poor little vampire. She must be exhausted from her untamed libido. I press a kiss to her hair and tug the blanket up around her shoulders as her steady breathing lulls me to sleep.

We continue snoozing throughout the day, waking only long enough for a slow, leisurely fuck or to use the bathroom. Once the sun sets, Naomi starts to feel better, and we work together to clean up the soup I spilled.

I have a pizza delivered for dinner, which I finish on my own while she drinks a bag of B negative blood with THC. Her fridge is filled with bags of each type, and I grow curious. "How does Quincy get access to all of this blood?" Does he steal it from blood banks? It seems unlikely he'd be able to accomplish that without getting in trouble.

"Quincy knows everybody," she replies. "He has a huge network of contacts across the country that he works with to maintain a steady influx of blood. Nurses, doctors, mobile blood bank drivers, and even just people who willingly donate their blood directly to him. I don't know the terms of their agreements, but I think it's a lot of trading favors and a few cases of cash bribery."

"How does he avoid getting caught? Or putting those he works with at risk of being caught."

A drop of blood gathers at the corner of her mouth after taking a large sip, and she swipes it away with her finger. I find myself disappointed I wasn't the one to lick it off. Blood has never been something I've incorporated into sex, but with Naomi, I'm tempted.

"It's happened once or twice, but that was years ago, and he's much more selective about who he works with."

Fascinating. Another non-human trying to operate on the outskirts of human laws.

"And I think the amount of blood each vendor sends him is too small to raise eyebrows, so he's getting a little from each one, contributing to a big inventory." She tips the bag back as she sucks the remaining drops from the bottom. "Ooh, you know what I have?" Her eyes are wide with excitement as she jumps up and opens the cabinet.

"Please tell me it's something you baked that has weed in it." I've grown quite fond of this routine. Sitting beside her as we laugh at ridiculous TV shows, getting high enough to let our minds take us to other places—nothing has ever brought me as much enjoyment.

She pulls off the top of a square plastic container, and I take a deep inhale as the scents of butter and sugar hit my nose. "My almond weed cookies."

I take three, knowing I'll love them. In just four bites, I've finished them off, so Naomi gives me several more. Time passes and the skies grow darker as we snuggle up together on the couch, and an idea starts to form in my head. It's hard to tell, but it feels like it might be the smartest idea I've ever had.

"My brother and his mate are throwing a Halloween party," I say. "I'd like you to come."

Her expression is unreadable.

"You mean, as your date?"

"Yes."

She tilts her head to the side. "As your date, or your girlfriend?"

"Either one."

Her brow furrows. "It can't be either one. They're different things."

I don't follow. If she comes as my date, she remains on my arm all night. I get to show her off and introduce her to my family. We have fun, or, we try to have fun. It all rests on Mylo's choice in music, I suppose. At the end of the night, we remove our costumes and pleasure each other until the sun rises.

If she comes as my girlfriend, everything that follows is the same. Maybe I should leave it up to her.

"Which do you prefer?"

She sighs. "No, no, no. You're the one asking me to the party. So you have to tell me which one you want me to be."

This is getting confusing. Perhaps I'm not being clear. Taking her hand in mine, I try again. "Naomi, I want you to be whichever one you want to be."

Ripping her hand away, she leans forward and rests her head in her hands. "Maybe we're too high to talk about this now."

Shit. This is my fault. When I thought of asking her, I was happy at the possibility she'd say yes. Now it feels like she wants me to leave. How did we get here?

"Wait," she says, her expression bright as she turns to face me. "Let me ask you this. Are you open to wearing a couple's costume?"

"What is that?"

"It's two costumes within the same theme," she explains. "Two things or characters that clearly go together to the point where it would look weird if one of us wore our costume without the other."

"An example of this would be…"

She leaps to her feet with excitement. "A squirrel and a nut!"

That is not what I was expecting her to say. "Would I dress as the squirrel or the nut in that scenario?"

"Good question." Naomi takes her time as she considers her answer. "The squirrel." When I look at her expectantly, she adds, "Because you're bigger."

"That's your justification? Because I'm bigger?"

She looks crushed. "You don't want to be the squirrel?"

"No, I'm fine being the squirrel. That's not why I think I'm more suited to wear it though."

Curiosity seems to brighten her mood. "Then why?"

I say the first thing that comes to mind. "Because I'm always looking for you, eager to gobble you up."

A fit of laughter seizes her body, pushing her into a sequence of wide-mouthed cackling and enthusiastic knee slapping. "Oh shit. I love that."

"So I will be the squirrel, then?" I ask, needing clarification.

"Yep. And I'll be your nut."

Another episode of *Veep* begins and something Selina says to Gary leads me back to the original conversation we were having. "Why does it matter that I'm willing to dress as the squirrel to your nut? What does it mean?"

"Huh?" she asks. It's then that I notice how hazy her eyes are. She is tremendously high. "Oh. It means you'd rather bring me to the party as your girlfriend than as your date, because no one is going to wear a couples' costume to a family Halloween party with someone who's just a date."

Now I'm back to being confused. Though I suppose it doesn't matter. If they mean the same thing to me but the title of girlfriend makes her happier, then I want her with me as my girlfriend.

"Right."

I reach for the cookie container and disappointment washes over me when I realize they're gone. Still feeling peckish, I go to the cabinet and start digging around.

"What are you looking for?"

I turn the cookie container upside down and pout.

Her smile reaches her eyes as she takes in my sad state. "I don't have any more snacks for you, I'm afraid. I guess I should start keeping some balanced meals on hand, right? You can't have cookies for dinner every night."

"Of course I can," I reply. "I'm three hundred and twelve years old. I can do whatever I please." Then I remember. I still have the orange Starbursts that Hudson left in my room. Plus, there's popcorn, and there's no greater bedtime snack than popcorn. "Let's go to my house. The perfect snacks await."

"Your house?" she asks, looking down at her long t-shirt and loose sweatpants. "It's late. Will anyone be there?"

I look at my phone and gasp. "How is it already midnight?" The only ones home will be Zev, Charlie, and Nia, but I'm sure they've all gone to bed by now.

"Let me change, and we can go," she says, rushing to pull on what looks to be one of her work outfits.

"It's late. You don't need to dress up for this. We're just getting snacks."

She shrugs. "I already had it laid out for today before the whole blood mess. It's fine." Then she pauses as she stares down at her bottle on the table. "Should I take it?" Before I can speak, she answers her own question. "Yeah, I'll take it."

As we step outside, Felix lands on Naomi's windowsill.

"Sorry, buddy," she says, waving to him. "We're on a snack run, but we'll be back soon."

"Where did I leave my car?" I ask, looking around the empty driveway. Then I spot it parked on the street. "Ah, there."

"Wait, you shouldn't drive. You're way too high." Somehow, she stumbles while standing perfectly still. "I shouldn't drive either."

"It's fine. We don't need to take the car."

She groans. "I really don't feel like running."

"We're not running, little nut."

"We're not?"

"No," I reply, before pointing to the stars. "Let's fly."

CHAPTER 15

NAOMI

My boyfriend is a motherfucking dragon, and I'm about to crawl inside his massive claws—which I'm sure are sharp enough to spill my innards onto the pavement with a single flick—and fly to his house for late night snacks. This must be how cool kids in high school feel all the time. I wasn't one, so this level of swagger is completely foreign.

For once, I'm not even jealous that these are snacks I won't be able to eat. It's all about the flight for me.

"Okay, so what happens now?" I ask when we reach the clearing next to my bridge. "How much space do you need to shift?"

He looks around, his eyes squinty with the weed still in his system, and suggests I wait on the bridge. I don't walk. I skip onto the bridge and bounce on the balls of my feet as I watch Kyan stretch his limbs and get into position.

A low growl pierces through the night sky as the air kicks up around his body. Leaves and branches swirl as if caught in a twister, and I have to duck to avoid getting staked by a few big pieces. His bones crack, and his features turn distorted as he grows. From the bottom up, Kyan transforms from a larger-than-average, smoldering, sex on a stick man to a blue-scaled beast with black spikes running down his back and feet the size of snowmobiles. The ground shakes beneath me as the dragon, my dragon, turns to face me.

Fear is absent from my mind, which is a nice surprise. I didn't think I would scream in horror, but I figured I'd at least gasp. But he's just so goddamn pretty that I can't even move. Most of his body, particularly the middle, is the same cerulean blue as when he's unmasked, but the difference between his two forms is that the shimmer is so much more pronounced at this size. It's like this dragon covered himself in body glitter. And the colors. My god, there are so many shades of blue I never knew existed. Each one so seamlessly fades into the next that you don't even realize the tip of his wide, spiky tail is turquoise until you look back at the front of him, which is mostly navy blue. What if this is all a dream? I don't ever want to wake up.

He offers proof that it's not a dream with a soft snuffle through his humongous dragon snout, sending hot air and spit across my face.

"Aww," I say, laughing. "Hi, big fella." I offer up my palm for him to sniff. He doesn't. Instead, his black lips curl back to reveal hundreds of teeth as sharp and as long as swords. A purr rumbles inside his chest as his jaws open and his long, black tongue emerges. My high is still strong, so I'm at peace with the possibility of him eating me. If that's my ending, at least I spent the day having the best sex of my life first.

Although would being chewed and fully digested kill me? Unless he's consuming wood on a regular basis, and a sharp piece stakes me as I travel through his digestive tract, I don't think it would. Is there a chance I'd be resurrected upon exiting his body? Along with a pile of waste?

Ugh. Then I would wholeheartedly choose death.

The tip of his tongue is the circumference of my head, and as it gets closer to my face, I notice the rough bumps along the top. They're pretty big, and I'm guessing they'd take a layer or two of my skin right off, so I hold up my hands, prepared to negotiate. "I think you want to kiss me. Don't get me wrong, I love that idea. However, I'm worried about my skin. It's always been on the sensitive side. I'd heal quickly if you scraped it off, but maybe we avoid that tonight?"

I think he understands me because he slowly withdraws his tongue.

Worried I've offended him, I quickly add, "Would you settle for an organic cotton-covered arm?"

The tongue surges toward me, and as gently as a ten-ton alien dragon can, he swipes the tip along my forearm. Then he immediately turns to the side and spits. I suppose cotton isn't for everyone.

He unfurls his front claw, and I quickly climb inside, eager to fly through the air without being surrounded by strangers and being told when I can and can't use the bathroom.

Kyan gives no warning. He launches off the ground, and suddenly we're blasting through the clouds, and my stomach is somewhere in my throat. He keeps his claws tight around me, so I can only see through the slim crack between his talons, but Sudbury looks incredibly small. It's also whizzing by below us, and just as I start screaming with glee, we land in the center of a tarped-off area between trees.

The shift back into his unmasked, two-legged form looks much less painful, and when the smaller Kyan emerges, he bows at the waist, holding out his hand. "I hope you enjoyed your flight this evening, Ms. Zhao."

"Mm, yes," I say, bowing too. "Five stars."

He wraps his arm around me, and we stumble into the house giggling. The light he turns on fills the entryway/living room, providing a soft glow to show off this massive, simply decorated space. The furniture and decor are very dude-like. Comfortable seating, muted colors, and lots of dark wood everywhere. The kitchen and living room occupy the same open-concept space, but with enough separation that it doesn't feel crowded. There's a long staircase to the second level on either side of the house, and on the main floor, it's clear that bedrooms exist on either side of the kitchen as well.

As I'm taking in the gorgeous mansion I find myself in, Kyan is making as much noise as possible in the kitchen. It doesn't seem intentional. It's more like when you're trying to be quiet in the kitchen and that's the moment the silverware ends up scattered across the floor.

"What are you looking for?" I whisper, trying to be mindful of anyone who might be asleep.

Kyan opens a top drawer, digs through it frantically, then does the same to the bottom drawer, but forgetting the top one is still out, he bumps his head. "Fuck!" he shouts.

That's when a child starts screaming.

After that, a lot seems to happen, and my mind has trouble keeping up. A man who looks like the grunge version of Kyan stomps down the hall toward us wearing a murderous expression. I determine this man is Zev, one of Kyan's brothers. They start yelling at each other, and the source of the high-pitched scream peeks out from behind Zev's leg.

"Ooh, it's a baby," I say in the same voice I use to talk to Felix. I'm filled with shame even before I'm done speaking.

Then a woman with luminous dark brown skin arrives at Zev's side and asks, "Who the hell are you?" She far too beautiful for having been woken up in the middle of the night and I'm a more than a little envious.

Trying to deescalate the situation and appear non-threatening, I wave. "Hi, I'm Naomi."

Kyan repeats, "This is Naomi." He keeps talking.

I decide to focus on my blood bottle, relieved that I'm full enough to lack even a snippet of desire to drain these two humans. This is why I always have it with me. "I'm his new assistant," I say, trying to be helpful.

The woman gives me the stink eye. "Okay, we get it."

Get what? Did I miss something? My hands clutch my bottle tighter. *Stay quiet. Keep your eyes on the bottle.*

The woman and her daughter leave. There's more shouting between Kyan and his brother, which leads to some shoving as well.

They're both dragons. Don't get involved. Let them sort it out.

When I look up again, Zev is glaring at me like I've overstayed my welcome, and Kyan is storming outside with a wine bottle in his hand. Confused, I hop off the barstool in the kitchen and scurry outside, trailing behind Kyan.

He empties the wine and throws the bottle against a tree, shattering it. I want to comfort him, but I'm not clear on what happened or why he's this upset. As soon as they started yelling at each other, I tuned it out. It felt like it was none of my business.

"Do you want to talk about it?" I finally ask as we step inside the hanging tarps.

"They just," he starts, shaking his head and looking so exhausted, I wish I could tuck him inside my claw and fly him somewhere safe. "They don't fucking respect me. At all." He throws up his hands in defeat. "Everything I do, and have ever done, has been for them. *They* wanted mates. *They* wanted families. I didn't. But here I am anyway, because I thought the least I could do was protect them."

He hasn't said much about his past other than the planet he came from, so I'm having trouble following the thread, but I listen and nod, because that's what he needs.

"So that's what I do," he continues. "I make it my sole focus to find a way to keep them and their families safe. My life's work is putting a system in place that punishes the criminals and avenges the innocent. I have to. It's the only thing that matters to me. Especially since law enforcement in this town doesn't fucking do anything."

I'm lost. Maybe I misheard him. "How does the company punish criminals, exactly?"

He waves a dismissive hand. "Never mind. Let's just go."

"Back to my place?"

"No, I have another idea."

Kyan doesn't provide additional details. He shifts into his dragon, I crawl into his claw, and he shoots us into the sky. This flight is much more enjoyable, as it lasts longer than two minutes. We fly over Concord, and I realize we're heading south when I spot 93 below us. When we land on the roof of the office, I'm prepared to protest and ask him to bring me home. I have no idea why we're here this late, but if he intends on blowing off steam by working, I'm out.

I cross my arms as he shifts back. "Why are we here?"

He holds out his hand, and his eyes are filled with sadness, so I take it and give him the benefit of the doubt. The door on the roof takes us down a stairwell that opens into…a closet?

I can't see anything since it's so dark in here, but the room feels small.

Kyan flips the light switch on the wall, and my eyes widen in shock. "You have a bedroom here?"

It's a small room, with nothing more than a queen bed and a nightstand with three drawers, but it's clean, and it's certainly bigger than the nook my bed is stuffed into, so it'll do for the night.

"Is that the only door?" I ask.

He smirks as he flips open a panel on the wall between the nightstand and the bed, and an entire segment of the opposite wall lifts into the ceiling like a garage door, opening into his office.

"You rich guys and your secret fucking doors."

He opens the nightstand and pulls out a black t-shirt and soft mesh shorts. "You're not impressed, then?"

"Well, I didn't say that." Of course I'm impressed. Every little girl dreams of living in a house with secret doors that lead to hidden passageways and dimly lit libraries. This isn't that, but it's still pretty cool.

I borrow one of his t-shirts and climb into bed next to him. We don't say much after that. The night turned heavy, and I just want him to sleep, leaving it behind once morning comes. His grip on my back and arm is tight, but not painfully so, and even when he drifts off, his hold doesn't loosen.

Soon after, I follow him into darkness, with the image in my head of the two of us in the middle of the sea when a storm hits. But in this vision, I'm not me. Instead, I'm a buoy, steadily bobbing above the surface as Kyan holds on tight. I can keep him above water as long as he doesn't let go. I know I can.

* * *

Halloween arrives, and it's not the fun, spooky celebration I thought it'd be. Kyan thought it was best for me to skip the party, since my introduction to his family got off to a rocky start. He said his sister-in-law, Vanessa, guilted him into attending even though he didn't want to, and I understood. Family is family.

In a petty form of protest, he bought a squirrel costume and told me he'd be wearing it to the party, and the shelled peanut he put in his pocket is to represent me, and how he'll be counting down the minutes until he can gobble me up once the party ends.

Since the confrontation with Zev, we've spent the week alternating between sleeping at my place and his secret room. I've noticed the suspicious looks Thea has started giving us at the office, but Kyan insists that all will be well, and I should just ignore it.

The only reason I can is because of the way things have shifted between Kyan and me. I've grown attached, and it feels like this could be something more than a taboo work fling. He makes me laugh, he loves my bird, and he's learned my body well enough that he can get me to come in under three minutes. Not that we're trying to beat the clock. The stamina of an alien dragon far exceeds that of a human man, and before I can catch my breath, he's ready for another round.

More than the incredible sex though, I genuinely like him. He's become my boyfriend and one of my best friends. We put each other at ease. I trust him, and there's no face I'd rather see before I close my eyes than his.

It's also the reason I'm standing in front of my trailer, waiting for Elaine to come outside so we can talk. I'm done with this spying charade, and I'm sick of living in fear. Fuck her and fuck Xavier. Let her call him. He'll have to get through Kyan to get to me, and there's no way he's getting through Kyan.

"Naomi, come here!" Elaine shouts from the door of the house. She's smiling. The sight makes my hair stand on end.

I don't want to have this conversation in the house. Wyatt and Mike are inside, and even though I don't think they'd gang up on me, I'm not certain they wouldn't. The yard feels like neutral ground, and I'd prefer it if those two bozos weren't watching as I tell Elaine to go eat glass.

"Can you come here, actually?" I shout back. "I need to talk to you."

I can see her scowl from here, but she ends up closing the door and walking down the driveway.

Before I can get a word in, Elaine blurts, "Check it out, I just learned how similar my singing voice is to Katy Perry's." Then she starts singing, and dear Lillith, it's horrendous. Her voice only sounds like Katy Perry if Katy Perry had been kicked in the throat by a donkey and chose to make a bunch of honking sex moans instead of singing her actual lyrics.

"Wow," I say, nodding with my teeth clenched. "So great."

She clears her throat. "Anyway, what'd you want to talk about? Do you have some new info for me? Burton won't get off my ass, so I really need something juicy. As in, week-old-baby-with-virgin-blood juicy."

Gross. It's time to end this.

"Yeah, I'm not doing this anymore," I tell her. "Every lead I followed turned out to be a dead end. The basement is just an office. I went in and that's all I found. He's an alien dragon shifter, like I said, but it's not like you can expose him without exposing us, so that doesn't hold much weight."

Her face twists into a hateful sneer. "That's it? You're just giving up?"

My hands start to shake at my sides, so I ball them into fists, hoping she doesn't notice. "Yup. That's it."

She chuckles and takes a step toward me. "You think you can tell me when you're done with an assignment?" I back up as she continues moving closer, stumbling a bit when I go from grass to pavement.

The longer I remain quiet, the angrier she gets. "Are you hearing me? Is English your second language or something?"

Is that…is she being racist? If so, it doesn't even make sense. "Elaine, I'm from Seattle."

"I run this cell, and you're a fucking toddler."

I notice her front teeth are smudged with red lipstick, and I know what's about to happen is going to suck, but that provides a little slice of comfort for me.

"You don't have any say in what assignments you do or don't take."

Now she's shouting, and any minute, Wyatt and Mike are going to come outside to see what's going on.

"So unless you want to abandon your pathetic sippy cup lifestyle," she stabs her finger into my chest as she backs me up against the side of my trailer, "and start sucking blood like a respectable fucking vampire, you do what I say, when I say it."

Stay strong. You knew this would happen. She's dumb and a coward. The chances of her calling Xavier to beg him to take me back are low. Call her bluff.

Pushing off the side of my house, I get into her space, lift my chin high, and shrug. "I'm not doing it. Call him if you want. It changes nothing."

Her hand shoots forward, and her fingers wrap around my throat as she lifts my feet off the ground. She smiles as her acrylics dig into the sides of my neck. I feel the skin break and it's becoming harder and harder to breathe. The only relief I get is when she hurls me across the driveway. My back hits the tree first, and agonizing pain slices through me as I curl in on my side, hoping the injury heals before she tries something else.

Those hopes are dashed as her kitten heels clack across the pavement, and she yanks me up by my hair. My back is still fucked, so I can barely get to my feet, and the second I do, she shoves her fist into my stomach, stealing any breath I had away from me once again.

I hear male laughter in the distance. It seems Wyatt and Mike have joined the chat. How lovely. Apparently, the bond I thought Wyatt and I shared by being former sex partners is meaningless to him. He has no problem watching me get my ass kicked.

Falling to my knees, I wheeze as I focus on breathing through my nose. If I can do that, I might be able to bob and weave until Elaine gets bored. She's way stronger than me, so I won't win a fight against her, but I'm fast. *Please let that be enough.*

She goes to kick me in the ribs, but I see it coming and crawl sideways to avoid the blow. Missing the kick makes her wobble in her heels, and I take that as an opportunity to roll toward the side of the trailer, where an old rusty lawn chair has been collecting leaves for years. Wincing, I reach for the chair and grab it by the legs. When Elaine rounds the corner, I heave it upward, and the back of the chair slams into her chin, causing her to land on her back.

The soreness in my spine starts to dissipate as I keep moving around the outside of the trailer. If I can keep her at a safe distance, she'll have no choice but to chase me around this trash heap until moonrise.

My good luck doesn't last long. As I peek around the corner, she sneaks up behind me, getting me into a headlock.

I have no more moves. She tightens her arm around my neck until I can no longer stand upright. I claw and scratch at her to let go, but she's wearing a fur coat and there's no exposed skin I can bite.

She screeches into my ear, and at first, I think it's an intentional form of torture, but then her grip loosens, and I fall on my ass. Panting heavily, I crawl on my hands and knees until her wrenching cries sound far enough away that I can safely turn around.

Elaine's sitting in a puddle of mud, clawing frantically at something lodged in her right arm. Wyatt and Mike race to her side, lifting her to her feet. It's a stick. A stick is coming out of her arm. How did that even happen? Did she fall on it?

Once Wyatt yanks the branch out, her pained expression morphs into fury. Her gaze lands on the roof of my trailer.

Felix.

He starts cawing loudly, almost as if he's laughing at her.

"Fucking trash bird!" Elaine yells. Then she takes off her shoe and throws it at him.

I curl in on myself, refusing to watch in case it hits him.

His continued caws tell me she missed, and they're quickly followed by about a dozen more. Several crows peek over the edge of my roof, high in the surrounding trees, and along the power line at the end of the driveway.

He brought friends. Within seconds, those friends start dive-bombing my cell mates.

Elaine, Wyatt, and Mike hunch down as the crows start to form a black cloud around their heads, flying in a tight circle as they continue their torment.

"He got me!" Wyatt shouts. "I felt his beak on the back of my head."

Mike bellows like a cartoon elephant who's just seen a mouse as he waves his hands around his face, trying to keep them away.

The three of them huddle together as they race back toward the house, but not before Elaine yells, "We're not done here."

Once their backs are turned, I hurry inside the trailer, throw some clothes and blood in a bag, grab the last jar of peanuts from the cabinet, and run toward the bridge. I don't bother calling for Felix. He saw me leave, and he knows where I'm going, but more importantly, he knows what's in my hand.

In the middle of the clearing, I pour the peanuts on the ground and spread them out. Then I look up. I see some of the crows. It seemed like there were hundreds back in the driveway, but maybe the rest were in the trees. Felix lands on the ground to my right. My eyes fill with tears as I stroke along his feathers. "I owe you, buddy. You showed up just in time."

He leans into my touch, and I know I have to make this quick before I start sobbing, and Elaine comes looking for me.

"I'm heading out for a little while. I don't know when I'll be back, but as soon as I can, I'll bring you and your friends more peanuts, okay?" It's not like he can talk, but I feel the need to provide more information. "I'll be at the office in Manchester for now, with Kyan. I'd take you with me, but this seems like a better place for you. Your friends are here, and I don't think they'd let me bring thirty crows into work, even if I explained your heroism today."

Looking up, I feel the need to address the rest of them. "Thanks for, uh, stopping by today. Keep an eye on Felix for me, yeah?" My gaze returns to him. "I'll be back. I promise."

Then I run, and I don't stop running until I cross the border into Manchester. I cut through the trees next to the highway and sigh as my feet reach cement. I walk the rest of the way to the office, and since I don't have my own keys, I take the elevator to the roof, and the stairs to the secret bedroom.

Once I'm settled, the perfect joke comes to me that I wish I had thought of when I was still face-to-face with Elaine. "Bitch, you just got murdered!"

Eh, I suppose it's not that funny.

Hours later, my phone buzzes.

> Kyan: Officer Burton was killed at the party. Freak accident. Charlie's ex, Nia's father, is a politician who was cozying up to Burton recently. He's also dead. Killed miles away. I'll tell you everything later.

> Is everyone okay? Charlie and Nia? Are you?

> Kyan: Technically fine.

> Technically?

Jesus Christ. What a mess. It's hard to process the news with such little information. And what little I have sounds bizarre.

> Kyan: I don't know what's going to come from this. We need to prepare for the worst.

CHAPTER 16

KYAN

I watch Naomi's chest rise and fall as she sleeps, wishing I could trace the curve of her lips without waking her. She's the epitome of radiance, especially like this, with the muscles in her face relaxed and her arms open at her sides. I'd like to slip back beneath the covers and hold her until morning, but I have work to do in the basement.

Burton died nine days ago. When his cruiser screeched to a halt outside of Mylo and Sam's house and he and his fellow officers drew their guns on us, I thought for sure someone would end up dead. I just didn't think it would be him.

Not that I wanted him to live a long, happy life. I kept his name off the pack's target list because he's always been *my* target. I've envisioned countless ways I'd like to end him, so many that him dying by my hand felt like an inevitability.

Unfortunately, I can't claim the credit. In the most unexpected chain of events, several of my family members participated in his demise without so much as lifting a finger.

Replaying the scene in my head has given me comfort over the last few days, and I'll take the few moments of peace I can get.

Burton aimed his gun at Zev and pulled the trigger. Zev, with his ability to communicate with machines, caused the gun to jam. Hudson, inheriting his father's ability to influence the choices of others, made Burton look down the barrel of the gun, and at that moment, Zev released the bullet.

Down the racist police officer went, clutching at the ravaged remains of his shoulder as he bumped into his car and collapsed belly first onto the road. Vanessa, with her newfound ability to move objects with her mind, shifted the car into neutral. I suppose gravity also played a role, as the car slowly started to roll down the hill Mylo and Sam's house sits atop, crushing Burton's body, one bone at a time.

It appeared as a series of freak accidents, resulting in his death. That's how the news first covered it, anyway. But as the interest in the story spread to larger outlets and across the country, it was later described, in carefully worded yet coded terms, that Burton perished, crushed by the weight of his own police car, after looking down the barrel of his own gun and shooting himself in the shoulder.

The pity and general embarrassment surrounding his death now serves as his legacy. I suppose any form of murder I fantasized about committing wouldn't have been this gratifying, so I'm glad it happened this way.

I just wish I didn't have this lingering feeling that trouble is still lurking around the corner. Burton was our biggest adversary. Now that he's gone, my family and I should be able to live in peace. I'm sure my brothers and their mates have been doing just that. But I can't, and I don't know why.

Naomi and I have been staying at the office. She hasn't left the building since the night Elaine attacked her. It took every ounce of control in my body to refrain from burning the top of the biggest tree I could find to a sharpened point and immediately impaling her on it, but Naomi begged me not to.

"If the IVA connects me to Elaine's death, I'm fucked," she told me that night. "Young vampires who kill or have their cell leaders killed get sentenced to death. I need to find a way to leave the cell legally, without hurting Elaine, which will be hard since I'm twelve years away from being able to live on my own. That's my only option."

If only the IVA had a justice system similar to that of humans. Then I could gather the pack and deliver my own form of justice to Elaine's doorstep. Along with that fucker Wyatt and the British prick, whatever his name is.

The upside to having her in my bed every night is how much closer we've grown. We've talked about my job as an assassin on Sufoi, and I've told her more about my brothers and how they met their mates.

She's shared many memories from her childhood in Seattle, told me all about her parents and the aspects of her Chinese heritage she continues to honor, as well as those she's chosen to let go of—learning how to play the pipa, for example.

"I'm never going to be good at it. It's just not in the cards for me," she said, with such ardent exasperation that I had to stifle a laugh.

Quincy has been delivering Naomi's blood supply. I met him briefly in the parking garage one night. He seems kind. Harmless. And he doesn't appear to be attracted to Naomi at all, which is why he still breathes.

The only times I've left the building are with the pack as we work through the target list, but I find myself distracted even as I watch my recruits grow into the savage vigilantes I hoped they'd become. I can't shake the feeling that I'm being watched, even in the secure confines of the building. No one is getting in or out without me knowing, so realistically, it's a figment of my imagination.

Things on the top floor haven't been going smoothly either.

Thea spent yesterday afternoon accusing me of sabotaging the potential of the company, phoning it in, and having inappropriate relations with Naomi. She's right about all of it, but I can't find the energy to care.

I feel guilty that I'm letting her and my employees down, but the future of Monroe Media Solutions is the least of my worries.

What weighs on me most heavily is the rift between me and my brothers. The only one I've spoken to since Burton's death is Luka, and he didn't know what to say. It was ten minutes of pregnant pauses, stilted chatter, and him asking how I am until I got sick of insisting I'm fine and hung up.

The only bit that sparked my interest was the news about Dante, our unwanted Italian cousin. Since he dropped the tree on top of Charlie's ex's car, killing him, and then made himself visible in dragon form while soaring over the town of Sudbury, local businesses seem to be embracing the buzz around the sighting of the mysterious big red bird that many are certain was a dragon.

As with Burton's death, larger news outlets have shared the story, sending cryptid enthusiasts into our town to gather eyewitness accounts.

The interest has spread so quickly and so far across the country, that I gave Andrei a two-week vacation from monitoring UFO sightings. The people who thought it was a cryptid reported it as a UFO, and then there were the people who thought it was actually a UFO and reported it as such.

Now there are restaurants serving Red Dragon Daiquiris and dragon-size sandwiches. Even the bar we frequent created a cocktail called the Dirty Dragon. I have no idea what's in it, but this town-wide excitement over spotting a dragon in the sky means Dante was right about the town not connecting us to the dragon sighting, and I find that infuriating.

The only other person I've spoken to lately is Hudson. He

hates that I'm not getting along with my brothers and sends me texts each day asking if he can come visit me here. I know Luka wouldn't approve, so I told him no. He is relentless, however, and I hate disappointing him. All he wants is to see me. I made it clear he can't shadow me for work. When I made the offer, Burton had just died, and the family was gathered to process what happened. Hudson was so proud of the way he helped stop Burton that I couldn't help myself. I saw him as a future member of the pack. He'd be perfect for it, but he's far too young, and Luka would slaughter me.

"Morning, Owen," I say when I enter the pack kitchen.

"Hey, boss. Supposed to be a beautiful day out there." He's still giddy from taking down his target earlier this week—a serial rapist who served just ten days behind bars, despite being accused by multiple women. The man only served a fraction of his sentence before being let out on a mere filing technicality.

When Owen dug his claws across the monster's neck, the man tried to scream, but all that came out was the muffled gurgle of a wretched degenerate drowning in his own blood. Owen shifted from his jaguar into his human form and wiped the man's blood on his chest in victory. Then he dedicated the kill to his late sister.

She wasn't his victim, but she suffered a similarly brutal attack, and the trauma of being silenced, not believed, and harassed weighed too heavily on her. The depression claimed her life six months later.

I pat him on the shoulder, unable to return his enthusiasm as I make my way to the lab.

Yvonne greets me with a nod as she removes her safety goggles and returns to her computer. "Yvonne, have you detected any long-term changes in their cellular makeup?"

"Too soon," she replies. "I see nothing yet."

We discuss changes to their diets and if any have shown feverish symptoms. She says no, then rolls her eyes at me.

"What?" I ask.

"Go sleep. Your face," her features twist in disgust. "Looks terrible."

I want to, but I can't. There's something I'm missing. I can feel it.

After checking in with the rest of the pack, I realize there aren't any pressing matters to attend to, so I return to my little vampire, still fast asleep in our secret room.

The bed dips under my weight, and that wakes her. A smile forms on her lips even before her eyes flutter open. "Mm, come here." Her voice is raspy from sleep as her arms open for me. I fall into them, careful not to crush her small frame beneath me.

I kiss along her jawline, down her neck, and across her collarbone, moving further down her body as I wait for further instruction. It's a new development to our Dom/sub dynamic, and I'm very much enjoying it. I let her know how much I crave her with kisses, and she directs me the rest of the way.

Reaching her breasts, I suck the tip of one into my mouth through her shirt, and she moans as her hands get lost in my hair. Her back arches as she sucks in a breath. "I love when you wake me up like this."

Her nipples harden into stiff peaks, and I lift her shirt to taste her skin. "How do you want me?" I growl as I flatten my tongue against one pretty pink nipple before applying the same attention to the other.

She lifts her arms, and I pull the shirt over her head. Her skin is flushed, and her eyes are swirling with heat as she lays naked before me. I don't know how I got so lucky.

Tugging me down by the collar of my shirt, she kisses me hungrily, immediately swiping her tongue across my lips. I brush the hair off her face, pausing to caress her cheek before meeting her lips with mine.

I feel her hips roll against me as she grips my hair. Her breaths turn ragged as I grind against her, giving her the friction she seeks. "Don't stop," she commands. "Make me come. Just like this."

I'm still fully clothed in a button-up shirt and dress pants. I'd love to remove the barrier between our bodies and feel the wet lips of her cunt slide against my cock, but this is how she wants me. I do as I'm told.

Her hands wrap around the base of my horns, holding on tight as I thrust. I feel my release begin to build, and I'm shocked that I might come from, what do the humans call it, dry humping?

I hear the subtle click of her fangs extending, and I offer her my wrist to bite.

Naomi's eyes roll back in her head as she comes apart, her fangs sinking into me. The skin on both wrists heals quickly, so there are no lingering marks from her previous bites, but the area has become a strong erogenous zone for me as of late, and a jolt of electricity zips through me at the feel of her fangs buried deep inside my flesh. Her entire body trembles with her release as my blood drips down her chin, and the sight of it has me following close behind. She pushes my arm away and pulls my face into the crook of her neck. I roar my release into the place where her neck and shoulder meet.

"It's okay," she whispers, her tongue tracing the shell of my ear. Our chests are still heaving as we come down. "Lay on me."

I lower myself on top of her, and she chuckles when I let out a contented sigh, resting my head on her breast.

"Comfy?"

"The comfiest."

I could fall asleep like this. If only we had done this hours ago.

The alarm on her phone goes off, and my hopes of taking a nap are dashed. I lift myself up and lean back on my haunches as she runs her hands all over my chest.

"I'm not done with you yet."

What? "Don't we need to get ready?" I definitely need to change my pants.

She shakes her head. "I wanted some extra time before people start showing up."

The time on her phone says it's seven, which means we have an hour before we need to worry about being overheard or interrupted. I'll take it.

I reach for her, but she scurries off the bed before I can catch her. She takes a moment to look around the room, forming her plan, and I admire the many mouthwatering dimples covering her luscious backside.

"We need a chair," she says, lifting the panel on the nightstand and opening the door to the office. Then she just strolls out as if she's not completely nude.

I panic. Launching myself off the bed, I wrap my arms around her from behind and cover the parts I want only my eyes to see.

"Hey!" she squeals. "What are you doing?"

"What are *you* doing? My office walls are glass. Anyone could come in and see you."

She turns in my arms, placing my hands on her ass. I don't mind it.

"But they won't, because nobody shows up before eight."

"Okay," I relent. "We should be fast though."

Naomi jerks back. "Are you in charge here, or am I?"

She's adorable. I press my forehead against hers. "You are. Always."

Slipping out of my arms, she struts around the room, her abundant flesh jiggling with each confident step. She grabs my desk chair and pulls it into the center of the carpet. Then she retrieves a tie from the closet next to the bathroom and drapes it around her neck. It hangs over her breasts, blocking her nipples from view, and I can't help the frown that tugs at my lips.

"Sit," she says, tapping the back of the chair.

When I do, she takes my hands and brings them behind my back, using the tie to bind them together at the wrists. Then she steps in front of me and starts unbuttoning my shirt. My mouth waters as her breasts bounce so close to my face.

"I'm going to fuck you in this chair," she says, removing the belt from my pants and opening them enough to let my dick spring free. It stands tall and already hard again, still coated in my come from before. Climbing into my lap, she straddles me, then takes my face in her hands, forcing me to meet her gaze. "You can watch, but don't touch."

"May I use my mouth?" I ask. *Say yes. Please say yes.*

Yes, more.

Oh, look who's awake.

She's about to give us more, I send back. *Be patient.*

"Yes," Naomi answers, "but you can't come until I tell you."

I nod. "I won't."

Bracing herself with one hand on my shoulder, she looks down between us and slides my dick between her pussy lips before guiding me into her channel. Her body adjusts quickly to my size, and she impales herself on my length, sinking all the way down until our hips meet.

She grabs hold of my horns as she sets the rhythm, and I can do nothing but watch the way her body moves as she takes what she needs. It's perfect. More perfect than perfect.

Perhaps the only word that fits her sheer exquisiteness is her name. Naomi.

Though if this is the rule, then no one else should be allowed to claim it, and I'm not sure how that could be enforced.

"Bite me." She brushes her hair off her neck and points to the exposed skin.

A hard knot forms in the pit of my stomach at the request. "I can't," I reply. It hurts to deny her, but I'm not clear on the specifics of how mate bonds for draxilios are solidified. When the two parts of us agree and accept that we've found a mate, our eyes turn red. That, I understand. To make the redness go away, the mate has to accept us—both halves. To solidify the bond, there is sex and a mating bite.

My eyes have not turned red. I have no intention of taking a mate. However, Naomi has seen my other form and adores us both. If I bite her during sex before my eyes have turned, would that make her my mate?

Do these events need to occur in order, or is the mating bite the final step no matter what precedes it?

I wish there was someone I could ask about this, but my brothers checked those boxes, albeit in slightly different orders, before engaging in the mating bite.

My movements have slowed since she asked for my bite, but Naomi doesn't seem to notice. If anything, she rides me harder and faster. My cock twitches within her channel, making it hard for me to think straight.

"Bite me," she repeats. "Make me bleed."

I'm tempted to do it because she feels so fucking good, and she deserves to get what she wants. The desperation to do it is also there, as I'm eager to take this blood play a step further than we have before, but I can't risk tying us together for the rest of our lives, especially since she doesn't know that could happen.

"Soup."

Everything stops. She freezes in my lap, still panting heavily, and pulls back to look at me.

"Soup?"

I nod, crestfallen that I have to use our safe word, especially since she seemed close to release. "Soup." If she asks about it later, I'll explain why, but I'd rather not right now. My dick is still inside her and hasn't softened. I just want to move past this and make her come. I'm not sure I'll be able to focus on work if I don't.

She grips the back of my head and leans in, brushing the tip of her nose against mine. "I understand."

I expect her to climb off me, untie my hands, and start peppering me with questions, not because she's nosy, but because she worries about me and wants to learn how my mind works. This is not a flaw of hers. It's something I appreciate.

But she doesn't do that. She presses a tender kiss to my lips, and her body starts moving. Before long, her pace returns to where it was prior to when I uttered the safe word, and our bodies slap together as we race toward completion.

I'm relieved. I thought hearing the safe word would ruin the moment, and she'd want to stop altogether. Instead, she respected my boundaries and moved past the brief pause.

"So good, Kyan," she moans. "Your ridges, your piercings. I love the feel of you."

A lightness inside my chest spreads throughout my entire body at her praise. My fingers and toes tingle as I thrust up into her, giving her what she needs.

The explicit squelch of our mingling juices joins the sound of skin against skin, and I wonder if we can be heard across the entire floor. With no one else here, I jerk my hips harder as I lean forward, licking every part of her chest I can reach.

As a result, her moans get louder, and her thighs start to shake.

"I'm close," she whimpers.

Fuck. I am too.

She must see it in my face because the next thing out of her mouth is, "Not yet, Kyan. Hold on for me. You can do it."

How? This is fucking agony.

Pinching my eyes closed, I try to slow my body down. I picture random household items: a towel, a bar of soap, a mop...then the mop turns into my cock and Naomi starts fucking it.

Okay, not a mop. I search my mind, and the only thing that pops into my head is a chair, like the one I'm sitting in as Naomi screams my name.

I don't realize she's actually screaming my name until her fangs sink into my neck just beneath my ear. Then her walls flutter around me and the growing flame in the depth of my belly grows once more.

"Come with me," she whispers, and I explode. The world tilts around me as I continue pumping into her. My body feels like it's floating through space and somehow anchored to her at the same time, and both sensations consume me in a way that has me struggling to breathe.

She reaches around and pulls on the tie, freeing me from my binds. My hands fly to her back, and I clutch her tight, seeking another layer of connection.

"Shh, it's okay," she whispers, pulling back to look at me. Her eyes are filled with worry, and when I look down, I realize I'm shaking. Not just my hands. It's my entire body. Even when I try to stop, I can't. This has never happened before.

"Are you all right, Kyan?"

"I-I think so," I stammer. "Yeah, I'm fine."

Her eyes search my face for another heartbeat or two until she's satisfied with whatever she sees. Then she hugs me, and I sag into her embrace.

"That was amazing," she says, her tone dreamy and content. "You were perfect. Just perfect."

The words reach me, but they barely register. I'm still buzzing from head to toe, and I can't figure out if this is a concerning symptom of an affliction exclusive to draxilios, or if it was simply the best orgasm of my existence. What I do know is that before I realized I was shaking, I felt free. Something shifted inside my head with that release. I felt like I left my body. I don't remember what happened. Those seconds are forever lost. But as soon as I was able to touch her, I felt like I needed to more than air.

Naomi takes me by the hand and pulls me into the bathroom, our strewn clothes covering the floor of my office. I keep a smile on my face as she turns on the shower and climbs in after me.

This isn't something she needs to worry about, and if she senses something off, she will most definitely worry.

I try to focus on her touch as she washes my hair, scrubs the blood off my chest, and coats my front and back with soap. Once I rinse it away, I return the favor, massaging her scalp as I work the shampoo through it. She moans, and it brings me back to the shakiness I felt just moments ago. My hands freeze, and she notices.

"You still back there?"

"Huh? Yeah," I quickly reply, coming back to myself. "Sorry."

We spend a little longer under the hot stream as she lets me massage her shoulders, then we towel off and start getting ready for the workday. Naomi goes back into the bedroom to get dressed, and I decide to push the unnerving experience away. Most likely, we reached a new level of intimacy that I was not prepared for, and my brain malfunctioned as it was trying to catch up.

We had sex. I came. She came. Nothing else matters.

I repeat the words in my head a second and third time I as tuck in my shirt. Naomi finds me in the bathroom and drapes a different tie around my neck.

"You should wear this one," she says, her smile bright as she pulls me down for a kiss. "It brings out your eyes."

"Very well." I don't know about the eyes, but the tie does match my pants, which makes the decision easy. Adding some hair balm to my fingers, I run them through my strands and push everything back the way I like it before masking up for the day.

Naomi takes two steps out of the bathroom before pausing on the balls of her bare feet. When she returns to my side, her expression is unreadable as she gazes up at me. "Hey, I..." the words die before leaving her lips. Suddenly, she looks nervous.

"What is it?"

Blood rushes to her cheeks. She shakes her head as if waging an internal battle, then swallows. "I love you."

My mouth falls open. It wasn't what I was expecting. I don't know what I was expecting, but it wasn't that. "You love me?" I ask, chuckling for a reason I can't determine. "Why?" The word is so heavy. So permanent. Frequently coupled with pain and loss. That doesn't feel like us to me. We are light, fun, happy.

Naomi stares at me for what feels like hours, blinking, waiting. Contemplating? I don't know. I have no idea what's going on inside her head, but if the crease between her eyebrows is any indication, the words I chose were the wrong ones.

"Why?" she repeats with a scowl.

Does she want me to answer for her? I have no idea why she loves me. That's why I asked. When I think of why she might, my mind goes blank. I'm a killer. She used to save lives. I used to end them. I still do. That part of me will never change. How could someone like her, so soft, so generous, ever love someone like me?

She crosses her arms over her chest, still waiting. Then it dawns on me, and I rush to get the words out, so she'll stop looking at me like I'm a failure. "Oh. I love you too. Yeah."

"Really?" she asks. I feel her shutting down, the distance growing between us. "That's your response?"

"Isn't that what you want to hear?" This seems like a riddle I'm never going to solve, much like the girlfriend-date couple's costume discussion. I found no differences between the words date and girlfriend, but Naomi had attached a rule I had never heard of to the definitions and expected me to follow the rule accordingly. The only thing I want is to say the words she wants to hear. I thought I did that.

"Not the way you said it. Like the words had no meaning."

It's not that the word love lacks meaning to me; I just don't find it to be the best term to describe the way I feel, mostly because of the permanence it implies. From what I've learned about human culture, saying I love you is as sacred as a wedding vow, and in Sufoian culture, the closest comparison I have is mate.

This is the part of my culture that I reject. It doesn't fit with who I am or my immediate goals. I can say the same about the word love. "It's not even a word I use, unless I'm describing food." The only reason for this exception is that food expects nothing of me when I express my love for it.

She looks crushed. "Wow."

"Naomi, tell me what you want," I beg, reaching for her. She sidesteps my embrace. "Please."

Her lip trembles, but she clears her throat as if to shove the emotions back down. "You know what? This is on me. I told you how I was feeling because I wanted you to know, and I shouldn't expect you to feel the same way."

Is she suggesting I don't care for her? That I wouldn't protect her from harm? If that's her assumption, she's wrong. "That's not—" I begin, but Naomi cuts me off.

"No, really. It's fine. I'm overreacting." She puts her hands on her hips and takes a steadying breath. "Shouldn't have rushed things with us."

"You didn't," I tell her. "I promise."

She smiles, but it doesn't reach her eyes. Running her fingers through her drying hair, she heads into the bedroom and starts stuffing her clothes into her shabby little backpack.

"What are you doing?"

Her nose is scrunched up when her gaze meets mine. "I think we should take a couple days and allow things to reset between us. Quincy will let me sleep on his couch."

Reset? I don't want to do that. I want her in my bed every night like she has been, writhing beneath me as I pound into her. We have a routine now. I'm not sure I can even fall asleep at night without making her come on my tongue.

"Don't go." The plea sounds as pitiful as I feel. I'm losing her. "We can fix this. Let me fix this."

She comes over and places her hands on my chest. Even through my shirt, my skin tingles where she touches me. I cover her hands with mine, afraid of what will happen when she lets go.

"Nothing needs to be fixed," she says, trying to reassure me. "We're not broken; there's just a little crack. Truthfully, I'm embarrassed I feel something that you don't yet, and I'll get over it. I can be patient. But right now, it's just too raw, and I need space."

"But I don't want space."

Naomi pats my chest. "We don't always get what we want."

Her body shifts away from me, but in a panic, I wrap my arms around her and cover her lips with mine. At first, she remains still, but slowly my tongue finds hers and they slide against each other in a heated dance.

This is the key. If I can make her come again, she'll realize words are just words, and what we have can't be defined by the misguided conventions of the human world. I'll show her that there's no one else who knows and worships her body like I do. No one else can give her precisely what she needs.

I groan into her mouth as my hands travel down her back, settling on her behind, my fingers digging into the soft globes.

A throat clears just a few feet from us. Thea stands just

outside my office door, her coat still on, bags in hand, and her expression horrified. "What the hell is going on here?"

Naomi pulls out of my arms, her cheeks a deep crimson as she wipes my kiss from her mouth. "I'm so sorry, Thea." Her voice is shaking. "We had no idea you were here."

Thea's mouth forms a flat line. "Because if I weren't here, this behavior would be perfectly acceptable?"

The judgmental gaze of my COO makes my blood boil. She's early. Much earlier than she usually is, and this is none of her business. I have nothing to apologize for, and neither does Naomi. This is my office. My entire building, in fact. She has no say in what I do when no one else is here.

Thea drops her bags at her feet. "How long has this been going on?"

"This doesn't concern you."

"Is that so?" she replies. "If you're in a relationship with your assistant, that's very much my business, actually, because it puts the entire company at risk."

Naomi shoves her feet into her shoes and hastily grabs her bag. "No. Naomi, you don't have to leave." I turn to Thea. "Let's discuss this later, shall we?"

Thea ignores me, approaching Naomi with the sorrowful expression one would wear approaching an injured dog. "Are you okay, Naomi? Because in a scenario like this, there's a clear imbalance of power, and if you felt pressured in any way…"

"Pressured?" I shout, aghast at her insinuation. Power imbalance? If Thea had shown up at seven, she would've seen me tied up and fighting an epic battle against my own body as Naomi ordered me not to come.

The look Thea gives me is vicious as she places a hand on Naomi's shoulder. "We can go talk in my office if you'd like. Where there's more privacy."

Naomi doesn't take the bait because there's nothing to talk

about. Not with Thea, anyway. "Actually, I think I'll take a personal day. I think that'd be best for everyone."

"Of course, dear," Naomi says. "If there's anything you'd like to share, you can always call me."

"Naomi, don't do this."

We exchange an appalled glance, one I hope Thea realizes is about her, and she says, "It's fine. Really. We'll talk later."

Thea doesn't wait for Naomi to leave the floor before she starts scolding me. "Kyan, when you hired me, you made it sound like this would be a partnership, and for several years, it was."

"Mm hm," I grunt.

After that, I stop listening. I pick up bits and pieces, something about how Naomi could sue the company, how I've been phoning it in, and other ways I've been a disappointment, but the majority of my focus remains on Naomi's back as I watch her get further away.

How did we get here? I went from having sex that left me shaking to losing my girlfriend. Naomi might say we're not broken, but it feels like we are. It all happened so fast.

As the elevator doors close behind her, my draxilio whimpers. *No more.*

CHAPTER 17

NAOMI

"Want to try the melatonin-infused A positive?" Quincy yells from the kitchen. "I've had some success with it. Got three bags in here." He's digging through the fridge trying to find me some comfort blood, but he's out of AB negative, and the other types just don't sound appealing enough.

"I don't know, Quince. At this point, I doubt anything short of heroin blood will cut it." Since I never dabbled with anything stronger than Adderall as a human, I doubt I'd have the ovaries to mess with it now.

He comes into the living room and hands me a tall glass of red with a dinosaur straw. "Try the melatonin. You haven't slept in two days. It's worth a shot."

I huff a breath and give in. "Fine."

"Still haven't heard from him?"

"No," I reply. "But I'm the one who asked for space. It seems like this is him trying to give that to me." Though the immature part of me wants him to ignore that request and blow up my phone with I love you texts.

"True. True."

Quincy puts his visor on and grabs his car keys. "All right, I'm working until six, so I won't be home until morning. Put on some background TV and try to pass out, okay?"

He tosses me the remote, and I scroll through his streaming channels. "Do you have Max?"

"Nah, just Netflix right now, but you know what that means…"

"Beef!" We shout in unison.

"Best show in history," I gush. "Nothing will ever top it."

"For real though."

I fire up the pilot as Quincy leaves, and a few minutes in, my mind inevitably drifts to Kyan. I'm just so goddamn embarrassed.

The whole thing could've been avoided if I had been patient and didn't let my post-coital glee plant these images in my head of me and Kyan buying a house together, maybe getting Felix a decked-out bird cage he can snooze in when he visits, and spending the rest of my days in the safety of his arms. I was so sure Kyan felt the same way I did, especially after we had sex in his chair and he looked all shaky and vulnerable afterward. That moment had the trappings of a man coming to terms with the depths of his feelings. Or so I thought.

I don't know what was going on in his head, but it had nothing to do with love.

The way I reacted was also embarrassing. His half-assed, "Oh, love you too," felt like rejection. Dismissal. My pride took over, and we ended up in a fight that never should've happened.

We'll recover from this. I know we will. It's just a cringeworthy blip that we'll laugh about down the road.

I should call him.

Two days is enough space. Besides, I sleep best when he's next to me, and Quincy's couch sucks. Kyan doesn't feel ready to go back to his house, and I certainly don't want to return to mine, so whether it's his secret bedroom at the office or somewhere new, I want to be where he is.

My throat feels dry as I scroll through my contacts. I take a sip of the melatonin blood to steel my resolve, and I press call.

It doesn't ring. It just goes straight to voicemail. That's odd, but maybe he's spending quality time with his brothers and doesn't want to be interrupted.

I debate on whether to leave a message, but when the phone beeps, I hang up like a coward. Instead, I send a text.

> Hi. I miss you. I know I said I wanted space, and you had to go ahead and respect my wishes, you thoughtful jerk. Anyway, I miss your lips, your horns, those piercings… 🫦 I miss all of you, and I want to get back to where we were. If you're open to it.

> Also, let me know if I should come into work next week? I never officially quit and as far as I know, I haven't been fired, so hopefully I can use sick time or personal days to cover this absence. Who do I talk to about that? Shelly in HR? Let me know.

Between episodes three and four of *Beef*, my eyes get heavy, and I curl into a ball on my side. Just as I start to drift off, my phone buzzes on the coffee table. I dive for it before I'm even fully awake, knocking the empty glass on its side in the process. I'm jumpy and scared as I turn my phone over, thinking it's a response from Kyan.

It's not.

A number that I don't recognize sent me a spammy text that says, "Is Linda still offering piano lessons?"

Disoriented, I delete the text and pick up the glass before settling into the couch indentation I've created over the last forty-eight hours. By episode seven, Ali Wong's performance has me sobbing, though it's probably a seventy-thirty split between the show's powerful character arcs and missing Kyan.

It doesn't take much for me to fall asleep after that, and when I wake up, the TV has powered down on its own. I pad into the bathroom to splash some water on my face and heave myself back onto the couch after turning off all the lights.

I check my phone, assuming Kyan hasn't texted back but needing to check anyway. A gasp escapes me as I see two unread texts from Kyan. Sitting up straight and buzzing with nerves, I open the thread, and find the first message is a picture.

The lighting is terrible, and the photo is heavily pixelated, as if the person taking it was far away and zoomed in as much as they could. I have to squint to determine what I'm looking at, but it seems to be a man with blood caked in his hair and pouring from several cuts on his face, with a bruised eye, swollen bottom lip, and slack jaw. His arms are spread wide, but I can't tell why, since his hands aren't in the frame. He looks passed out, but is somehow standing and holding his arms up, which doesn't make any sense.

He wears a white, V-neck t-shirt that's stained with blood and what looks like grease, and on his bicep, I see the curve of a black tat—

"Holy shit!"

It's Kyan. Someone beat the hell out of him and now they're sending me photos. I check the text that came after the photo.

> Kyan: Eye for an eye, trailer trash. Your boss is about to pay the ultimate price for fucking with our food.

I leap off the couch and shove my feet into a pair of Quincy's sneakers before racing out the door.

When I make it onto the street, the three dots appear. Elaine has him, and she's fucking taunting me. I expect her next message to be a selfie next to his severed head as she throws up a peace sign, but it's an address.

Dropping it into my Maps, I get directions and haul my ass through the woods toward the abandoned textile mill.

My dragon is leaving that mill alive. I don't care what it takes.

CHAPTER 18

KYAN

I cry out in agony when the hot poker sinks into my back, the skin sizzling as the heat burns it away. My vision is blurry in one eye, and I can't open the other, but I see the outlines of two people on the other side of the room I'm in, hovering inside the shadows. I can't make out their features, but one has a cloud of puffy yellow hair and is roughly the shape of a pink bell resting atop two sticks. The other doesn't have much hair at all, given the way overhead lights bounce off their scalp. This one is bigger than the bell and more of an oblong shape.

There's nothing familiar about them, which makes me wonder why they've brought me here.

And why they keep burning holes into my body.

I wait for my draxilio to growl in anger at the situation, but he gives me nothing. In fact, I don't even feel his presence in my head.

Hey, wake up. We have a problem here.

I wait and wait. Nothing.

We don't have to communicate, but we do need to work together to find a way out of this. I need to shift, set my fire on the fuzzy blobs, burn this torture chamber to the ground, and get out of here. Through shallow breaths, I try to ignore the pain that radiates across my face, down my back, and is spreading to my wrists as I picture his form. His scales, his claws, his impressive size—I bring these images to the forefront, as I always do when I shift, but nothing happens. The air doesn't even change around me. Why can't I shift? What have they done to me?

I suppose I need to think backward a few steps to find the answers I'm seeking. Who are these people? That's what I need to find out first. Once I know that, I'll have a better idea of their strengths and resources. A relative of one of our targets, perhaps. I'm sure the justice we've been serving up across New England has upset a few people.

Or maybe members of the police force, on a mission to avenge Burton's bizarre death. If not them, it could be members of Burton's family.

Burton's nephew, Travis, raped Sam and Vanessa, but Axil tore him apart months ago, and I don't remember any other known family members besides his uncle.

Dante's punchable face pops into my head, but he's more annoying than evil. I wasn't exactly welcoming when we met, but it seems unlikely he'd want me dead over poor manners. And if he's out, then so is the Scottish *tikano*, Ronan, as well as the one from Iceland we still haven't met.

Dante is responsible for the death of Charlie's ex, and from what I heard, he and Charlie didn't get along before he died. So one of his family members could be looking to take me and my brothers out.

Scanning through my memories, I recall the man Harper went on a date with before she and Luka were mated. This was when we lived in Boston. When she rejected him, he snuck into her house and tied her up, intent on killing her. We stopped that from happening, though, and Harper's three-legged rescue cat saved the day by jumping onto his shoulder, scaring him enough to fumble the gun in his hand and pull the trigger. That fucker didn't even get to die with his face.

Hm. I suppose we've made some enemies over the years.

Despite my current circumstances, standing barefoot on a wooden platform with my feet chained to the floor, my arms pulled tight to either side like the thin man with the beard who wears the thorny crown, and countless cuts and bruises covering my body, I have no regrets. The men I've made suffer caused enough suffering of their own to last a thousand lifetimes. Given the chance, I'd do it all again with a smile.

That is, until I hear Hudson's screams.

I don't need to see his face to know it's him. "Kyan!" he cries, followed by a long, low whimper.

Surging against my chains, I push toward the sound of his voice. "Hudson!" I roar. Fury pumps through my blood at the thought of my nephew being harmed. "Where are you?!"

He doesn't answer my question, just continues to shout my name. Though I doubt he even knows where he is. I certainly don't. Trying to scan the room, I see a dark, wide space. Large, rusted machinery sits on the far end, and there are wooden barrels, ropes, and rectangular metal cages scattered around the platform. The walls are brick, and on one side, there are hundreds of small square windows, most of which are broken. The sounds I hear are scattered drips, the rattling of metal—which seems to be coming from the direction of Hudson's voice, so he might be in a cage of some kind—and the dragging of chains whenever I try to take a step.

Then I hear laughter. It's a feminine snicker, brittle and harsh. The pink bell shape approaches across the platform and as she gets closer, I realize the bell is a dress, and the sticks are her legs.

"Release me." The growl that emerges is low, quiet, but the warning is clear.

"No, I'm not going to do that."

Not clear enough, it seems.

"Release me!" My roar rattles the shards of glass that were once windows, and I catch her slight stumble backward at the sheer volume of my voice. She hides it well, but I terrify her.

"Again, no."

I jerk toward her, straining against my binds, unable to figure out why they aren't snapping beneath my strength and why my draxilio feels dormant. I *need* to shift, and my body isn't cooperating.

"Wow, so angry." She circles me, and I follow the clack of her heels to where she stops directly behind me.

I feel her lift the back of my shirt, and then a pinch on my right side, just above the hem of my pants.

"We've got big plans for you, Kyan Monroe."

We? There's more than one of them. I knew that already, but how many in total? Knowing my full name isn't a surprise. Anyone intent on torturing me would've been able to learn my name.

Her fingers thread through my hair, and she yanks my head back. She whispers against my ear, "You can thank Naomi for that."

My legs give out beneath me as the walls start to move. Her laughter returns, but now it feels like it's coming from all around me, in the distance and tickling my neck. "S'happening?" The word comes from me, but it doesn't sound like me. I don't mumble. Why am I suddenly so tired?

My arms feel like they're being slowly torn off my body, my muscles tearing as my body sags. The only things holding me up are the thick, coarse bands that are chafing my wrists.

"Nnn-omi."

The word feels like acid on my tongue. Is it a word? No. A name. *Her.* The reason I'm here. Contempt wraps around me like a blanket as the world fades away.

* * *

Help.

The plea is soft. Coming from somewhere far away. No, not far. Close. Inside my head. My draxilio. He's with me, but something's wrong. Very wrong. He's scared. Why would he be scared? There's nothing he needs to fear. No enemy he can't conquer.

I hear his whimper again just before my feet leave the floor, my legs floating in front of me as they balloon into a horrifying partial shift. There are patches of pale skin on my arms between blue scales, a sharp claw next to a stubby human toe, and my bones begin a cycle of snapping and shrinking, snapping and shrinking, as my body is yanked between my two forms.

There's no part of me that isn't in excruciating pain. At one point, something erupts from my mouth. I assume it's a roar of fury, but when my cheek is shoved into something wet, I realize it was vomit. Between the violent changes of my body, I hear my captors speaking to me. They poke me with the hot prod as they tell me about Naomi and how she was sent to spy on me. Learn my secrets.

"Ahhh!" I bellow as a dull blade sinks into my arm.

"She didn't even apply for the job. I made her résumé. It's total bullshit."

This must be Elaine, the leader of Naomi's cell. Every story that Naomi has told me about Elaine makes her seem like a demon in kitten heels. In place of her heart is an endless black hole of misery, so there's no reason for me to trust her. Certainly not while she's cutting me open.

"Officer Burton was kind of our go-to guy for blood sources, and man, he did not like you. Or your brothers. He wanted us to dig up some dirt on you and your family, so I passed that task onto Naomi. She became your assistant, got close to you, and from just walking by her trailer," Elaine says, chuckling, "it sounded like you two became *very* close."

The hot poker is plunged between my ribs, and I curl in on myself, a steady whimper escaping me as I wrap my free arm around my stomach. "No more."

"That was all part of the act," she continues. "She did a great job, don't you think? I mean, she really sold it. Inviting you over for cupcakes, introducing you to that little rat with wings she lets into her house."

Wetness pools beneath my arm, reaching my elbow. I feel damp everywhere, actually. I hope it's sweat, but I know there's also blood. Lots of it. The clothes I wear are sticking to me like glue.

"Anyway, since Burton died, we haven't been able to connect with his successor," Elaine says. "He's not answering my emails. This is a problem, you see, because for decades, vampires all over the country have had an unspoken partnership with local law enforcement. They give us names and addresses of newly released convicts, and we hunt and drain the ones the public will care the least about. The drug addicts, the homeless, prostitutes, anyone from a high-crime neighborhood, you know. The cops love it. We make their cities and towns safer, and they reward us with more convicts. Everybody wins."

It sounds remarkably similar to the way the pack is set up, except for the glaring distinction between targets. We're seeking to avenge the ones hurt by violent criminals who use the system to their advantage, and they're hunting the people repeatedly criminalized by a system designed to keep them destitute.

She laughs. "Those people die, and it doesn't even make the news."

What I wouldn't give to summon the strength to slowly plunge a wooden stake into her heart right now.

"Why me?" I ask. My voice is so hoarse from screaming, I wonder if she even hears me. "And this."

She leans down next to my head. "Because you're going to tell me what you're keeping in that basement in Manchester. I know it's not just an office. Burton died before we could figure it out. We owe him this. Tell me or that sweet boy in the other room won't make it out of here alive."

I swallow, trying to lubricate my throat enough to speak. "If I tell you, you'll let him go?"

"That's the deal."

I don't want to tell her. If I do, she's going to find the pack and will probably kill them. If I don't, she might kill Hudson. Either way, it seems likely that I'm going to die here, so I need to decide who to save. My pack, or my family?

On the other hand, I don't trust her to keep her word and let Hudson go. What's to stop her from executing him immediately after I reveal the truth?

End? My draxilio whispers. I wish he were seeking permission to take over and make these bastards pay for what they've done, but that's not what he's asking. He wants to know if this is it. If this is our final chapter.

Any other day, I would be certain it's not.

However, any other day, he wouldn't even ask.

I don't know. I send back. *It might be.*

I feel another pinch at my lower back, and tears stream down my face, knowing it's about to get worse while wondering how that's possible.

My body is thrown forward, and I land on my stomach as my wings jut out from my shoulder blades and expand behind me. When I look down, I see my blue, five-fingered hand on the floor above my head. Somehow, I've been pushed into a partial change that shouldn't even be possible.

Flap, I send, hoping he has control over the wings. Nothing happens when I try it. *Fly us out of here.*

He doesn't get the chance, because a loud, mechanical rumble fills the air seconds before a massive blade slices through the center of my left wing.

* * *

"Kyan."

It's a soft voice that comforts me.

"Kyan, over here."

My head pounds with a thousand aches. I can't move it, so I try to follow the sound with my one good eye. Saliva fills my mouth as a wave of nausea hits. I can't see anything. It's all a blur, except for the glaring fluorescent light directly above me.

"Oh god, Kyan," I hear her say. It sounds like she's crying. "What have they done to you?"

Her small form emerges from behind one of the barrels, her hands covering her face as she approaches.

"Naomi," I try to say. It comes out as a crackling whisper. A cough racks my body, and muscles I didn't know existed clench and burn with the fire of the Sufoian sun.

I wish I could hold her, apologize for that horrible day in my office, and tell her that I truly do love her. The word meant different things to us. In my mind, it carried too many expectations that often lead to disappointments. Expectations that I wasn't sure I was ready to meet. That was, until yesterday, when my views changed.

Hudson showed up at the office, hoping to shadow me. I declined, knowing Luka would be furious. I offered to buy him lunch instead. We picked up our sandwiches from the restaurant, and I took him to a park close to the office. It was empty. No one in sight. He sat across from me at one of the picnic tables, and we talked.

I told him about Naomi, and how worried I was that I'd ruined everything. He listened as he ate, asking questions about my feelings for her, and why I was so upset if I wasn't ready to say the L word.

After explaining my point of view, and how I wanted a term that meant more perfect than perfect, and that "love" didn't feel like it fit, he replied, "Why don't you use *Moonavi?*"

"Moonavi." A Sufoian word.

"Yeah, Dad's teaching me how to speak Sufoian fluently. He told me about that weather event that only happened on Sufoi every three hundred years, where orange and blue lights would shoot across the sky, and how, when you were looking out onto the sea—"

"It looked like fire was colliding with ice," I finish.

He nods. "Exactly. That sounds so awesome. And she sounds awesome, so, wouldn't that be a better word to use?"

I hadn't thought about *Moonavi* since we came here. "It was," I tell him. "Do you know why it's called *Moonavi?"*

"That's not the scientific name for it?"

"No. I can't remember the scientific name, because no one ever used it," I explain. "The event was seen by our ancestors as a miracle. A sacred joining of forces so polarizing that they could only meet every three centuries. The ancestors called it that because of how rare it was, that two things so vastly different could still find each other and connect, despite the perceived impossibility of it."

As I recall the history of it, I can't believe it took me this long to see how aptly it fits.

Hudson smiles, the mirror image of his father as he gives me a knowing glance. "That's what she is to you, isn't she?"

I nod. "The ice to my fire."

After we finished eating, we started walking toward the office. We never made it back. Out of nowhere, I was tackled from behind. A black bag was thrown over my head, and I felt a pinch at my hip. Then I woke up here.

Naomi ducks down until I'm done coughing, trying to stay out of sight. I don't know where Elaine is, and I don't hear Hudson. All I can hope is that he still lives.

She creeps toward my cage.

I'm in a cage now? I suppose it doesn't matter. Now that my wing has been destroyed, I can't fly. I can't even shift. My body has returned completely to its flightless form.

She sticks her hand through the bars and reaches for me. I wince at her touch, and she immediately pulls away with a gasp. "I'm sorry."

Losing the feel of her skin hurts almost as much as the stinging lacerations that cover my hand. Almost. "You're here." Seeing her settles my insides. I didn't think I'd get to see her beautiful face again. Though marred with sadness at the moment, she radiates warmth that her body temperature lacks.

As I look at her now, standing in front of my cage, crumbling at the sight of me, I wish I had the strength to relay the story of how Hudson brought this word to my attention. To tell her that, yes, I love her, but *Moonavi* is more. *Moonavi* represents how I feel, and what she is to me. In the end, all I can get out is the word.

"*Moonavi.*"

She doesn't hear me.

Tears stream down her cheeks as her shoulders begin to shake with the force of her sobs. "I'm so sorry. This is all my fault."

"What?" My eyes start to itch as she tells me about Elaine, and how she was forced to spy on me. It takes me back to the haziness of earlier, as Elaine was revealing the truth about how

Naomi and I met while using various weapons and substances to send my body into a state of complete self-destruction.

I didn't want to believe it, but is it possible Naomi was actually using me?

"I can't believe they did this to you. When I agreed to it, I had no idea this was the potential outcome. If I knew she was capable of this…"

"Wait," I say, gently rubbing my eyelids to make the discomfort go away. "So you *were* spying on me?" My question comes out as a muffled rasp, but this time, she hears me. "None of it was real?"

"What? Of course it was real," she replies, sounding offended. "I mean, my résumé wasn't, but I told you I used to be a doctor. Everything that followed, everything that happened between us *was* real. I swear. I love you."

How am I supposed to believe that most of it was real when some of it wasn't? Simply because she swears? What weight does that hold? I'm locked in a fucking cage. My nephew is being tortured, and I can't do anything to help him. My brothers will never forgive me, and my pack might be in danger. And she *swears* that she loves me?

"Kyan, stop scratching your eyes."

I ignore her. This is worse than the hot poker. Besides, I'm completely useless as a draxilio now anyway. What do I need eyelids for?

"Why are the whites of your eyes bright red like that?"

Maybe because I'm slowly dying? "My eyes are bleeding. That's why."

"Oh damn. Kyan, they're…blinking."

Shit.

Right on cue, I hear the purr of my draxilio, right before he whispers, *Mate.*

I don't have time to panic about what this means, or to yell at

Naomi for the situation we're in, because the echo of Elaine's sharp cackle bounces around the walls, making my headache worse.

Naomi scurries back behind the barrel before Elaine comes into view, the oblong-shaped man at her side.

"Kyan, I wanted to share the good news."

If she's expecting me to ask, she's going to be disappointed. I'm not playing her game.

"Your office building has been destroyed."

Fear chills me to the bone, giving a momentary but miserable reprieve from the itchy eyes. "What do you mean?"

Oblong pulls a blowtorch from behind his back, and his eyes sparkle like a madman.

"We set it on fire. The fire department came but couldn't put it out in time."

Oblong decides to get in on the fun. "Hope you didn't have anything important in that basement, because it's a pile of ashes now."

My throat seizes up, and I can't speak. "S-ssurv-survviv... were there surviv–"

They walk toward the doorway without even pretending to listen.

"By the way," Elaine says. "Your nephew is next."

CHAPTER 19

NAOMI

I text Quincy from my hiding place behind the barrel as Elaine tells Kyan about the office.

> EMERGENCY: Meet me near the textile mill. At the edge of the woods. Elaine has Kyan.
> It's bad.

Slipping into the shadows, I crouch down and crawl toward the old machinery in the corner and crawl through the hole that leads to the woods. I start running through the trees toward Kyan's house. His family needs to know where he is. I also need their strength and fire if I'm going to take Elaine and Wyatt down. Quincy meets me on foot at the edge of the clearing, two blocks away from Sudbury Road.

"I'm going to get his brothers," I tell him. "Head over there and stay outside. Don't let her see you."

"Okay, got it."

"I'll be back in five minutes. Hopefully with more dragons."

We take off in opposite directions. I don't stop running until I reach Kyan's front door, and I press the doorbell at least eight times as I wait for someone to answer.

"Come on. Come on." I'm bouncing on the doorstep. This is taking too long. Clearly, no one's home. I remember Kyan telling me that his brothers live on either side, so I head to the one I can see and frantically ring the doorbell.

The face that greets me is Charlie, and she is not happy.

"You. What the fuck are you doing here?"

Several voices start speaking at once, and a crowd of people fill the room behind Charlie.

Zev gently nudges her to the side, his expression less murderous. "Naomi. Have you heard from Kyan? He's missing."

"Of course she has," a booming voice adds. A man with fair skin, neat, tightly cropped light brown hair pushes his way forward. It's one of his brothers. No doubt about it. I just don't know which one. "She is the reason my son is also missing."

Luka.

He grabs my arm and squeezes as he grits his teeth. "If you do not tell me what you have done with my boy and my brother, so help me—"

"The abandoned textile mill," I interject, refusing to waste any more time. "Kyan and Hudson are both there and are being tortured by two vampires."

A collective gasp fills the room.

"I don't know how much time they have left, and I can't save them on my own." They can blame me for Kyan and Hudson's abduction later. I'm certainly always going to blame myself, but now isn't the time. "Please. Help me."

The woman in the very back with long, curly dark hair and warm tawny skin surprises me by coming to my defense. "She wouldn't come here alone begging for help as part of a trap. Hear her out."

The brothers move into a circle, seemingly forming a plan without speaking. Can they read each other's minds?

The one in the flannel shirt must be Axil. He takes the lead.

"Ladies, you need to stay here. We'll be back with both of them shortly."

"Are you fucking serious?" A blonde woman steps forward, leaning heavily on her cane. "You think I'm just going to sit here while my son is being tortured? Just wait around while you guys get to take out the bastards that hurt my baby?"

I quickly gather that this is Harper.

Luka takes her face in his hands and presses his forehead against hers. "It's safe here, *ledai*," he says. "I cannot focus on freeing Hudson if I am worried about you too."

"I second that," a very pregnant woman with a short, brunette bob adds from the back, next to the one who stood up for me. "Harper, I need you alive to bring this little beast into the world soon. Also, because I love you."

Harper rolls her eyes. "Fine." She pokes a finger into Luka's chest. "Make 'em suffer." Then she addresses the only guy in the room who doesn't look like an alien dragon shifter. "Ryan, go with them and take the med bag."

"Will do, doc," Ryan says, leaving the room momentarily to retrieve a black apothecary bag.

We don't bother walking back to Kyan's house for them to get inside their designated shifting area between the hanging tarps. I crawl into one of Zev's claws, and Ryan gets into one of Luka's just before they launch into the sky like a formation of four stealth fighter jets.

In under a minute, we land in the woods behind the mill. Luka shifts back into his flightless form, but once Zev releases Ryan, he launches back into the sky. "Here is the plan," Luka begins. "The three of them are going to circle the building. They can avoid detection as long as they stay in the air. Do you know where they are inside?"

I point to the left side of the building. "Kyan is in a cage over there. His injuries are," I shiver as I picture how I left him, "really bad. I don't know where they're keeping Hudson. From inside, it looked like Kyan's area was one big room. Elaine and Wyatt came from the northeast corner, so I think that's where he'd be."

Luka nods as he takes in my directions. "Okay, how were you able to get in?"

I show him where we can crawl through. "It's a tight squeeze, but we can fit. That whole section doesn't have any lighting, so once we get inside, we can hide behind the machines as we make our way toward Kyan."

"Ryan," he says, turning to the man with the bag, "I want you at least twenty feet from the building, okay? I will throw a rock at one of the windows once we are inside, and the guys are going to start busting through walls."

"Makes sense."

Ryan smells like a human, but without an offensive, artificial odor. I expect him to look more afraid than he does, given he's the only one tagging along who'll likely die before he reaches one hundred. Hell, depending on how the night goes, I might join that list. He must be used to these kinds of dangerous dragon missions.

"I will call for you once the threat is neutralized, and we know what we are dealing with in terms of injuries." Luka looks between me and Ryan, I think to assess our mental strength. "Ready?"

We say yes, and I lead the way toward the mill. When we get inside, I hear Elaine talking to Kyan. Peeking around the edge of what looks like a tractor with a conveyor belt, I notice that Kyan is lying on his side, looking far too still for my liking. Blood continues to seep out of a deep gash down his back, and it looks like a pool of it has formed around his entire body.

It would explain why Elaine is leaning against the bars of the cage. There's no way she'd get that close if he were conscious. I can't hear what she's saying, but her tone sounds mocking.

We creep along the wall, behind the barrels, and when we're safely behind the closest barrel to the cage, Luka grabs a rock off the floor and hurls it toward the wall of windows next to the tractor thing. Glass shatters, causing Elaine to jerk her head toward the noise and then stomp in that direction.

She circles the machine, looking confused when she finds nothing. Before she can return to this side, a blue wrecking ball smashes through the bricks, leaving a dragon-sized hole in the wall and roof. She screams as chaos rains down around her.

I race to Kyan's side, whispering his name to get him to wake up. Luka throws another rock at the glass only a few feet from where we just were, then there's a ball of fire, and another Monroe brother uses his body to blast through the bricks.

Elaine cries out in horror as the roof caves in above her head, and her kitten heels fail to get her out of the danger zone before debris crashes down on top of her.

Luka uses the opportunity to charge toward the section where I think Hudson is being kept.

A ball of fire lights up the sky, casting a menacing glow in every dark corner of this miserable torture chamber. More glass breaks as another wall is toppled, leaving Kyan and me in one of the few remaining untouched parts of the building.

"Please wake up, my love," I whimper, noticing the dull blue shade of his skin. I'm worried about fever, sepsis, and so many things. I just know I can't lose him. Not now. Not this soon after finding him.

"Hey," Quincy whispers, emerging from behind another barrel.

Fuck, I totally forgot he was here. "Quince," I shout, as quietly as a shout can be, gesturing for him to come toward us.

"Jesus," he says, looking around at the mess with raised brows and a playful smirk. "Those fuckers are crazy."

"Yeah, they don't mess around."

He leans against the cage next to me. "How is he?"

"Not good. I just need them to help me get rid of Elaine and Wyatt so they can get their doctor in here."

"They have a doctor?" Quincy asks. "Like, for dragons?"

I nod. "I assume so. That's why they brought him along."

"Baller."

Axil and Mylo emerge from the back rooms. Mylo has Wyatt's arms locked behind him as Axil holds a sharp wooden stake to his throat. Luka follows close behind with what I assume to be Hudson draped across his arms. He's awake, but barely. His long, lanky body is covered in bruises, and there are cuts all over his face.

"Ryan!" Luka roars.

Ryan leaps over piles of brick and shattered glass with surprising grace for a human, and he rips open his bag as Luka lays Hudson gently on the floor.

Wyatt's face is red with anger, and I can't suppress the smile that forms at seeing him like this, especially after he watched Elaine beat the crap out of me and just laughed.

Mylo and Axil lead him over to us, and Quincy and I step to the side as they reach the front of Kyan's cage. "Open the cage," Axil growls, pressing the tip of the stake against Wyatt's chest.

Wyatt trembles. "I can't. I don't have the code."

Axil's not buying it. "Open it!"

When he yells, you can't stop your body from shaking. The whole room does. He's one scary dragon.

Wyatt decides this would be a good time to yell for Mike. "Mike! Hel—" Mylo and Axil immediately get him on the ground, covering his mouth as they search his pockets. Axil pulls a phone out of Wyatt's pocket as Mylo kneels on his arms, keeping him immobilized. He tries kicking them but can't reach and just looks ridiculous.

"Well, the British one is dead," Zev says as he strolls through an opening that used to be a wall. He notices the stake on the floor and grabs it, taking Axil's place as he holds it against Wyatt's chest.

"Give me the fucking code!"

Wyatt refuses, probably because there's not a big enough threat to his life.

"Wait, we don't need him for that," Zev notes, handing the stake back to Axil. Zev steps toward the front of the cage and his gaze narrows as he stares at the keypad.

Seconds later, the keypad lets out a pleasant beep and the lock clicks open. I don't know how he just did that, but I also don't care.

Ryan finishes tending to Hudson's most immediate needs and climbs inside the cage once the door is open.

I hover at the opening, silently praying Kyan will pull through.

A pile of bricks topples over, and Elaine leaps out from beneath it, covered in dirt and dust. She's barefoot as she charges at me with lightning speed, clutching a splintered piece of wood in her hand.

Wyatt somehow wiggles free while the guys are distracted by Elaine, and Kyan's brothers become a tangle of limbs as they try to tackle Wyatt and pin him to the ground.

Elaine's eyes are wild, and she's screaming like a madwoman, holding me in her sights.

Luka covers his son's body with his own, shielding Hudson from the violence erupting everywhere.

I'm shoved sideways, my shoulder slamming into the side of the cage before I fall to the ground.

When I pull myself up, I see Quincy lying in front of the cage, his eyes open, and his body still as Elaine climbs off him, leaving the wooden stake lodged in his chest.

A piercing wail is wrenched from my throat as I fall to my

knees at his side, my hands wrap around the stake, trying to remove it. "No, Quincy. No," I sob, refusing to accept that my friend, my brilliant, generous friend is now gone.

Because of me. He sacrificed himself to protect me from Elaine.

I already owed him so much for just being there when no one else was, and now this. It's a debt I will never be able to repay, no matter how many decades or centuries I'm given the opportunity to try.

Pulling the stake free, I drop it at my side as I lay my head against his chest. "I'm sorry."

Out of the corner of my eye, I see Elaine circling Zev, Axil, and Mylo as they continue fighting with Wyatt. The moment one of them gets Wyatt on his back, he slips through their grasp.

My eyes are trained on Elaine's back as she moves toward Kyan's brothers, and I start to tally all the ways she's caused me pain. She forced me to spy on Kyan while working with a corrupt cop to learn secrets about Kyan's family. She tortured my loving, magnificent dragon and his nephew. And now Quincy.

Rage darkens my vision, and something inside me just snaps. My hand finds the stake without looking down. I leap over Quincy's body and throw myself headfirst into her side. We hit one of the barrels and it splinters beneath us. Punches are thrown as we wrestle for dominance. Eventually, I end up on top.

Then…

I don't know. Time skips ahead, and I don't realize what's happened until I'm driving that stake through her heart, over and over, in an attempt to seek justice for what she's put me through. Big hands clasp my arms, and I'm lifted off her.

"It's okay," Zev whispers as he pulls me away and holds me against his chest. "Breathe, Naomi."

I stand frozen in shock as he rubs my back, trying to calm me. At one point, his arms loosen, and I tumble forward.

"Okay," he mutters. "We're not there just yet. It's okay. Shh."

I hear Axil's deep rumble to my right. "She's gone, Naomi. Elaine is dead. You're safe now."

Just beyond the leveled walls of the mill, tires screech, and four burly men charge inside, followed by a frail-looking blonde woman.

"Hey," Luka says, pointing at the woman. "You're the doctor, right?"

"Yes," she says, putting her hand on her chest. "Yvonne."

Wait. *This* is Yvonne? The mysterious texts to Kyan came from her?

The men survey the scene and seem pleased the hard work is done.

Gesturing to the men, Luka asks, "Who are these guys?"

One of them steps forward, offering his hand. "Owen, sir."

Luka shakes it, a smirk tugging at his lips after being addressed so formally. "Owen."

"I'm a member of Kyan's pack, a jaguar shifter." He nods toward the other three. "These chuckleheads are the rest of the pack."

Mylo tilts his head to the side. "His pack?"

Yvonne pipes in. "Yes, we live in basement of office building."

The basement. So that's what he was hiding down there? A group of shifters and a shady-looking doctor?

"Were you there tonight?" I ask, remembering Elaine bragging about arson. "When it burned down?"

"No, we left before," Yvonne says. "I see two shady men in parking garage on smoke break. They act suspicious, so I pack up lab and boys and leave."

"Kyan?" I hear Ryan say, and I break free of Zev's embrace to race over to the cage. "Can you hear me?"

"Mm," he groans, his eyes slowly blinking open. Everyone

surrounds the cage. His brothers, his pack, me, and Yvonne as Ryan shines a flashlight into each of Kyan's eyes. "Yeah," he croaks, and my heart soars.

"Kyan," Yvonne says, "I secure finances and get out of building before fire. Boys are okay. Everything okay."

"Mm, thas good," he replies, so groggy and out of it I wonder if he understood her.

Axil and Luka exchange a questioning glance at Yvonne's words, clearly confused about her role in Kyan's secret life.

As Ryan lifts one of Kyan's eyelids, Mylo shouts, "Whoa, is that what I think it is?"

Axil leans in and starts chuckling. "Yep. They're blinking."

"Are you kidding me?" Luka asks, shocked. "Kyan? I never thought I'd see the day."

Zev's hand covers his mouth as he shakes his head. "I did."

Then they all look over at me. "I don't get it."

Luka puts a hand on my shoulder. "Welcome to the family, Naomi."

What the hell am I missing?

The members of his pack seem just as confused as I am.

Axil seems to be the only one willing to spell it out. "You're his mate. The final Monroe brother has met his match."

CHAPTER 20

KYAN

Agony is ever present in my mind and body once I awaken in my old bed at Zev's house. Luka told me that I've been asleep for two days, and in that time, the most superficial cuts I gained during Elaine's torture session have healed, and the more significant ones show signs of improvement.

Still, I can't even breathe without wincing. There is no position that provides additional comfort, either. If I lay on my back, the massive tear down my left side where my wing was cut sends blinding pain through my upper body. Laying on my stomach is better, but only marginally, as the pressure on my three cracked ribs quickly becomes too much to bear.

Harper and Ryan have me on a schedule of thirty minutes on each side before I flip over. They check my wounds each time the alarm goes off, and Harper gives me the strongest pain meds she has, which helps with the physical pain but does nothing for the crippling shame I feel at having to be rescued by my brothers and pack.

It never should've come to that. I am the fiercest among us. A monster made in a lab and designed to kill. What am I if I can't defend myself, or worse, my nephew, from those like Elaine, who wish to harm us? I've spent my entire time on Earth preparing for the day when I had to use my body, my fury, my fire, to protect those I care about, and when that day came, I was utterly useless.

I don't know what to do with these feelings. Telling my brothers isn't an option, as I've embarrassed myself enough already.

Each time I close my eyes, there's a significant part of me that doesn't want them to reopen.

Zev knocks on the door before letting himself in. "Guess who's here?"

Naomi steps into the room, a big smile on her face as she takes me in. "Wow, you look so much better." She turns back to Zev. "Look at the color in his face."

My blood boils at the sight of her, despite the gleeful purr of my draxilio inside my head.

She betrayed us, I send to him. *She is the reason Hudson got hurt. They could've killed him because of her.*

Mate is his only reply, which makes me want to crack my skull open and remove the part of my brain that allows him to speak to me.

Zev nods. "Yeah, he's on his way." He looks between the two of us for another moment before excusing himself and closing the door behind him.

Naomi comes to sit on the side of the bed and gently places her hand over mine. "I'm glad Zev called me. It feels like I've been waiting years for you to wake up."

My throat is scratchy and dry, and even though I can speak, I choose not to. I don't even know where to begin with Naomi. Technically, she is my mate, but I can't stand the sight of her right now.

"I just want to make it clear to you that I love you—you and your draxilio," she clarifies, "and I accept you completely in both forms." She lets out a contented sigh. "I'm honored to be your mate."

I pull my hand from her grasp. "I can't discuss this now."

My draxilio growls in anger as Naomi's face falls. "What?"

"You spent weeks lying to me, trying to get close to me just so you could relay the information you learned to Burton."

She jerks back, her expression pained. "Not...not directly."

"It might as well have been. You told Elaine, who told Burton, the man who has spent the last year terrorizing my family."

Her eyes fill with tears. For a moment, it looks like she's going to protest in an effort to defend her actions, but then she pinches her eyes shut and nods. "You're right. What I did is unforgivable, but you have to know that, once I got to know you, I felt terrible about it. And I did stand up to Elaine. I refused to keep helping her. That was before we started staying in the secret bedroom at the office."

"It doesn't matter," I shout, though it comes out as a hoarse whisper. "The very idea that you spent any time simply trying to learn information that could be used against me, against my family, has me questioning all of it."

Her bottom lip trembles.

"Every look, every touch, every kiss. None of it feels real."

Tears stain her cheeks as she reaches for me, but then pauses before her withdrawing her hand. "Kyan, I'm so sorry. I'm disgusted with the part I played, and how it ended," her voice cracks. "I almost lost you. And..." She takes a moment to wipe her nose. "Without you, I don't know where I even belong in this world."

Now I'm responsible for her outlook on life? What do I owe her after the pain she's caused? I don't think I owe her anything, and I'm in too much pain to feel pity right now. "Stop being so afraid to be happy, and I'm sure you'll find your way."

Her nose scrunches up in disgust. "What are you talking about?"

I shift in bed, my ribs sending radiating waves of pain down my body as I try to lay on my side. It hurts so much, I struggle to take a deep breath. "Elaine's dead. You have the house to yourself now."

"And?"

"All the obstacles keeping you miserable and aimlessly floating through time have been removed. Use this time to figure out how to live as a vampire, rather than moping about and acting like the world is out to get you."

She gets to her feet, her eyes filled with rage. "At least I'm not afraid of my own emotions."

I was created to feel a constant wave of anger so intense that I obliterate anything that steps into my path. I couldn't be *more* in touch with my emotions. It's how I was designed. "That makes no sense," I reply, rolling my eyes. What little energy I had is waning, and I have no interest in continuing this discussion.

"As long as you can put all your focus on blaming society for its failures and punishing the evil men of this world for their actions, you never have to make time for the people in your life," she says, her cheeks turning a deep shade of red. "You can just stay busy and angry, working eighteen-hour days, training your pack, and killing your targets, instead of spending time with your actual family, because god forbid you experience even a moment of genuine affection and intimacy with one of your brothers. Anger is the only emotion you know. It's ruining your life, and you can't even see it."

"Enough!" I shout, my chest heaving. It sends me into a coughing fit, and it takes several minutes before my breathing returns to normal. "This is how I was made."

She shakes her head. "That may be true, but you actively feed this part of you. You're choosing your anger, even now, when a happy future is standing right in front of you."

No. That can't be true. I don't seek it out. Anger is simply the most dominant part of my brain. It's not my fault, and it's not a part of myself I can deny. A throbbing pain appears between my eyes, and I want more than anything for this moment to end. "I think you should leave."

Naomi looks crestfallen. Her mouth falls open as I adjust the pillows beneath my head.

"Harper," I call out, hoping she'll give me another pain pill.

"When can I come back?" Naomi asks, hope filling her gaze. "Tomorrow?"

"I don't know," is all I can give her. I know she's my mate, but I can't think about that right now. My mind is a mess of agonizing memories from inside the mill, my body broken from the abuse.

Harper and Ryan come in, and I hold out my hand for a pain pill. She gives it to me then hands me a glass of water to swallow it down.

The two of them help me onto my back as Naomi leaves my room, and I can't help but take a long look at her retreating form not knowing when I'll get to enjoy it again.

CHAPTER 21

NAOMI

*D*ays pass. Kyan is slow to heal, but Ryan and Harper are hopeful he'll make a full recovery. Their only concern is his wing. Because it was so badly injured during a partial shift, and he's been too fragile to shift since, they aren't sure if he'll be able to fly again.

I'm not sure how to make up for the pain I've caused, so I settle with baby steps, bringing him muffins and cookies during my visits. Despite the way he dismissed me after our fight, he has allowed me short visits—five or ten minutes—before he says he wants to go back to sleep. I'm not expecting forgiveness or any sort of declaration of love. Ultimately, I just want to keep him in my life. Even if he's just a friend.

When I'm not at Kyan's bedside or baking him treats, my grief threatens to send me to my knees. The house next to my trailer is empty, but because I still have so much hatred for my late cell mates, I can't even step inside without feeling nauseous. Quincy is dead. My only friend is Felix, who stops by my trailer to check on me in the morning and right before bed. Kyan's brothers seemed to accept me in the mill after learning I was

Kyan's mate, but with Kyan unsure if he can forgive me, they haven't spoken to me much since.

And their mates flat out despise me. They seem even more protective of Kyan than his brothers. I get dirty looks from them constantly when I'm at the house, and Harper doesn't hide her hatred when I'm around. She blames me for what happened to Hudson, despite leading the guys to the mill and aiding in their escape. Hudson has made a full recovery, but the scars of her son's pain are etched into her soul forever.

When I knock on the door to the house the next day armed with a basket of freshly baked brownies, Zev opens it, and his expression makes my stomach twist. "Hey, Naomi. I'm afraid Kyan isn't here."

"Not here?" How can that be? He was still mostly bedridden yesterday.

"He woke up this morning able to move around much better and went over to the house Yvonne and the pack are renting out."

"Oh, okay. Do you know when he'll be back?"

His eyes swirl with pity. "Here's the thing. Before he left, Kyan said he didn't want you coming by today."

My shoulders sag. Now he doesn't even want to see me.

"I don't know how he'll feel tomorrow, but today he wants space."

Space. I suppose that's only fair. He gave me as much as I needed when I asked for space. The least I can do is return the favor. "Will you give these to him?" I ask, handing over the brownies.

Zev takes them and encourages me to stop by tomorrow.

I thank him and slowly trudge back to my place. The dark cloud that seems intent on remaining above my head just got a little bigger. I don't know what to do, or what my purpose is.

There's no job to show up for anymore, so other than my trips to see Kyan, I curl into a ball on my bed and cry. I cry for Quincy mostly. He was on the verge of a breakthrough discovery with his work on artificial blood, and now he'll never get to finish it. He helped as many Sippers as he could to feel normal, seen. I doubt I'll ever come across another vampire with such a kind soul.

Elaine might be dead, but somewhere out there, Xavier still lives. I'm sure he'll hear about what happened soon enough and come looking for me. If he isn't already, that is.

The only bright spot, the one thing that has made me feel somewhat useful, are the video calls I've had with a woman named Oya, who is President of Vampire Relations for North America for the IVA, and we've had a standing call every day at three to go over the details of what happened in the mill.

As I'm the only surviving vampire of my cell, and the only vampire eyewitness from that night, she's relying exclusively on my account to process the paperwork surrounding the deaths of Mike, Wyatt, Elaine, and Quincy, to determine how best to proceed. There is a chance I'll have to pay a fine for killing Elaine. Vampires are strictly prohibited from staking another vampire, but Oya is confident she can have it waived.

She was not a fan of Elaine. Oya made several unsuccessful attempts to collect past due fees after Xavier dropped me off here. Xavier gave her enough money to cover my yearly fees until my twentieth fangiversary. I saw it. Apparently, though, that money never made it to the IVA. I don't know what happened to it, but if I had to guess, I'd say it paid for the contents of Elaine's closet.

There have been mandatory seminars that Elaine never showed up for as cell leader, emails never answered, and calls not returned over the course of six years.

When I told her about Elaine's ties to Burton, Oya rolled her dark brown eyes.

"No. That's being phased out as a food resource all over the world," she said.

"Really?"

She gestured to herself, nodding. "Honey, I'm leading the charge. Me and the presidents for the U.K. and Germany. Our black asses don't want to be associated with continuing that archaic alliance."

It was such a relief to hear that those in power are actually trying to fix things.

When her face pops up on my phone, I answer immediately.

"Hi, Oya."

"Hey, Naomi." She wastes no time. "Okay, so this will be a quick session and likely our last."

Disappointment washes over me. "Oh. Okay."

Her puffy afro fills the screen, framing her round face. My eyes are drawn immediately to her eye makeup. It's always a bold color, with a swipe across her lids and a line along the inner corners, and today is no exception. It's a glittery blue shade that reminds me of Kyan's draxilio. Absolutely gorgeous.

"So I had a quick conference with the supreme leaders," which are the three vampires that oversee the planet, all over a thousand years old, "and they don't see a reason for you to be sentenced or even pay a fine."

I suck in a breath. "Really?"

"Yeah, they see it as open-and-shut. If Elaine were still alive, she'd be sentenced to a public staking for her litany of crimes." She flips a page in the notebook in front of her, going over her notes. "They're also very impressed with the work Quincy did in seeking a blood alternative for Sippers. It's a movement that's trending upward, and the supremes see it as the best way to secure the future of our kind."

This is true vindication. I wish Quincy were alive to hear it.

"I've been given approval to help you fund a laboratory in Quincy's honor."

I pause, wondering if I heard her correctly. "Wait, s-seriously?"

She smiles. "Yes, seriously, and any equipment you need, tools, staffing, I've been authorized to use the full resources of the IVA to get you what you need."

I'm breathless. This is amazing, and I have no idea what to say. Tears spill onto my cheeks. I try pushing them back, but they become a river. "Thank you. Thank you so much."

"Aw, honey. Don't mention it." Oya closes her notebook. "Keep me posted on the progress and shoot me an email with a number. I'll wire the funds to your bank account within twenty-four hours."

When we disconnect the call, I crumple into a ball on the floor of my trailer, and my body quakes as I sob. After a while, the tears run dry, and I find myself wandering through the woods, ending up at the bridge, climbing the guardrail, and standing on the highest beam as I watch the flow of the river below me.

Lately, I find it calming, tracking the ripple of the current, hoping to spot a fish now and then. It no longer holds the intense hopelessness I used to feel when I came here, despite how uncertain things are with Kyan at the moment. Maybe it's because of how peaceful Kyan looked when we came here last, and the memory of that gives me comfort. I don't know. The bridge is more of an optimistic place for reflection now. It really—

I'm thrown sideways by sheer force, my feet leaving the rail as I tumble through the air. Strength circles my waist in the form of thick arms just before I slam into the ground. I land on top of Kyan's wide chest.

"Kyan, what the hell?"

He looks so angry as he pushes us off the ground, lifting me into his arms. When we're standing, he settles me on my feet and grips my shoulders so tight it hurts.

"What were you thinking, Naomi?"

I've never seen him like this. He's standing, with only light scars running down his cheek and neck, but his expression is twisted in anguish. I open my mouth to speak, but he does it first.

"I can't believe you could be so reckless!" he shouts, releasing me and pacing in a tight circle. He looks feral, his movements jerky and aggravated. "You were going to jump? To what end? You wouldn't die, so what…you just wanted to hurt yourself?"

Oh. I suppose from his perspective, that's how it must've looked.

"No, I wasn't going to jump."

He shakes his head disapprovingly as he takes me in, sizing me up. For what, I don't know.

Groaning, he runs a hand down his face. Then, in a quiet, tortured rasp, he says, "I'm fucking miserable without you."

My breath lodges in my throat. A sliver of hope threatens to bloom in my chest.

"I can't take it anymore." He throws up his hands. "I was mad, and I'm still mad, okay? But I don't fucking care about any of it anymore. It felt good to punish you for putting my family at risk. Until it didn't. The vengeful part of me wanted to keep it going, just to see how long you'd be willing to grovel." He sighs as his gaze lifts to the sky. "Then you had to give me fucking space."

A soft chuckle escapes me. "It's frustrating, isn't it? When the one you're mad at gives you the chance to miss them."

His eyes meet mine, and I see one side of his mouth curving up ever so slightly. "Infuriating."

"Listen," I begin, knowing I should probably keep my mouth shut about what happened, given his apparent change of heart, but I need him to understand why I did it. "When Elaine told me to take the job as your assistant, I didn't feel like I had a choice. It was that or be sent back to Xavier. She made me feel powerless."

He nods as he shoves his hands in his pockets.

"But getting to know you made me realize how much power I

actually possess. *You* make me feel like I can do anything. Be anything. I didn't think I'd ever feel that way again after I was turned." My eyes sting with tears as I recall the brush of his hand, the way he looks at me, the way we swap roles in bed. I can't lose him. "You've given me an incredible gift, and I can't thank you enough for that. And no matter what happens between us, I'll always be grateful to you for helping me come back to myself. The person I was. The woman I am."

Kyan's expression is unreadable, and because I don't know what's going on in his head, I just keep talking. "I spoke to Hudson, you know. After one of my visits with you, he ran up to me in the driveway."

"What did he say?"

"He told me he forgave me for what happened. That he didn't think it was my fault." I understand why he's Kyan's favorite. When he hugged me that day, it felt like he already saw me as a member of their family.

Kyan nods, looking proud. "He's the best among us."

I clear my throat as I continue; my hands shaking with nerves. "Then he told me about *Moonavi*."

Kyan's nostrils flare.

"About the history of it. Where the name came from." I kick at a leaf next to my foot, unable to meet Kyan's gaze. "How it was so rare that everyone on Sufoi stopped what they were doing to experience it. And how those lucky enough to have a view of the sea thought it looked like the collision of fire and ice."

He remains still and doesn't speak for what feels like forever. "That's what it means, yeah."

"Then he said the reason you didn't like the word love is because it felt like the wrong word. It didn't match how you felt about me."

Kyan nods. "True."

I step toward him. "And that *Moonavi* felt like a much better fit."

His chest rises quickly as the distance between us starts to close. "Fire and ice."

I place my hands on his chest, and my knees buckle at the force of the connection. God, I've missed touching him. "Do you still feel that way?"

Suddenly, I'm in his arms, my feet no longer touching the ground as his lips crash into mine. I grip his shoulders as his tongue rubs against mine, and I moan into his mouth. I don't know how long we stay like this. A while, but still not long enough. I'm the one that breaks the kiss though, because there's something I need to know.

"Where do we go from here? How can we move forward?"

He cups my cheek as his eyes dart between mine. "I don't care about the lies. The secrets. You weren't the only one guilty of it. My most important work didn't happen in the office where we met. It was in the basement. I kept that from you. The pack and Yvonne, even Andrei."

I learned about Andrei from Yvonne the day after the rescue, and I still can't believe the work he does is legal. The U.S. government allowing him to erase UFO reports—crazy.

"But how can you forgive me?"

He kisses me again, then cradles the back of my head as his forehead presses against mine. "You can come with me right now."

I pull back. "Come with you? Where?" I'll go anywhere.

"To Axil's. Vanessa's water broke. She's in labor."

"What?" How exciting! Then I remember she hates me. "Are you sure I should be there?"

He nods, his mouth forming a grim line. "You need to be there. The baby is sideways, and Harper and Ryan have never performed a c-section. Harper says it's not an emergency, but still urgent. We need to go now."

"No." The word comes out on its own, firm and laced with fear. "I can't. Kyan, I haven't performed a c-section in close to nine years."

"You have to."

"No way." I can't be their only option. If so, I feel bad for them. They deserve an obstetrician who isn't rusty. "You need to get someone else to do it."

"Who?" Kyan shouts, panic etched into his features. "It's a half-alien, dragon-shifter baby. We can't bring her to the hospital."

Fuck. I want to help them, but I don't know if this is still a skill I possess. Then there's the bigger concern. "The blood, Kyan. What about the blood? It's too dangerous."

"Naomi," he says in a stern tone as he grabs my shoulders, "you have complete control over your thirst. When was your last sip?"

I think back. "An hour ago. I drank a full bag."

"Then you're fine."

It seems like a huge risk, but I find myself considering it.

Kyan crooks a finger beneath my chin, lifting it until I can look nowhere but directly into his magnetic gray eyes. "You can do this, Naomi. I know you can. You know it too."

I still don't totally believe him, but I also can't stand here while a mother and her baby are in distress. "Okay. Let's go."

CHAPTER 22

KYAN

Since I can't fly, we drive. I speed through the country roads that separate my house from Naomi's, not caring if one of the Sudbury cops clocks me. Let them turn on their sirens and chase me back to Axil's. A house full of stressed-out dragons awaits them.

We get inside the house and head straight for the basement, where Harper and Ryan have set up a makeshift delivery room. Vanessa is hooked up to multiple machines, her forehead creased with worry as she watches the monitors, her hand in Axil's.

"Naomi, thank god," Harper says, relieved.

Naomi is clearly taken aback by Harper's tone, as it's a drastic shift from the way she was treated before. When Harper determined that the baby was sideways, she was terrified she wouldn't be able to deliver Vanessa's baby successfully as she had planned. Relaying Naomi's extensive experience in Seattle, Harper instantly set aside her mistrust and begged me to go retrieve her.

"She's in the transverse position. I tried shifting her position with my hands, but it didn't work. You can scrub up over there," Harper says, pointing to the sink against the far wall.

On the opposite side of the room from Vanessa, couches and

chairs are placed in a line, and every seat is occupied by a member of my family, all anxiously looking on.

"Did you administer the epidural?" Naomi asks.

"Yes," Ryan replies. "Ten minutes ago."

Harper and Ryan don their gloves, gowns, and masks, and once Naomi's hands are clean, I help her into the spare gown.

I can tell she's nervous as she approaches the foot of the hospital bed and surveys the tray of surgical tools.

Axil leans toward Naomi. I've never seen him look so afraid. "You're certain you can do this?"

She sighs, then nods. "Yes."

Sam gets to her feet and crosses the room, reaching Naomi's left side. "Look, I'm pulling for you, and not just because you're a vampire. Sure, I had no idea your kind existed beyond Stephanie Meyers's sparkly version of Forks, Washington, and I'm not gonna lie, I'm a little starstruck." She lowers her voice, "But if you fuck this up and hurt my best friend or my niece, I'm taking you down."

Naomi's back straightens, and the unshakable confidence that I've only seen Naomi have in the bedroom washes over her. "Understood," she says to Sam. "But you're not human. Not anymore."

Sam jerks back, not expecting that response. "What?"

Naomi assembles the surgical tools in her preferred order, no longer paying much attention to Sam and her threats. "The only humans in this room are Ryan and Nia. The rest of you smell like dragons."

Chatter arises among the group, the women discussing their newfound dragon abilities. I knew this strange biological shift had occurred, but I didn't realize it would make them smell nonhuman to vampires. It's a relief. As long as Charlie, Vanessa, Harper, and Sam are alive, they'll be protected from predatory monsters by the change in their scent.

Naomi lifts her gloved hands in front of her chest, takes a slow inhale, and then says, "Let's begin."

I stand in awe about two feet behind Naomi as I watch her cut a horizontal line just beneath Vanessa's stomach, amazed by her focus. She's working so quickly, it's hard to tell each step of her process. Ryan and Harper hand her the tools as she asks for them, offering support as the procedure progresses.

Forty minutes pass, and I have to remind myself to breathe. I'm anxious to meet my niece, and even more to see Naomi do what she was meant to do. To complete this procedure and know her skills have not been lost. She was a good enough assistant, but it's clear by her commanding presence and calming aura that this is her destiny.

I seethe at the thought of her maker ripping her from such a promising future, taking from her the thing she loves most. Xavier needs to pay for his crimes.

A high-pitched wail breaks me from my murderous thoughts as Naomi lifts the goo-covered newborn in her hands. "Here she is. A healthy baby girl."

Being present for the birth of Hudson and Cooper, I knew Axil's baby girl wouldn't have any obvious draxilio traits, apart from a pale blue tint to her skin. The rest will come later. She also has a full head of dark brown hair, and ten perfect fingers and toes.

Vanessa's smile is so big, I can see almost all her teeth. Her euphoric laughter quickly transforms into a steady weep as she reaches for her child.

Tears of pride run down Axil's cheeks as his eyes are locked on the baby, and then his mate, as Naomi wraps a towel around the newborn and places her in Vanessa's arms. His mate continues to cry as he presses soft kisses along her sweat-covered forehead.

"She's incredible," he says to Vanessa.

Vanessa nods as the baby wraps her impossibly tiny fingers

around Vanessa's pointer finger. "I'll always protect you," she whispers to her daughter.

"Me too, sweet girl," Axil adds. "For the rest of time."

When I look over at the seating area, everyone is crying, except for Hudson and Cooper. They're young and seem more astonished than anything that they just watched Naomi pull a baby from the hole she cut in Vanessa's stomach.

Naomi, Harper, and Ryan clean the baby, then complete the procedure by removing Vanessa's placenta and stitching her incision closed.

I take a turn holding the baby as the three of them dispose of the bloody medical pads and sheets. Ryan cleans the surgical tools in the sink as Harper pulls Naomi aside.

"Thank you so much. I don't even want to think about what could've happened if you weren't here."

Naomi's cheeks turn pink. "Oh, my pleasure. It felt good to get back on the horse. I'm surprised it all came back to me so easily."

"You're a fantastic surgeon, and if you ever want to start a practice with me and Ryan, let me know. I think there are others like us, who exist between the human and monster worlds, who need quality care."

My mate's lips part, stunned by the offer. "Wow. Um, yeah. I'll think about it."

I take her hand as we go back upstairs, leading her outside. "I want to show you something."

Turning left out of Axil's driveway, we talk to the next house. It's a smaller cottage painted dark green with white shutters. There's a short, paved driveway, and a fenced-in yard.

"What do you think?" I ask.

She stares at the house, puzzled, then back at me.

"It's ours."

Her hand goes in front of her mouth as she gazes at the cottage in disbelief. "Ours? You and me?"

"Well, and Felix too, I assume."

"Oh my god."

"It's a little small," I add, "but the primary bedroom has its own attached bathroom. We might need to expand the kitchen. I don't know if it's big enough." I cross my arms over my chest as I envision the layout and recall the changes I plan to make. "Or we can knock it down and build our own. Whatever you want."

She jumps on my back unexpectedly like a woodland creature, wrapping her legs around my waist and gripping my shoulders tight.

"Thank you, Kyan."

I try spinning my head around for a kiss, but I can't reach, so I end up spinning both of us in place as I seek her lips. Eventually, she hops down and comes around to my front. I pull her into my arms and moan against her sweet, plush mouth.

I guide us into a small copse of trees between the two properties and press Naomi's back against the white bark of a thick birch as I push her coat off her arms and tug her shirt over her head.

She moans into my mouth as I unhook her bra and pinch her hardening nipples.

Her pants and shoes require more focus for me to remove, but once they're gone, I push her already soaked panties down her legs.

My pants remain on, but Naomi pushes them down past my knees before wrapping her fingers around my cock and stroking me just the way I like.

This is my opportunity to officially make her mine, and I have no patience for foreplay.

I lift her into my arms and push her against the tree, her legs wrapping around my waist and her arms tight around my neck. "Hold on tight, sweetheart."

Her breath catches as I sink into her channel, her walls gripping my cock as our hips meet.

A tingling builds in the depths of my stomach after only three thrusts, letting me know I won't be able to last very long. "You feel so good," I tell her, hoping she won't make me hold out for too long. "I'm close, Naomi."

Her eyes are already rolling to the back of her head as I pound into her. It's clear she's close too. "Ss'ok, same," she says through heavy pants. "Fuck me hard."

I give her everything I've got, to the point where the tree shakes so violently that I worry we're about to snap it in half.

My sac tightens against my body, and I whimper, "Can I bite you?" against her neck.

She pulls back to look at me. "Huh?"

"Once I bite you, you're mine forever. It seals the mate bond."

Mate, my draxilio purrs. *Our mate. Perfect mate.*

Her eyes widen as she realizes why I used the safe word previously.

"Last chance to back out," I warn.

She gives me a predatory smirk as she runs her tongue along my throat. "Never."

I resume my thrusts, my gaze drifting to her long, elegant neck and the spot just beneath her ear that I plan to sink my teeth into.

"Oh fuck," she cries as her thighs shake against me. "Bite me, boss."

I feel her fangs sink into my neck as the walls of her cunt flutter around me, milking my cock until I can't see straight. Just as I'm about to come, I bite her neck, the taste of copper flooding my tongue, and it's enough to send me soaring over the edge. My vision blurs as I hold on to my mate's soft body, my head filled with the triumphant roar of my draxilio.

Our mouths find each other as we start to come down, the taste of our blood mixing as her tongue slides against mine.

When our lips part, she gazes up at me with those captivating eyes. Those wide set, trusting eyes that make me forget where I am, and she whispers, *"Moonavi."*

Nodding, I repeat the word that perfectly captures the way my little vampire has forever changed me, making me a better man. *"Moonavi."* The ice to my fire.

CHAPTER 23

NAOMI

The week that follows Axil and Vanessa's daughter's birth is extremely hectic. I spend a lot of time at their house with Harper and Ryan, checking in on Vanessa and little Mona Monroe. Vanessa's healing remarkably well, which I assume has a lot to do with her altered DNA. From what I can tell, this is happening as a result of the mating bite, or through the brothers' sperm. It's a discovery Harper and I are excited to learn more about.

Kyan and I are staying with Mylo and Sam, since the four of us are the only ones without kids. My mate and I have started planning the renovations we want to make to the new house, and Mylo begrudgingly agreed to let us crash with them until the house is done.

After the office fire, Kyan resigned as the CEO of Monroe Media Solutions, promoting Thea to the role. She agreed to take it, especially after Kyan offered her a two hundred thousand dollar signing bonus as an apology. He told her she can sell the company if she wants. It's her choice to make. His employees were set up to work remotely during Covid, so until they can find a new office to lease, the entire team will work from home.

My relationship with Kyan's family got a fresh start after Mona's birth, and the girls have invited me over for lunch every day since. They're all such unique, fascinating women. I'm thrilled to finally have a core group of female friends again. I didn't know how much I missed it until they took me in.

Kyan and I take our nightly walk together back to my trailer to visit Felix, and I bring him a jumbo jar of unsalted mixed nuts, dumping it out on the floor next to the fridge once we get inside. "Don't eat it all at once, and share some with your friends, okay?" I say as I open all the windows.

The trailer is a mess, but that's because I've let Felix take over. It's his house now, and if he wants to leave peanut crumbs on the floor for several days, that's on him.

My hope is that I can lure him to the new house once we're settled and set him up with a really cushy cage/greenhouse that makes him feel at home. I know he's a creature of the woods, but he also deserves a soft blanket and gourmet food whenever he wants.

When we head back and climb into bed at Mylo's house, Kyan lets me cover his eyes with a blindfold while I run my tongue all over his body. I take his cock deep into my throat and moan as his piercings scrape along my tongue. His grip on my hair tightens as he fucks my mouth, my scalp burning slightly. Knowing his strength and how easily he could overpower me though he chooses not to is so fucking hot; I feel my pussy gush as he throws his head back, letting out a guttural groan. He tastes of salt and musk on my tongue; as I massage his balls, and I can tell he's close. I tap my fingers twice on his stomach, letting him know he's allowed to come, and he does. Hard.

I swallow as much as I can, but it's too much. When Kyan rips the tie off his eyes, he sees the come dribbling down my chin and wipes it away with his finger, then uses that finger to trace the outline of my lips.

Using a damp washcloth, I clean the stickiness from our bodies before climbing in bed next to him. I fall asleep listening to the sound of his steady breaths as I watch the snow falling in fluffy, fat flakes out the window. Winter is officially here, and everyone in the Monroe clan has begun their holiday preparations. Sam and Mylo decorated immediately after Halloween, and even our bedroom has little Santa figurines along the dresser and a plastic tree in the corner.

At some point during the night, my sleep turns restless, and I can't seem to get warm enough, despite the thick blankets piled on top of us and the fact that my body isn't supposed to experience the sensation of being too cold, since I'm technically dead.

A darkness hovers above me, an ominous presence that makes my skin prickle. Tossing and turning, I try to shove it away and fall back to sleep.

"Naomi." It's just a whisper, but not only do I hear it, I feel it. The voice hisses again, "Naomi."

I wake with a gasp, sitting up so fast that it makes Kyan jump. He looks around the room, ready to attack. "What? What is it?"

Wheezing, I struggle to catch my breath as my gaze turns to the window looking out over the backyard. "Xavier," I whimper. "He's here."

Kyan leaps out of bed, throwing clothes on before opening my closet and grabbing the first sweatshirt and pants he can find. I hastily get dressed as he runs down the hall to wake Sam and Mylo. They're already up. Mylo sensed something around the same time I did.

"Ready for battle?" Mylo asks as the four of us head downstairs. From the umbrella holder, he grabs two hand-carved stakes Kyan made and tosses one to his brother.

"You're staying here," Kyan says to Mylo as a wicked grin spreads across his face. "I'll be handling this one on my own."

"Kyan," I say in protest. "Please let Mylo go with you. You need backup."

He strides toward me on his long, powerful legs, never breaking his gaze. Grabbing me by the chin, he kisses me hard, leaving me dizzy when he breaks it. Stroking a finger down the slope of my nose, he says in a growl, "No, sweetheart. This is what I'm best at. You keep bringing new life into this world." He takes my lips once more, this time softer. So tender. "I'll keep taking it out."

Snow is dumping on us when Kyan steps outside, and I can see the terrifying glow of Xavier's eyes from where he leans casually against a tree.

"I believe you have something that belongs to me," he says with a sneer. I had almost forgotten how basic Xavier is. His hair hangs in limp black strings, hitting the center of his chest. Black makeup is smudged around his eyes, and if it's not made of leather, he doesn't fuck with it. He looks like a vampire who just got a gift card to the goth store at the mall and shopped for quantity over quality.

I think it's his form of rebellion. He looks so much like a typical vampire that he dresses like one, as if daring anyone who sees him to make the assumption. He encourages confrontation and always has.

Kyan stops in the middle of the yard, dropping his stake in the snow. "I'm afraid you're mistaken. She's *mine.*" I wait for the shift, but it doesn't come. Kyan remains in his flightless form, which makes me anxious. As a dragon, I'm almost positive he can take Xavier. Like this, I don't know.

"You have a choice, friend," Kyan says, holding his arms out, practically begging for a fight. "You can leave here now in one piece and never come back."

Xavier walks toward him, leaving about five feet between them when he comes to a stop. "And the other option?"

"I shower you with enough fire that you beg for a stake."

Xavier opens his mouth, showing his extended fangs before charging at Kyan. He's a blur of shiny black as he cuts through the falling snow, and when he launches himself through the air, I stop breathing.

Kyan still hasn't shifted, and his feet remain planted in the same spot. I know he regained his ability to shift the day after Vanessa gave birth, so I'm not sure why he isn't right now.

What the fuck is he waiting for?

I hear commotion behind me, but I don't turn around to see what it is. I can't take my eyes off my mate.

"What's happening?" Julian says next to me in his slithery, velvet voice. "Does he need us?"

The pack is here. I don't know how they knew Kyan was in danger, but they showed up to support him.

I'm about to send them outside to gang up on Xavier, but just as I open my mouth, Kyan catches Xavier by the neck in midair and slams him onto the ground hard enough to cause a shaking beneath our feet. It's hard to tell what happens next, they both move so fast, but I smile when I count the many punches Kyan throws into Xavier's stomach, ribs, and face.

"No," I finally answer. "I think he's good."

I hear the arrival of Axil, Zev, and Luka, and we all crowd against the doorway as we watch the battle unfold.

Xavier gets the upper hand at one point, shoving Kyan to the ground and crawling on top of him. He uses his spindly legs to pin Kyan's down as he opens his mouth wide, ready to strike, fangs first.

That's when the air starts to change. The crisp white snow whips into a tornado around the two men, and before long, Xavier is a hundred feet off the ground, perched on top of Kyan's head like a fly on a horse.

Laughter fills the room the moment Xavier realizes how fucked he is. He scrambles to climb down but Kyan plucks him off with one of his claws and slams him onto the ground. He does this several more times, and I wonder if there will be anything left of Xavier to kill. By now, he's probably as flat as a pancake.

But Kyan isn't done. His shimmering blue wings extend behind him, the injured one still split in the middle and looking like a torn flag. My heart squeezes at the sight, angry and devastated he has to live this way for who knows how long.

That's when he shows off his draxilio's versatility. His wings flap as he pushes off the ground. He doesn't shoot into the sky like before, but he gets high enough to spit a ball of fire on the top half of a tall, thin tree on the edge of Sam and Mylo's yard. The house shakes when he lands, but he quickly jumps again, burning the branches off and molding it into what looks like a ten-foot-tall spear with a deathly sharp point. As the flames continue to lick down the length of the tree, Kyan adjusts Xavier's position inside his claw, and once he's in the air, Kyan raises his claw and slams it down onto the tree. The tree becomes a skewer, and Xavier a sad, lonely kebab.

Xavier's lifeless body hangs in the middle of the tree trunk, his chest completely hollowed out and his insides coating the charred, splintered edges of the top.

Kyan shifts back and can't hide the smile on his face as he stomps through the snow. His gaze is heated and remains fixed on my face. I hear cheers and applause as he sweeps me off my feet and kisses me like he hasn't seen me in years.

"You're free, little vampire," he says, rubbing the tip of his nose against mine.

"Because of you," I reply, wondering how I ended up with such a remarkable man to spend my days with.

"Are you sure you're okay with this?" he asks, tucking a lock of hair behind my ear. "Me doing the things I do? Being the way I am?"

My answer comes easily. "I wouldn't change a thing." *Moonavi.*

EPILOGUE

KYAN

ONE YEAR LATER...

"I still don't know how I feel about it," Zev says, gnawing on a piece of pizza crust. "You used your DNA to alter the genetics of the pack. That's what they did to us on Sufoi."

"Yes, that's true, but my intentions are different from our handlers', and every member of the pack is free to quit whenever they want. They live in their own houses, and I pay them handsomely. Julian even has a mate."

"That's the key to this whole debate," Mylo says. "The freedom."

Over the last year, Mylo and I have reached a place of mutual respect. He defends me now, and when those occasional disagreements arise, they're more playful than cutting.

"I think this is a brilliant thing you've done. Giving these boys a way to bring meaning to their lives while protecting their communities," Dante says, taking a long sip of his Red Dragon Daiquiri. "Bravo, Kyan. Bravo."

Our Italian cousin is growing on me. I hate to admit it, but he's charming, never seems to take anything too seriously, and loves coming to see us.

"This is something I think I might consider for my people. They don't need more protection than their handsome red dragon," he jokes, fluttering his eyelashes in a silly, seductive way, "but it would be nice to take a holiday every now and then."

"Listen," Luka pipes in, picking a pepperoni off his slice and tossing it into his mouth. "It's a good idea. I support it. But you can't let Hudson join, do you hear me? I don't want him going on your dangerous missions for Oya or hunting sexual predators across state lines."

"I won't," I vow, "until he's eighteen."

Luka stops chewing to glare at me.

"He's an adult at eighteen, brother," I remind him. "You have to let him make his own choices."

He shakes his head as he lets out a long groan.

"Do you have a new mission scheduled with Oya?" Axil asks.

I nod. "We're heading to Canada next month. Saskatoon, I think. She hasn't given me many details on the targets. All I know is that it's a trio of vampires who are responsible for the deaths of six Indigenous women."

Oya has hired me, Yvonne, and the rest of the pack to take on missions on a per-contract basis. She wanted us to take on a full-time position, but I declined. The *wrathenol* is working, but I don't want to push the pack too hard. Besides, my list of human targets is still quite long, and I have no intention of putting that aside to kill a bunch of law-breaking vampires.

Every species has its fair share of monsters.

There's a vengeful gleam in Axil's eyes. "Make them pay."

"You know we will."

The six of us finish eating, and I offer to pay the bill. Dante says his goodbyes in the parking lot. He's flying home to Siena today.

I wonder if Naomi would be interested in a trip to visit him sometime. I'm eager to see how a charismatic dragon lives when the public knows about him. What are his days like? Perhaps we can stop by Scotland and Iceland at some point too, to visit our other European cousins.

When I get home, Naomi is sitting at the kitchen island scrolling through her phone.

"Hey, you," she says, hopping off the stool and wrapping her arms around my neck. "How was lunch?"

"Good. Dante wanted me to tell you he misses you already."

"Aw, he's such a sweet meatball."

"How was your day? Did you finish setting up your office at the lab?"

"Yes, finally," she says with a breath of relief. "I don't know what I'm going to do with all the volunteers though. I knew Quincy had a million friends, but I didn't expect them to move here after he died."

Oya made good on her word to pay for Quincy's lab, sending Naomi money whenever she needs new supplies, is considering a dedicated wing for a specific aspect of research, or wants to hire additional staff. In the wake of Quincy's death, there was an outpouring of support on Facebook. Naomi didn't realize how many lives Quincy had touched until he was gone. There were vampires from all over the country who credited Quincy with saving their life, simply by offering support in their darkest moments. Several of them have since moved to Sudbury to volunteer at the lab, eager to dedicate their remaining days to developing artificial blood.

"If you don't have enough work for them at the lab, you could see if they want to help out at your practice."

She considers this. "That's true. I know Yvonne could use a

hand with the new recruits, and Ryan certainly deserves a promotion. He's still doing all the work of an assistant with the skills of a doctor."

That's long overdue indeed.

"Even Betsy has been coming by to help. She mostly complains, but I like having her there."

"Betsy?" I ask, searching my mind for the name.

"You know," Naomi says, "the old Cuban lady from my Sipper meetings."

Her face pops into my mind, along with a rather unpleasant interaction at the lab when she yelled at me for taking her seat. "Yes, Betsy. I remember."

"I wouldn't let them volunteer though. I'd want to pay them."

"So pay them. The practice can afford it, right?"

She nods. "Yeah, I think we can make that work. I'll talk to Harper about it."

I stand behind her and wrap my arms around her neck. "Well, if you need a cash infusion, don't hesitate to ask."

Naomi chuckles as I kiss along the shell of her ear. "Mm, that's convenient. I like having a dragon who's so liquid."

I doubt she meant for that to sound as dirty as it did, and I can't stop myself from replying, "So much liquid. Gallons."

She throws a crumpled napkin at my head. It bounces off my nose and lands in the sink.

The flutter of wings draws my attention to the covered porch. "Hey, Felix," we both call out to our frequent avian visitor.

Since it's winter, we keep the windows closed, but Axil crafted a sealed circular tube made of wood that serves as the bird version of a doggie door, allowing Felix to come and go as he pleases without our house dropping to freezing temperatures.

The entire porch is his domain, with a luxurious oversized bird cage, plenty of blankets, a fountain that only serves filtered water, and a crystal platter the size of a truck tire for his fancy peanuts.

My phone buzzes, and I see Naomi pick up hers at the same time. I don't bother reading the text, since it's clearly on the family text chain. She'll tell me what it says.

"It's Charlie." Then she squeals with excitement. "Oh, Caitlyn won the election!"

"Caitlyn?"

"You know, the one Sam and Vanessa went to high school with. They were enemies but settled their drama when Charlie and Caitlyn started becoming friends."

"Oh, yes." This is the woman who would often have too many drinks at Tipsy's and start petting my chest, asking if I'd like to be her Carlisle Cullen, whoever that is. I found her to be somewhat irritating, but from what I've heard, the many nights spent at the bar are behind her. Charlie helped run her campaign, and with the influx of so many new vampire residents who all seem to hold progressive views on how Sudbury should be run, Caitlyn apparently emerged victorious. "That's great."

The afternoon fades into evening, and Naomi and I settle on the couch in the living room, her with a bag of weed blood, and me with a stack of her famous almond weed cookies. The drug settles into my blood quickly, and we turn on the TV. Naomi found a new sitcom she likes, and we've been watching it every night this week.

Her laughter will forever be my favorite sound, and when our nights are spent like this, completely relaxed with our arms wrapped around each other, giggling about everything and nothing, I finally understand why my brothers were so desperate to find mates. The companionship, the knowledge that there is an entirely separate person with whom I share the same soul—it makes the darkness of an unjust world easier to bear.

"Did you have an appointment with Charlie today?" I ask, remembering it was scheduled for some time this week.

"I did," she says with a bright smile. "Baby's fine. She's officially in her second trimester now."

"Was Nia there?"

"Oh my god, that baby is so cute, I want to squeeze her little head until it pops."

What an odd inclination. "I don't think you should do that."

She laughs. "Yeah, Nia was there. Zev too, obviously. Nia is thrilled to have a baby brother. She wouldn't stop talking about it. How she's going to give him her stuffed dragon to keep him safe. It was adorable."

My mind drifts as I think about my brothers and what incredible luck we've had since coming to Earth. Our mates are very different, as are we, but in a country of over three hundred million people, we found our mates in the same general area. It might've taken over a decade, but we're now living in the same place too.

Luka and Harper bought the house on the other side of us, and theirs has a large, inground pool, which made Hudson and Cooper very happy. Ryan bought a condo in downtown Sudbury. Yvonne is renting an apartment near Tipsy's. Even the pack has moved into their own houses, just two streets away.

The doorbell rings, and I growl quietly as I pull myself off the couch and go answer it. I know it's not an unwelcome presence on the other side of the door, but I hate having my nights with Naomi interrupted.

"You forgot your credit card at lunch," Mylo says when I open the door.

"Ah. Thank you."

I go to shut the door, but his feet remain planted.

"Was there something else?"

He smirks. "Decal."

Decal? "What?"

He throws his head back, laughing loudly, and that's when it clicks.

"The fucking Wordle?" I send my fist into his shoulder. "You dick."

Mylo shrugs. "Now we're even."

I shut the door when he leaves, still stewing. Even? I'm not sure about that.

"Who was that?" Naomi asks, snuggling deeper under the blanket draped across her lap.

"Mylo," I growl. "He gave away the Wordle."

Naomi covers her ears. "Don't tell me! I still have three guesses left! La la la, I can't hear you."

I remove her hands. "You think I would do that to you? I'm offended, little vampire. That's just cruel."

The next episode begins, and Naomi notices the scowl on my face. "Still mad at your brother?"

"Yes," I grumble.

Her expression turns thoughtful. "He's not so bad."

No, he's not. Despite all the trouble we've given each other, he might be the best man I know. Well, one of four. Actually, the pack too. So one of eight.

"I never thought I'd be here," I say, stunned at how many people I willingly have in my life. This was not how I pictured my time on Earth to be spent, surrounded by people I'd die for. I look around our house, and then down at Naomi. "Or any of this. There's so much joy everywhere I look."

"You deserve it." She leans her head on my shoulder. "We all do."

I suppose my brilliant mate is right.

ALSO FROM IVY

ALIENS OF OLUURA

Saving His Mate

Charming His Mate

Stealing His Mate

Keeping His Mate

Healing His Mate

Enchanting Her Mate

(This series isn't finished. There's plenty more to come!)

STRANDED ON EARTH

Her Alien Bodyguard

Her Alien Neighbor

Her Alien Librarian

Her Alien Student

Her Alien Boss

FROM IVY

When I started outlining Kyan's story, I was worried being inside his head would put me in a dark headspace. He sees the world as an unfair, evil place, and thinks humans are too annoying to be considered worth his time. The few exceptions to this are his brothers' mates, of course.

I thought, *how am I going to carry such a miserable outlook for however long it takes me to write this?*

Then my mom got sick. She was diagnosed with Acute Myeloid Leukemia, and helplessly, I watched the disease steal decades off her life, cutting my time with her far too short. She died two weeks before the release of this book.

Kyan's rage made a lot more sense. I slipped into it easily the sicker she got.

The problem with our morally gray hero, however, is how certain he is that he can rid our society of all the evils and injustice he comes across. This isn't realistic of course, but that's what makes it fun! It's an escape.

In *this* world, Kyan and his band of vigilante bruisers snuff out some Seriously Bad Dudes and things do get better. And despite his gloomy-colored glasses, this dragon has layers. Writing him as an arrogant CEO who listens to Dolly Parton and loves being dominated was so healing for me. He was a delight.

Then there's Naomi, Kyan's complete opposite, and perfect match.

I've often seen vampires written as extremely confident, vicious sexpots. Even the ones who don't love the lifestyle still get to be all hot and broody and popular. But what happens when a newly-turned vampire is socially awkward as hell and flat-out refuses to suck blood? What about the inner conflicts of a vampire who's still ruled by their humanity? Then I realized that if one vampire felt this way, there had to be others. A whole community of fanged immortals seeking a better, more peaceful way to coexist with humans, lead by an unassuming owner of a Dunkin Donuts who's secretly a brilliant chemist.

I know Quincy's death was horrible, and I promise you, I didn't want to kill him off. Unfortunately, it had to be done, because I needed Naomi to snap. Throughout the book, she avoids confrontation, and can't summon the strength to stand up for herself against Elaine. This changes little by little when she's around Kyan, especially when they get to explore the Dom/sub aspect of their relationship, but she needed that final shove to see herself clearly. To understand how much agency she actually has. Watching Quincy sacrifice himself for her sent her hurtling over the edge into vengeance, and wasn't that so satisfying?

I hope you also enjoyed Naomi's crow bestie, Felix. In a setting filled with shifters, you probably wondered if he was one too. I considered it, but since crows are such brilliant, loyal creatures, it made more sense to keep him as a bird who comforts Naomi when she needs it, but also comes and goes as he pleases even after Kyan and Naomi get their happily ever after. He's their pet, but also a wild creature they aren't trying to tame, and that felt like the most authentic version of how they'd care for an animal.

Since this is the final book in the series, there were lots of loose ends that needed to be tied up. I hope I got all your faves!

Even though Kyan spends most of his time away from his brothers, I loved bringing them back into the fold and showing you where they ended up.

In terms of what's next...I'm leaving that up to you, my lovelies. The Monroes may have found their mates, but there are three European dragons who haven't. There are also a few shifters—a werewolf, a polar bear, and a jaguar—who just moved to town, and can now breathe fire. That's a pretty cool first date trick, if you ask me.

So if you'd like to see HEAs for the European dragons and the new members of Kyan's pack, let me know! I want to write stories that you want to read! If there's enough interest in these characters, I'll give them their own happy endings.

Tell me what you'd like to see next. DM me on Facebook, Instagram, or TikTok. Mail me a strongly worded letter. Have it written across the sky. Shout it from the rooftops. Send a carrier pigeon. Whatever it takes! Ask, and you shall receive.

Love,
    Ivy

P.S. - A huge thank-you to my sensitivity reader, Angel. Your notes were insightful and incredibly helpful. Properly honoring Naomi's culture and lived experience is not something I could've done without you. I appreciate you so much.

P.P.S. - My team has carried me through this awful time by propping me up when needed, and offering flexibility when the timeline seemed impossible. To my editors, of this book and the entire series; Chrisandra, Mel, Jenny, and Tina: I'd be lost without your brilliance, your patience, and your empathy. To my PR team; Kelsey, Sarah, and Nikki: I've had so many panicked moments of *HELP! WTF DO I DO?* and you're always right there, talking me down. I love you so hard.

RESOURCES

National Suicide Prevention Hotline
1-800-273-8255 (call or chat)
suicideprevention.org

National Domestic Violence Hotline
1.800.799.SAFE (7233)
thehotline.org

SAMHSA (Substance Abuse and Mental Health Services Administration Hotline)
1-800-662-HELP (4357)
TTY: 1-800-487-4889
samhsa.gov

RAINN (Rape, Abuse, & Incest National Network)
1-800-656-4673 (call or chat)
rainn.org

ABOUT THE AUTHOR

Ivy Knox has always been a voracious reader of romance novels, but quickly found her home in sci-fi romance because life on Earth can be kind of a drag. When she's not lost on faraway worlds created by her favorite authors, she's creating her own.

Ivy lives with her husband and a neurotic princess pup in the Midwest. When she's not reading or writing, she's probably watching *Superstore, Bridgerton, The Fall of the House of Usher,* or *What We Do in the Shadows* for the millionth time.